Light Step

by Jessica Ferrara

Tea With Coffee
— Media —

Acknowledgements

<u>**Giving Thanks!**</u>

Writing, marketing, and especially publishing, don't happen in a vacuum. Getting Light Step out into the world has been a group project of the best kind and I'm so grateful to everybody who had a hand in the work.

I'd like to give a big thanks to:

- Tyler Wittkofsky for your monthly marketing lessons, revising my biography, blurb, and also for your constant support of my work and social media pages.

- Kelsey Ann Lovelady for your marketing lessons, for hosting monthly self care sessions, and for formatting Light Step.

- Victoria Moxley for taking my cut-paper illustration into consideration with regards to, and ultimately designing, the book cover.

- Sarah Faeth Sanders and Grace Witt for editing Light Step, and Grace Witt also for beta reading it.

- Kaitlyn Kalor for reaching out to me about potentially submitting my work to Tea With Coffee Media in the first place, and for all of your help with the book since.

- Rebecca Popp for animating the preview for Light Step, and I'd also like to thank Dennis Kambury for narrating the clip.

- My Tea With Coffee Media family for believing in the success of Light Step so much that you agreed to publish it. Thank you for bringing me on as an author. I'm sure there was a lot of work and organizing going on behind the scenes that I barely gleaned the surface of so thank you to everyone involved, and I'm sorry to anybody I forgot. You all did a fantastic job!

- My family, and friends (both virtual and in-person), for being so supportive throughout my creative journey. I'd like to especially thank my sister Domonique Nacovsky, my aunt Dawn Nacovsky, my cousin (basically sister) Michelle Santor, my father-in-law Pasquale Ferrara, and my dear friend Marissa Mendes for always asking about my writing projects. There are too many of you to name here but I love you all and appreciate you!

- My husband, Daniel Ferrara, for everything, always. Without you, there would be no book.

And thank you to everybody who reads this book or who follows me online. I'm just another creative following a dream, but with your support, it's becoming a reality. So thank you everyone!

Contents

Chapter 1
No Rest For The Smitten

"I hope you're not planning on sleeping here!"

Blinking, Hugo looked to the speaker, but the guard had already passed his cubicle. Glancing at his computer screen, he agreed it was time to head out. He'd been alone for a while, the ambient sound of typing long gone. Logging out of his terminal, Hugo gathered his things, namely his wallet and a light jacket, and headed for his car. Had he errands to run? The cleaners were closed, had been for an hour, but he had no desire to return to his empty house. In the passenger seat were the last two novels he'd opened but failed to finish.

"Best return them," he muttered, setting the engine to rumbling.

There was minimal traffic, the journey brief. Pulling into the library lot, he found it nearly empty. Still, the windows shone bright against the violet sky.

"Shit. Hope they're not closed."

The hours listed showed that if they weren't, they would be soon. Without his watch to check, he turned the handle, and when it gave, slipped inside.

"Can I help you?"

Turning, Hugo saw a bald Black man coming his way.

"Hey! The door was open," he replied, impressed by the approaching figure. The man looked more like a bodybuilder than a librarian, muscles shining past his tight button down, its sleeves rolled up.

"So it was. Returning these?" the man asked.

Hugo tried to read the name tag but struggled to identify the letters through the fluorescent glare. Handing his meager pile over, his shadow cut the shine, allowing clarity. Ogoun? Best not to attempt pronouncing that, he decided. Any corrections would only slow their interaction, and Hugo was sure he'd intruded after closing. The least he could do was minimize any inconvenience.

"Yes. Sorry for coming in. I could've left them in the slot."

"What sort of book were you hoping to take out?"

Slightly taken aback, Hugo considered. "Ah well, anything to get away. Fantasy, sci-fi, maybe a historical fiction." He added, "Work's been dry," in case he sounded depressed. Work was the universal bane, the complaints of which were met by knowing nodding, not pity.

"Excellent! I've got the perfect book."

Rather than guiding Hugo past rooms of densely packed and carefully labeled shelves, Ogoun stepped around the front desk and bent low. When he stood up, he was holding a thick volume, doubtless an antique given the fading hard cover and yellowed pages. The spine was barely holding on by a few stubborn strands of thread, the ancient glue having lost its stick.

"Thank you," Hugo replied, accepting the book, which was heavier than it looked, *and it looked heavy.* "I'll just check this out and be out of your hair."

Flinching at his choice of words, Hugo retrieved the laminated card from his wallet and placed it in Ogoun's hand. There erupted a sudden slam, and Hugo swung around to spot the source.

"Don't worry about that. Door stopper must've been misplaced. Here you go."

Thanking him, Hugo took his card back and left. On the drive home, he wondered what the story was about, having missed the title in his rush. When he finally arrived, he settled in with tea and turned on his desk lamp before delving in.

"Storm Of Souls huh?" he said, reading aloud. "Never heard of it."

The story began at sunset, the tropical setting indicated by the intense heat, which forceful gales failed to allay—much at odds with Hugo's brisk New England abode. The birds had gone, off or to rest, but swarms of insects cried on, heeding not the incoming storm. The men wiped sweat from their brows, speaking little as they stood waiting. They rejected the implied safety, both physical and of secrecy, that an indoor gathering would have provided. When they first sent out word that it was time to prepare for what could only be a harrowing war, the air had been still, the sky blue. From the afternoon onward, the very light took on the dull gray of smoke as the sun was concealed by fast moving clouds. Already, the leader, Boukman spotted lightning shooting horizontally above the horizon. It bode well that the heavens too assented to the imminent violence. The rain came hard and sudden, the drops so large another would have doubted that the onslaught might persist past the hour. Not only was the battering constant all through the night, but so too the slaves and maroons trickled in alone or in pairs, and sometimes as whole families. They strode forth from between the trees and stony ridges, what distant light of settlements lost to their backs, their expressions hard.

With a crowd numbering at least a hundred, Boukman presided over all, shouting to be heard. There were no pleasantries, no kind greeting, and given the necessary volume, he couldn't have affected gaiety with his speech. Instead, he announced what all present knew, airing cruel grievances generations in the making. Others called their accord with every accusation, as there were none among them ignorant, nor spared. He called on the gods of his ancestors to arm his people against their oppressors. His plea had hardly concluded when lightning flashed, illuminating a plump woman who suddenly stood beside him. Her face was scarred, yet handsome, her hair tucked under her headwrap. She called upon those gathered to sing and, though it was unclear from what authority she spoke, the crowd acquiesced. What began as a series of melodies merged into a chorus that had all the instinctive familiarity of a retired wet nurse to the infant long grown. Not knowing how they knew the words, they sang, and the woman danced. She moved between the many, coaxing them to follow, and soon all were swept up in a music of such depth it seemed to come from beyond their throats, the stomping of their feet, and the clapping of their hands.

Then, with no warning, she pulled a large black pig up onto a stony outcrop. He wasn't perched but for a moment before she sliced his throat with a gold dagger pulled from a sheath at her belt. Another, younger woman, was immediately beside her with a rough hewn cup. She held it to the beast's neck and once the cup bore the wet darkness, she handed it to the person nearest to her. He drank, and offering thanks, handed the cup back. She filled it and passed it off to each and every soul gathered there, empowering and bonding them, as much to one another as to their mighty crusade.

Hugo usually lacked the stomach for gore, but aside from pausing to remove his glasses, carried on reading. He needed them to drive, and so left them unfolded beside his wallet, hoping to forget neither come morning.

In time, the first woman was introduced as Dantor, a warrior matriarch, and the other, her daughter Anaïs. It fell to her to spread messages from one rebel camp to the next. Thus far the narrator followed her journey over that of those heading the rebellion, and through her communications, emphasized the vastness of their alliance. The setting was Saint-Domingue, some centuries prior, but Hugo didn't know off-hand where that was on a map, only assuming the Caribbean, because of the once-prominent slave trade there.

When next he glanced from the book, it was at motion on the periphery of his vision. Distracted from the aftermath of a bloody skirmish by what had appeared to be a woman, he turned to watch her full figure spinning just past the edge of sight. Rubbing his eyes, he rose, putting down the novel to follow, though he knew himself alone. Looking back to the book, he blinked, recalling that the heroine had kohl skin, high cheekbones, eyes black as obsidian, a shaved head, and a curious pale heart-shaped birthmark, rippled as though stitched, over her left breast. Obviously tired, given the illusion, Hugo yawned, flipped off the light, and went to bed.

In the dark however, there was nothing to distract from her voluptuous silhouette as she danced always just off to the side, swaying to a song unheard. The night was long. When he felt himself on the verge of sleep, there she was, silently passing by, sharing with him neither word nor glance. The sun was creeping in when he finally drifted off.

When Hugo awoke, he did so suddenly, ripped from his dream with such force it was lost at once. Mouth dry, lips tender, and throat hoarse, he sat up, coughing into his elbow. Then he read the clock on the nightstand.

"Shit! The time!"

He must have hit the snooze button. It was too late to jog. Hugo barely had a moment to brush his hair, let alone his teeth, cursing without curiosity as he shook red petals from his copper waves. Showering, shaving—they'd have to wait. Grabbing his keys, wallet, glasses, a banana, and a sandwich from the fridge, Hugo ran past his late-blooming dwarf pomegranate tree. His momentum carried its secrets through the doorway, over the patio, down the walkway, and to the car. Unconsciously brushing the crimson ribbons from his work shirt and pants, he donned his eyewear and pulled away from the curb. The sky shone scarlet. He blinked, anticipating the aura preceding a stroke, but no, the very air was pink.

"Wasn't that an Edith Piaf song?"

Glancing at the rearview mirror, he gave himself more of a once-over as traffic lulled. His lips were split, bloody. He'd have to pick up chapstick.

Human Resources didn't care about phantoms in the night, no matter how captivating. So, Hugo had no time to wonder about the strange visions before collapsing into the swivel chair at his mahogany patterned particle wood desk—doubtless put together by a laborer in a for-profit prison, purchased in bulk by his employer. Cheap, fake, and tainted with undisclosed suffering—like a life, or like his life anyway. No, that was melodramatic. His life was fine. How many times had he been told he came from *good stock?* And he had received a decent education, graduated with minimal debt, thanks to the once-upper middle-class pockets of his folks. He paid his bills on time and didn't so much as suffer from the seasonal sniffle that plagued his office mates. Hugo was lonely, but could he really complain? "Children are starving in Africa," as his ma would say.

He lacked the freedom to ponder the hows or whys of *Her.* Work, work, work. Hugo had a job to do, a paycheck to earn, and a reputation to maintain. If he couldn't cut it, somebody else would, and then he'd be flat out of a job. Instead of peering inside to admire those mysterious dark eyes tattooed along his core, or sketching that angular face, he calculated mortgage costs for potential home buyers.

Could he get them a better deal? No, he could not. No more than he could pause his morning to dwell on her rhythm could he re-calculate that price, recalibrate their credit. It was a no-go. The numbers left no room for dalliance, whims, or favoritism.

Lunch was spent alone but equally occupied. There were charts to fill and mounds of creditworthiness to verify. His team was out of overtime for the month and Hugo had only his best to give. That's why Janet in Human Resources ignored the occasional complaint in the bi-monthly surveys his more motivated clients filled out and turned in. How could he be blamed for staring when that broad's skirt barely covered her crotch? And in what universe was it his fault that an eighty-year-old couldn't understand her loan request was denied? What?! Was it his job to teach her how to read, too? Jesus Christ. Thankfully, he'd been coming in on the weekends since Claire left. He would've minded Nate's request not to clock in those extra hours, but spending every weekend confined to his couch wasn't exactly preferable. That's why he was the Mortgage Loan Officer of the Month four months straight. It would have been five if Veronica hadn't been sleeping with one of Alek Walton's bastards, he thought, adding another column to the livelihoods lining his monitor.

God damn Veronica and those magnificent breasts. Rumor was, Girls Gone Wild funded those melons back when she was a freshman in college. Nosier peers stalked her social media accounts, proclaiming the modesty of her pre-collegiate chest. He'd have believed the rumors too had he not once sat with her mother, tallying the numbers for a monthly payment on a new condo. Shame. He could have used the spite. The pride. But no, those bundles were genetic. Apparently illegitimate Walton junior was a breast man. And who could blame him? Her face wasn't anything to scoff at either. She just wasn't Hugo's type. Something about her garish lipstick, drawn past the plump, or the way she drew out her long A's, didn't sit well with him. No matter. He hadn't expected to be Employee of the Year anyway.

Hugo glanced from his work as shouting arose from the bank lobby. Well, that's what Security was paid for. He turned back to his calculations, taking a bite of a baloney and mustard sandwich.

After work, he ran to the dry cleaners, stopped off at the grocery store, picked up a fertilizer pack from Home Depot, circled his block to prolong the drive, and finally hopped out, steeled for silence. Flicking on the lights, he fed his suddenly recovered pomegranate tree. After a month spent wallowing, dry and grim, he'd assumed it was on a hunger strike, rebelling at having been posted inside.

Of their plants, the tree alone had survived without Claire's care, and he was grateful for the company. Striding from room to room, he rid the air of darkness but couldn't chase away the gloom. Hugo located the book but put it down after glazing over the same paragraph thrice, retaining not a word. The space between statements was filled with *her* face, head high, turning as though to face him, then peering coyly beyond before their eyes met. Scowling, Hugo found a notebook, a pen, and sketched. Like a song circling his skull, with a listen, she'd leave him be.

Except Hugo was no artist and he drew without skill, tearing out page after page of painstaking line work. And while the shape it was taking was face-like, that face wasn't hers. Frustrated, he quit, set the kettle on, and plucked the TV remote from between crumb-crusted cushions.

Right away the commercials cut into the sitcom and a breaking news bulletin intruded on the rest. The weather alert wasn't relevant to his area, and with a sigh, he turned it off.

"May as well check my voicemail," Hugo said, the ominous flash catching his eye. "Let me guess. Telemarketers?"

He almost missed the door-to-door vacuum salesmen of his youth. They'd been easier to ignore, less persistent than the magazine, insurance, and vehicle warranty cold callers who never left him a day's peace.

The first message was a play-by-play of his mom's afternoon. Doctor Cornwall-or-whatever didn't think the mole was cancerous, but it was safer to get it biopsied and her insurance would cover it, so why not? Also, her friend's daughter was starting up a business consulting firm. Would he like her number? It sounded like a better fit than that backwater bank he was working for.

He considered returning her call, but the kettle screamed.

"Where there is tea, there is a way," Hugo murmured.

Though, a way where? He didn't chuckle at his half-hearted humor, retrieving a bag from the nearest box without glancing at the label. The tea cabinet was packed with flavors from big names to local holistic brands, all forgotten by Claire, and likely expired, if tea could expire. Seated and silent, too polite even to slurp, he waited for his drink to cool. The fridge groaned and a breeze caressed the windows, shaking them within their frames. He shivered in the draft. There was a scratching on the roof, then again down the siding. Doubtless, the fat squirrel infamous for robbing his neighbors' bird feeders was hoarding nuts it would never remember the location of. Hugo could just see the full-bellied furball squirming, shooing mildewed leaves from his gutters, blocking them instead with snacks for later. The scratching followed the downspout. Whatever. It was just a rental.

Inside, Hugo peered up from his chipped "Used To Bank But Lost Interest" mug and examined his meager furnishings. No nuts, but the couch matched the curtains. That was something. A burglar wouldn't have assumed he was some frat boy, no siree. Not with the paisley throw blanket draped over the love seat. It was too much stuff for one man, too tidy for a family, too messy for a matron, and too worn for a yuppie. He was an in-betweener, in between the working and middle class, and in between relationships.

There remained a feminine influence in the doilies he'd never gotten around to throwing out but couldn't bring himself to use. The wine rack was classy, or would have been, had it not housed what beers wouldn't fit in the fridge. As for the fridge—it was a wreck.

His inner penny pincher had run amok again, buying bulk ingredients at a discount because *a self-starter has no qualms against cooking from scratch.* So many cookbooks, so little motivation. That idealistic chef lasted about three nights before he was ordering in again.

"Soon the cream cheese will have gone bad," he remarked.

The cold wasn't magic after all. Hugo rose and moved two tinfoil-wrapped cubes from the fridge to the freezer, pulling out the ice trays so they'd fit.

"I never had these problems when Claire was here," he said out loud. *I never talked to myself then, either,* he continued within.

More than six months had passed without an explanation from her. No, that wasn't true. She'd given her reasons. She'd dropped and slopped her feelings like batter from the pan, wildly flipped. He wasn't there for her, invented excuses not to come out with her friends, didn't care to travel, and always had something to say about her drinking. He was stuffy, dull, and she needed freedom to thrive. To breathe, without inhaling the fumes of stagnation, *decay*.

"What am I? A zombie?!"

Only if he meant the crawling kind, she explained, having already called her girlfriends in Seattle.

"But I'm a jogger!" he'd argued, and she said he missed the point.

Upon learning her friends had room to spare, she bolted. Would he have tried, had she given him more notice? *Maybe?* He could have put up with the slow-witted ruminations of her shallow troupe. Had she been willing to compromise on how much she drank per outing, he would have let the frequency go. Europeans had a glass of wine with every meal. So could Claire, had she stopped there.

"Do you see a future with me?" she used to ask, and he'd evade.

Would he have married her? Had he ever wanted to father Claire's babies? That he had no answer was an answer, but it irked that he wasn't given the choice. She could have communicated that there was a time limit, a deadline to respond by, before parting. How was he supposed to know if he wanted to spend his life with her? Most days he didn't know what he wanted for dinner until the wrong meal arrived at his door.

He wouldn't have lied to her, led her on. He wasn't that guy anymore, the idiot frat boy who promised the world, jumped in head after dick—not since divorcing Riga. What, five years ago now? God, that woman was a nightmare.

Could he be blamed if he didn't want to map a route with another so soon? Maybe not, but nor could he condemn her for seeking out someone better-able. Had he known she was on her way out, he would have tried, but instead, he hadn't smelled the burnt toast until the roof was ablaze and the walls had given way. He wondered if she liked Seattle.

Her mom called him a month after she'd left, confessed Claire was prostituting herself to get by, and begged him to talk sense to her. Terrified that he was the cause of another soul-rendering meltdown, Hugo did exactly that. He contacted her through her roommates, his sleeves wet with apologies. Of course, this would be his fault too. Just like Evelyn—but he was mistaken. Claire was doing very well, *"Thank you very much,"* as a model, and she wasn't fucking for money—not that it was any of his business. So, he and her mom could go straight to hell. *Click!*

And what was trying, when marriage and a family were off the table? What was the compromise? They'd been living together. Was there a step between cohabiting and marriage? She was right; she made the move he couldn't. He hoped she was as happy as she claimed, posing naked for the camera. "Someone should be." Happy, he meant.

Hugo poured himself a mixed bowl of the two off-brand cereals he had left. Despite the illustration on the one box, there wasn't a matchbox car inside. Upon further inspection, he found he had to cut a postcard from the interior, fill it out, and mail it in. That was too much effort for a cheap plastic trinket. Hugo shook his head, scoffing at the marketing ploy. He could remember when cereals advertising a toy had it packaged within, safe in a sheer wrapper. So too, he could recall when soda caps bore prizes, needing only to be turned in at the corner store counter. Not codes he had to type into a website, no personal information logged. There was a reason he no longer drank Mountain Dew, and it had nothing to do with his weight. The milk was sour, so he dumped it, eating the bowl dry.

That night he couldn't sleep under the weight bearing down on his chest. Alone, his mind no longer busied by credit scores and monthly incomes, his hands no longer tied by bureaucratic expectations—he was free to want, and want he did. He wanted her. Not Claire, not really. He wanted Anaïs. He wanted more than glimpses of her shifting away, wanted her in bed beside him, his arms wrapped around her, mouth on hers. And more. So much more.

Had some novel incited this futile infatuation? Or had he seen her before and put his interest aside as an impossibility then, stifling his heart? Perhaps she'd belonged to another? Or he had? Or was she an actress, one of many faces on screen, her character now forgotten in the cascade of visual media, with just the impression remaining? Had the tale of this heroine called her repressed visage home? Try as he might, he couldn't guess where he might have seen her, met her, but such perfection surpassed his capabilities for invention. Swiping through his closet, he scanned for a patterned button-down. If he walked to the bar, there was bound to be a pretty face with whom he could spend an evening, perhaps the night. But he had work at eight a.m. sharp. Tardiness resulted in write-ups, hurting him when raises and promotions were assigned. He bit his lip on instinct, then flinched, debating.

So it was that Hugo lay awake, chapstick reapplied, one foot out of the covers, for what felt like hours. Finally, his mouth grew too dry to ignore and he rose for water. Checking the clock over the oven, he saw that it was after three. The witching hour, he observed. Did he have any NyQuil left? None behind the bathroom mirror. None under the sink. None in the hall closet. Damn. Had Claire left her Benadryl? If so, where would it be? There—in her abandoned drawer were over-the-counter pills, vitamins, their bottles barely legible, smeared with eye shadow once spilled. She *had* left in a hurry.

How much Benadryl would knock him out? Two pills? Three? Assuming the doses were similar to those of Aspirin, he swallowed with water and returned to bed. Any sleep was better than none.

He awoke unrested, the sun tucked away. Anaïs' striking profile turned with her hand raised, as though pressed against the invisible waist of her partner. If only she would speak!

"Say something," he begged. "Anything at all," he whispered.

After that first sleepless evening, Hugo picked up NyQuil, earplugs, a noise machine, and a couple of pornos. Unexpectedly, the drug did not induce sleep so much as enhance visions of his muse the moment he closed his eyes. He couldn't bear the pressure of the earplugs for long. They reminded him of his bouts of swimmer's ear as a kid, and the noise machine made his head hurt. While the women on his DVDs were delightfully acrobatic, willing, and sultry—his woman had been more than sex. The others brought him pleasure, but no joy.

Despite his best efforts, her shadow against the night, its indentation on his mind, became more pronounced, her waking absence, profound. Hugo wished he'd never opened the book. He brought it to the library counter to return it, only for the clerk to shake her head, loosening a curl from her bun.

"I'm sorry, sir. We don't have any record of this in our system."

"But I borrowed it days ago. Are you sure?"

"Absolutely. We don't have that title here. Nor the ISBN. Could be we used to have it in our collection but after a couple of years without being taken out, it was cleared from our logs."

"Except I just checked it out."

"Or you thought you checked it out, just as we probably thought we'd removed it from our shelves as well as the catalog. Either way, it's yours now."

"But I don't want it."

"That's a shame. We're not accepting donations at the moment, though you're welcome to try back around Christmas. Books tend to be *misplaced* then, and we should have space."

He tried and failed to send it off to a few other libraries before tossing it in the clothing donation shack outside of McMart. Hoping that'd be the end of his obsession, Hugo raced home. But he found himself mistaken, her silhouette present in every shadow, hands flashing, hips swiveling, eyes glancing always past.

No sooner would he collapse of exhaustion in the wee morning hours than his alarm would startle him awake. Hugo could see the fatigue in his reflection. Beneath hazel eyes lay bags like termite-hollowed branches weighed low under ice. Creases cornered his sandpaper mouth, and his complexion was ghastly, freckles gone. Even his strawberry-blond waves fell limp, the roots ginger, untouched by daylight. Unlike his face, which tanned with the sun's exposure, his hair paled during the morning jogs he'd been neglecting.

Thank goodness it was Friday. One more shift, then he could focus entirely on rest, recuperation. Except when he showed up to work ready to punch in, he found that it was Wednesday, not even close to Friday, and his friend asked if he was coming down with something.

"Maybe," Hugo said, throat dry, voice a rattle.

"You should take tomorrow off," Esteban advised.

"That might be good advice," Hugo admitted.

Blinking back sleep during his lunch break, he ate vending machine chips, afraid to patronize a drive-through in his condition, fearing he might hit the curb, speaker box, vehicles, or passersby. Fingers gritty with crumbs, he googled the local news, scanning headlines listing criminal activities until he landed on a story that featured an artist's sketch of the suspect. More luck, the artist had signed his work: *Christopher Malcolm.* Another search failed to reveal a means for reaching out, but all was not lost. Locating the non-emergency number for the local police, Hugo rang and requested the contact information of their go-to sketch artist.

"Why do you need to talk to Chris?"

Hugo peeked into the neighboring cubicles, confirming the guys were out to lunch.

"I was reading this book, see, and when I put it down, I swear I saw the protagonist in my house. It was just for an instant, but now she's stuck in my head. I need the artist to get her out so I can sleep at night."

"Oh, sure. We've all been there. How about I take down your number and we pass it along to him. Sound good?"

"Sounds great."

Hugo gave his home number and email, thanking the officer for his willingness to help a lonely man out. Not five minutes later, his desk phone trilled. It was the artist. He'd be available later that day if Hugo could afford his commission. Without asking how he'd gotten his work number, Hugo agreed, jotting down the when and where.

That afternoon, he caught a number of mistakes as he double-checked his earlier work, and it was a relief when he was off the clock. At last, no one and nothing relied on him, and thank goodness, because he could not be relied upon. He needed to sleep.

But first, he had to stay awake and alert long enough to get from point A to point B. Mooching stale coffee from the communal pot, Hugo chugged a mug of battery fluid before running out to his car.

"Time to get that song out of my head," he said.

In a flash, Hugo parked, concluding a drive he'd already forgotten. He peered up at the red brick house, admiring the floral design painted on the backrest of the wooden bench on the porch. Though the wrought iron bars shielding the windows hinted at a history of burglaries. He buzzed up from a cracked panel beside the front door.

"Coming!" responded a voice that was more static than man.

Hugo heard footsteps and saw the blurred outline of a figure through the frosted glass spanning the door an instant before it opened, letting him in.

First, he confirmed Hugo brought the money. Then the artist said to call him Chris, and led him up the stairs. The building's interior was more rundown than its shell hinted. Every step creaked, and Hugo found himself pressing on the corners, where dust devils softened his step, cutting off the echo and muffling the crunch of roach carcasses. Reaching his floor, Chris unlocked the door with a large, likely antique, key. The patina plate listing the apartment number hung upside down from a bent nail beneath the peephole, clattering as the hinges screamed. Stepping inside, Hugo was able to see the whole of the studio apartment. Barely a hint of wall separated the kitchen-living room combo from the bedroom. Only the bathroom door afforded any privacy.

Centered in the kitchen-living room was an easel, hoisting a large sketchpad. Before it sat a stool, and beside it, a stepladder propping up a tackle box of supplies. Chris instructed Hugo to sit on what he called a couch but was clearly a dilapidated loveseat, and they got to work. Hugo described Anaïs, detailing her facial features, expression, and posture as she danced a path from the secrecy of night to the revelations of day. Chris focused on the project at hand, asking only for clarification, conveying no judgment. First, he sketched her as a whole, flipping the pad around so Hugo could see and confirm the accuracy. Aside from minor repositioning of the hands, feet, the pale birthmark on her chest, there was little to alter. Returning to his work, making the necessary changes, Chris had Hugo approve them before focusing on her face. Hugo struggled to articulate the features he could see so clearly with his eyes closed, and Chris flipped the image back countless times until, at last, they were both satisfied the sketch was an accurate reproduction of Hugo's imaginary lover.

"I could stare at her forever," he admitted.

Chris made Hugo an offer. He could accept the piece as complete and pay the agreed-upon rate, or, if he had the time and the funds, Chris would add color.

"That would be great," Hugo said.

Carefully tearing the drawing from the pad, Chris carried it to the largest light table Hugo had ever seen outside of a collegiate art department. He watched while Chris traced the figure on a new sheet, her leg extended beyond the other, gliding forward, a hand on her hips and the other raised in invitation. Chris lightly indicated highlights with dotted lines, faintly cross-hatching to shade the sky above. Then he carried the new drawing to his easel, clipped it to the sketchpad, and resumed his questioning. Black eyes? Was he sure? Well, it was his dream. Paler bottom lip than the upper, almost scarlet? How about her complexion? Fine, he would go darker. And what of the shade—was this the right brown? No? How about this one? Perfect.

When Chris turned the finished piece around, Hugo had to stop himself from sharing that he would have happily paid double for such a treasure. Thanking the artist for his excellent work, Hugo paid, and Chris stepped away, returning from his balcony with a frame.

"This piece is already very dark, so I'd suggest against hitting it with a fixative."

So saying, he eased the painting into its sanctuary. Then, weighed down by the vision, he walked Hugo to his vehicle, making certain the piece would be safe in transport. Judging Hugo's ancient Renault Alliance tidy, Chris placed the painting flat in the trunk.

"Be mindful of smudging if you want to swap out the frame," he warned.

They exchanged goodbyes and Hugo left.

Stopping home, Hugo hung the fragile beauty in the walk-in closet before heading to the pharmacy for sleeping pills. There would be no more allergy meds. He needed the good stuff. Eight straight hours of rest. Heck, more if possible.

At the convenience store, Hugo was interrogated by the pharmacist, who judged him inebriated. Once he'd convinced her he was safe to drive home, she directed him to the appropriate aisle. In case he'd been wondering, yes, he looked just as bad as he felt, and *he felt terrible.* Hugo's neck was stiff, his thumb half numb, and his eyes and mouth both felt like he was mid-trek across the Sahara. Pills in hand, he drove home wide-eyed, afraid to blink in case the lids sealed shut.

Luckily, the distance was brief. Soon, he was seated at his kitchen table with a tonic in one hand and a bottle of pills in the other. Initially, he'd intended to continue as he had, taking the meds right before bedtime. However, given the circumstances, sleep couldn't wait. Popping the sleeping pills, he followed them up with a gulp of Sweetwater. Slamming the plastic bottle on the table so hard foam splashed up the lip, Hugo wiped his mouth, then the table with a napkin. Dinner could wait until tomorrow. Hunger was hardly the issue.

Under the flickering closet bulb, Hugo jerked off to the woman he loved. Staring until, having imprinted her form on his eyes, the wall beyond showcased her inverted image when he glanced from her portrait—he scoffed at his own idiocy, then washed up. This was foolishness. She wasn't real, and all dreams, even daydreams, came to an end. But the more Hugo tried to bury her image under thoughts of work and other women, the more she stood out, until he could just see her standing beside him, brushing her teeth, shaving one day's stubble from her smooth, shining skull.

Rubbing his eyes and stifling a yawn, Hugo retreated to bed, acknowledged her following, joining him therein. Under a heap of blankets, arm tucked beneath his pillow, he successfully fell asleep imagining he held her curled back, heard her faint breathing as she relaxed into him—only to wake a mere three hours later. At this point he took more pills, which proved ineffective, resulting in those same waking dreams he recognized from the NyQuil. Eventually, he drifted off, but awoke no more energized Thursday than he had Wednesday.

Hugo called his manager. Without any preamble, he explained that he was unwell and wouldn't be in to work that day, nor the next. With luck, he hoped to have recuperated by Monday. Nate admitted he'd expected as much, remarking on Hugo's countenance the day prior, and so approved the time off without requesting a doctor's note, despite company policy. "Feel better," he said, and hung up.

Chapter 2
Riptide Away

How many pills could Hugo take before he was doing more harm than good? He had a hunch he should seek a diagnosis, note or no. Except, what was he supposed to tell his go-to guy, Doctor Meyers? "Hey Meyers, my man, I fell in love with the perfect woman in a day-dream earlier this week and now I can't sleep for thinking of her?" Meyers would toss him in the loony bin, where the song might well haunt him forever. Did they let patients have porn? He doubted a psychiatrist would see the value of the masterpiece in his closet.

Still, what if this restlessness was a symptom of a larger ailment? He vaguely knew of a genetic disorder that reared its malignant head through permanent wakefulness and resulted in sudden premature death.

He was being crazy. He wasn't sick. He wasn't dying. He just needed to go to bed and maybe Meyers would have the means to make that happen. Sleeping pills didn't work. Putting the song down on paper, while worthwhile, was not the cure. Hugo needed to tackle the problem from another direction.

After his morning coffee, he called Dr. Meyers' office. The receptionist said he would be free at eleven if that worked for Hugo. It did. Chugging another mug, he staved off creeping blips of microsleep. He didn't want his two thousand pounds of speeding metal careening into a passing crossing guard, baby carriage, or dog—or all three—a crossing guard, pushing a baby carriage, while walking their dog.

If a pharmacist thought him drunk in his sleep-deprived state, in effect, he was. As if to emphasize the thought, a line of cars honked at his back when he failed to pull forward as the light flashed green. Waving an apology none knew how to interpret, Hugo hit the gas, letting the roar of the engine overtake the curses flung his way.

Naturally, Hugo had left his wallet at home, but Meyers' office had both his card and insurance on file. The appointment preceding his bailed early and he was called in. Meyers had lost weight since his last visit. Between his newly firmed face, brown wavy hair, swirled mustache, and trimmed beard, Meyers was looking more and more like the Burger King with every passing year, though sounding more like Colonel Sanders. Leaving out the book, the painting, and all things sexual, Hugo described the extent of his insomnia, as well as the methods he'd been using to treat it. He then listed the consequences of his exhaustion, namely the mistakes at work, but also his driving concerns.

"Do you have any advice?"

Well, that was tricky. Was Hugo sure he hadn't been experimenting with mind, and perhaps mood, altering substances? Indeed, he was. Hugo hadn't smoked a joint since college, more than a decade ago. Did he drink? Yes, socially, but he hadn't in the past week. Not one beer.

Why would he lie? Had he been engaging in unprotected sex? No. Next question. Did he drink caffeine? Well, yes. Now that the doctor mentioned it, almost every beverage Hugo drank had some caffeine in it, be it coffee, tea, or tonic.

"Well, there's your problem, son," Meyers said. Hailing from Texas, perhaps Meyers called every male patient son, regardless of their age. Hugo dimly wondered at the female equivalent. Darling? Pumpkin? Sweetie, maybe. "Cut out the coffee, the caffeinated teas, and cokes. I'm going to prescribe you melatonin, but don't take it if you don't have to. Stick with herbal teas and water, and you might not need it. I'm giving you a note, too. No work tomorrow. You shouldn't even be driving. If we call you a taxi, is there anyone you can send to pick up your vehicle?" Meyers didn't mention Claire. She'd been a patient of his too, up until she took off for the opposite coast. "Not really," Hugo answered honestly. "I haven't been social lately."

That was true. He'd met Claire through the bank, and while her circle spanned the entire continental U.S., he lacked her outgoing nature. Those few friends from his college days that he used to call rarely answered, too busy with work, kids, and errands to meet up. Not one of them called him.

While he had work friends, he wasn't close enough with any to ask a favor. When Hugo told Esteban that Claire was out of the picture, he'd taken to inviting Hugo out for drinks after work, to bars on Saturday nights, and to his flat for football Sundays. Mostly, Esteban went out to meet women, and Hugo made a fine wing-man. But, with occasional fleeting exceptions, Hugo wasn't looking for a girlfriend. Esteban was as likely to call as Hugo was to decline, especially now that he'd witnessed perfection only for her to be unattainable.

"Would it be okay if I left it parked here overnight and came to pick it up tomorrow?"

Meyers considered the option. "Yeah, sure, but not tomorrow. Wait until Sunday or Monday. I'll make sure you don't get towed. Get some sleep. You're in rough shape, son."

Hugo thanked him and accepted the prescription. He taxied to the pharmacy, then home. The car would be fine.

Cold-turkeying caffeine was painless initially, and the melatonin bought him five hours rest, his record for the week. Friday, his head killed. Nestled fully under the covers, blocking out the sizzling light, Hugo clutched blindly for another hour or two of rest. He wiggled and writhed where he lay, groaning. Finally, accepting sleep wouldn't come, he dragged himself to the bathroom. A swig of tap water later and he'd swallowed more Aspirin, which failed to vent the pressure in his skull. In his youth, whenever Hugo was unwell, he'd sleep the hurt away. Likewise, that was how he'd handled breakups until now. Anaïs, his dream girl, not-real-girl, was the first woman whose absence robbed him of the abyss. It made no sense.

"I wish she were real," he said. "If only she were real," he whispered, close to sobbing. The hours marched on, and he begged a god he didn't believe in, to breathe life into the she that had to be, for otherwise, he would flounder, flicker, blink out, wasted as a story untold.

Noon came and went under the throbbing of his temples, and he downed more pills. Sorely tempted to brew a nice dark pot of sweet, *sweet* bitterness, he refrained on behalf of the stack of loan requests, doubtless experiencing a growth spurt, awaiting his return. The doc said no coffee. Sure, Meyers hadn't exactly warned that caffeine withdrawal was akin to a bitch of a hangover, but maybe the doc figured he'd already known that. Or, to the doc, pain didn't matter. And did it? Hugo had slept the night before. Wasn't sleep worth the headache?

As the pounding counted down the seconds, minutes, hours since he'd awoken, Hugo lost confidence in that assertion, and the TV offered nothing entertaining with which to distract himself. What else was new? Goddamned reality shows had taken over every channel. It was that, televangelists, or infomercials. Why did he even pay for cable? Hugo had a used paperback he'd been looking forward to delving into over the weekend, but he feared the eye strain would aggravate the throbbing in his temples. By dinner time, he'd written the day off as a total loss. Hugo nibbled at cold cuts, took his melatonin and went right back to sleep.

He dreamed of his angular-faced beauty. Hers wasn't the glamor to headline a magazine. She didn't have that gaunt figure, the hand-drawn lips, pencil brows, nor bleached hair that were in vogue. What he'd seen of her body bore nary a tattoo nor piercing. The nearest to a blemish was her birthmark, ridged like it had been lined with stitches.

More importantly, who was the *she* he'd based this fantasy on? From where did he know the model his psyche had costumed?

Asleep, he stepped into the story. He knew himself to be unconscious, recognized the setting as the vivid tropical swampscape of Saint-Domingue. His beloved led him through the muck, past reeds that slashed at their legs and over sharp stones that sliced the soles of his feet, to a wide patched tent hidden between palms. There, a plump woman perched, lit by the glow of dozens of tall red candles, bravely planted not a foot from the canvas walls. Two long scars crossed her cheek, highlighted rouge and flickering. To meet with the sitting matriarch was an honor, and he bowed low in her presence, though it was her daughter with whom he'd have wished to speak, to pursue, whose tent he wanted to share.

The woman barked a command he was duty-bound to accept. Rising, he gave an affirmative and made to leave, alone. Regardless of his desire, Anaïs couldn't be spared to show him the way, even if he had forgotten the path, which he had not. Still, be it instinct or lust, Hugo turned back, just for an instant, and was shocked to witness the silhouette of a large man towering over the figure of the matriarch, the telltale shape of shears in his hand, poised to strike.

There was a cry that became his alarm and he sat up. Stretching, he breathed, allowing himself a moment of introspection, to feel his body, diagnose himself. Was he well?

Not mentally. His mind and heart brandished retroreflective Out-of-Order signs. But physically, how was he holding up? His head didn't hurt *yet*. Although, another hour or two without coffee and that would change. No matter. He'd preemptively popped some Aspirin, and could it step it up with Excedrin. His eyes stung. He rubbed them, blinked, gaze tracing his striped comforter, wandering from the hardwood floors to the dresser that matched the bed frame, to the closet door, ajar. Focusing was no trouble and his skull felt fine. Just fine.

Hugo stood, walked to the bathroom, and checked the mirror. Still pale, but his sockets were no longer skeletal, and his flesh shone with the suppleness of this decade, not the next. He was healing. Getting close to the streaked glass, he smiled, then frowned. Those lines weren't gone, but faint. He may have been so marred for ages and not noticed until insomnia spurred him into self-consciousness. Or he might have aged overnight. Hugo relieved himself. His piss was a moody yellow, but no more so than while chugging coffee and its many substitutes.

Would he be going to work Monday? No. He had the note and, fuck it, when was his last vacation? Fully awake, Hugo called his manager and left a message on his work phone. Then he plugged in the fax machine, waited while it started up, and faxed a copy of his doctor's note to Nate's cubicle.

Two Exedrins later, he looked in his refrigerator for a potential breakfast. His usual was coffee and a bagel, the latter purchased on his way into the office. A home bagel either wasn't a bagel at all or was very stale. Hugo pulled his lucky quarter from where it lay beside his wallet on the counter, considering alternatives. There was a pack of chicken breasts on the top shelf. He had the ingredients for a chicken scramble.

"Tails, I offend some birds," he said, flipping a coin and catching it, displeased by the harshness of his voice.

When the timer went off later, he poured his meal onto a plate and slouched over the porch steps, eating a warning for passing fowl. After, he tidied and took a shower, Hugo heard the phone ring, but naked and wet, he ignored it. Only after having rinsed the suds off, did he turn the current off. Reaching for his towel, he'd barely wiped his front when the phone rang again. Curious, he wrapped himself, heading to the living room.

"Hi?"

"Hello. Is Jacques there? We were supposed to meet for coffee this morning," the caller said in a low voice. She spoke slowly, as if choosing her words with care.

"My name is Hugo and I don't know a Jacques. Sorry. Are you sure you have the right number?"

The woman apologized and recited the number she had on record.

"Odd. That's my number."

"So, I didn't dial wrong then?"

"Nope. It doesn't sound like it. Could it be their handwriting?"

"I don't see how. It's essentially block letters. Would you mind if I gave you my number? So you can get in touch with me if Jacques realizes his mistake and happens to call you?"

Hugo was cooperative, jotting down her number and wishing the stranger good luck on her Jacques hunt. She thanked him and hung up. Hugo got dressed, immediately shrugging off the mystery of the girl and her missing fellow in favor of time alone with the painting of his beloved.

He wasn't in the closet long, and after catching a glance of his darker-than-average mop, he figured a day in the sun, on the water, would help him recuperate more quickly. Burlington framed Lake Champlain, so there were plenty of small beaches to choose from. Packing a lunch, towels, sunblock, and the like, Hugo considered which area wouldn't be too crowded. Then, double checking MapQuest to make sure he remembered the way, Hugo headed out to Pebble Beach. He and Claire had celebrated their anniversary there the previous year, drinking wine over a platter of chocolate-covered fruit, watching the sun set over Malletts Bay. Of course, while they'd been snacking, he'd provided a four course meal to every mosquito within a five mile radius, judging by the bites. That was not a mistake he would make again.

Arriving, he applied ample sunblock, spritzing such a thick mist of bug spray over top as to constitute a shower. Memorizing where he'd parked, Hugo turned, keeping to the sidewalk until the waterfront was in view. The beach was as small as it was packed, and judging by the food trucks parked at even intervals spanning the lot he crossed to reach the sand, he assumed some festival was the cause. Shrugging, he kept on until he'd left the sand behind and was trekking along the tree line, his feet just before the water. Come to think of it, they'd ditched the actual beach last time too, and for the same reason, laying their blanket under the foliage while they watched the sky shift across the bay, painting the waves with sunset, then night.

He dropped his bag when he could no longer hear the revelers at his back, spreading out a towel for laying on and another to shield his belongings from the ground. The breeze wreaked havoc on his hair, and he wondered how the women were fairing in their covens, whether they minded wisps slipping into their eyes, slapping their faces. The effect was romantic on screen, much less so in reality, as the limited field of view encumbered all forward momentum.

Hugo brought neither book nor music, so he sat quietly, thinking. He wondered what his next lover would be like as he unwrapped and bit into his sandwich, then took a swig of tart juice from the bottle. His legs fell asleep, so he stood upon finishing and stretched, pacing along the water's edge, glad to be moving after his long, restless rest. Once the ice daggers dissipated, he paused to look across the water, where Red Rock Point should be. Instead, he had the oddest sensation that he was seeing the mirror image of himself and his own shore, squinting at a distant figure of like posture in a bright green top.

Peering down, he confirmed he was in fact wearing his old Nirvana concert T-shirt. Neon, he half expected it to glow in the dark when he purchased it in the nineties. Scratching at his hair, Hugo backtracked to his bag and pulled free his binoculars. Better armed, he inched near the waves that lapped almost to his sneakers and examined that coast opposite.

Sure enough, he zoomed in on himself, the binoculars masking his face and that of his match, so they appeared as insectoid monsters, though limited to two arms and legs as opposed to six of the latter. He waved and the other him waved back. They jumped in unison. *Uncanny*, he thought. Scanning what could only be a mirage, he checked each tree and shrub, seeking inconsistencies. It was as he was panning after a horseshoe crab or perhaps a piece of driftwood, that he saw the wave rise up, slapping down not far from where the other him watched, and the naked woman that stood in its place after the mighty claws of the sea receded.

"It can't be!" he breathed, staring at Anaïs. More incredibly, she stared back, her eyes firmly on his. The other Hugo was gone.

Letting the binoculars fall, he peered to his left where she should have stood, according to the reflection he alone seemed to acknowledge. Except, where she belonged just before him, sopping wet, yet resolute, her back straight and head high, stood no one. Hugo shook his head, as if the slight motion might revive his good sense. Bringing the eye pieces to his face, he turned again to that distant shore. There was here, but she was there, and apparently comfortable with her nudity. It seemed a shame society might demand otherwise. What value had laws, common standards of decency, when beauty paid the price?

Without another thought, word, question, Hugo kicked off his shoes and lunged forth, plodding through freezing torrents as they rose from ankle to knee to chest, at which point he ducked under and swam, shoving his head above water with every other stroke. He didn't feel, refused to acknowledge the cold, and silenced the niggling worry over how far he could swim. He was separate from the blades piercing below each rib, another entity entirely from he whose lungs quaked, shuddered, as a sudden wave pulled him low. It wasn't Hugo who coughed upon emerging, hacking with such ferocity the lake filled with his lunch, breakfast, last night's dinner. With every stroke he brought himself closer to her, and he told himself she'd warm him, love him as he must her, that she had to—for why else would he have seen her in every shadow, at the edges of his sight and nestled in each lid before he drifted off to sleep? And especially when he could not, for dreaming of her.

The current was dragging him away from the bay, away from Colchestor and Burlington both, towards the true Great Lake. He fought to maintain his direction, shifting to swim diagonally, never losing sight of the coast. When he felt himself freed from the stream, he reoriented at once, and kept on.

Hugo pushed himself through the frigid waves and the air that froze what the sun failed to heat, forcing his arms and legs to move even as his chest grew tight and his breath came in bits and puffs, until finally, he was crawling across the sand, spitting out the muddied water and collapsing before feet too light to be hers. Though he swore his eyes were open, told himself to lift his hand, to stand and bask in the glory of his hard won prize, he hadn't the strength to continue. So said the blackness creeping from the edges of his vision, a true dark, and not that of his favorite silhouette.

It was impossible for him to say how long he was unconscious, but he awoke with a start, found himself sitting up, his mouth layered with acid, nostrils on fire, body all a-shiver.

"Thank god! Buddy, I didn't think you were gonna make it. The hell got into you, crossing the bay like that? Didn't anybody tell you it's October? Lucky if that water's above freezing. Christ, man! I nearly jumped in after you, sent Curt here to grab my board!"

Turning to the speaker, letting his eyes adjust to the bright daylight, Hugo took in the upper-middle-aged man with the life jacket over his sweater and assumed him the lifeguard. As for Curt, his near-savior was gesturing to a younger guy, more freckled than tan, with a faint cataract clouding his left eye.

"Did I make it to—is this Red Rock Point?"

The lifeguard shook his head emphatically, bewildered and looking to Curt for support.

"Naw, man. This is Pebble Beach. You're in South Colchester."

Hugo nodded, recalled the mirroring and his purpose in crossing the bay. Standing so fast he nearly bumped faces with the guard, he spun around, looking for Anaïs. The towel they must have draped over him slipped to the ground and onlookers from all sides stared unflinchingly back, some having crowded near, feigning concern. Hugo hopped up, peering over shoulders, but she was gone.

"Wow pal, settle down. It's best you don't move too fast. You fainted, remember?"

"There was a woman. Black, stunning, with a shaved head, nude. She came up from the water. Did you see her?"

"Did you—man, I think you might have hit your head coming in. Or swallowed too much water. I don't know. I've got my truck about a block out. I can give you a lift to the emergency room."

"No! She was here! I swam out to meet her."

The lifeguard and Curt exchanged concerned glances, but Curt shook his hands both physically and of the situation.

"Well, you seem fine now. I've got to go, Jim. See you later for drinks."

The lifeguard, whose name was apparently Jim, bade his friend a fun spin class before turning back to Hugo.

"You sure you don't want to go to the E.R.?"

"Yeah. I'm fine now. I've got to run too, catch her if I can."

"Look man, any woman who doesn't wait for you after you've crossed a bay to meet her isn't a woman who's gonna meet you halfway, ever. Let her go, get home, dry up, and have a nice warm meal. You'll feel better with hot food in your belly and a mug in your hand. Alright?"

Hugo thanked the man for his help, his advice, and for not calling him crazy. Then he waltzed across the sand, past the nosy onlookers who ranged from obvious to subtle, sneaking peeks between their hands, looking over their shoulders, until he'd gone from their view.

With no sign of her on the beach, nor in the woods, he made a truce with fate. Just for today, he'd leave love be. Tomorrow was a new day, and having seen her once, not a figment this time, he was sure, he would see her again. Then, locating his shoes, towels, bag, he packed the lot and backtracked to his car before dawdling home.

"So close."

Chapter 3
Whiskey, Vodka, Larger, Cider

Tuesday morning, Hugo was an hour early to work, having jogged twice around the block, then showered. He'd normally have run farther, for longer, but given the state of his back after his big swim, he didn't want to over-exert himself, and anyway, he was busy. He'd been right about those loan requests. No one had pulled from his load. Rather someone, probably Nate, had added to his stacks, leaning papers precariously over the edge of his desk, in danger of being wafted by the gentlest breeze—over, onward, and downward, into his waste bin.

If only, Hugo thought with a sigh. Then, knuckles cracked and three treks out to the coffee pot later—each brief journey concluding with the silent affirmation that yes, he was still taking a break from the sultry springs of liquid energy—Hugo sat his ass down and got to work. The empty mug cooed from its corner perch until he swept temptation into a drawer, instead taking more Excedrin. Esteban was pleased to see his color had improved upon arriving, and Nate was relieved the towers were depleted by several stories.

It was Esteban, black hair swept under a grey newsboy hat, scarf tucked into his beige V-neck sweater over belted slacks and polished shoes, who convinced the far less stylish Hugo out for lunch. One quick trip to the cafe wouldn't dent his numbers.

"—and, anyway, you just got over being sick. You should be easing back into the workflow. Not skipping meals, working without breaks. Those forms will still be here when you get back. Come on. Stick season is coming. Leaf peep while you can."

Shrugging, Hugo donned his jacket and followed Esteban past neighboring cubicles, the break room, into and out through the bank lobby, which was strung with bat-themed garland and plastic pumpkin bins offering goodies (best ignored) beside each window. The rosy-cheeked teller with the cat eyeglasses gave him a wave, which he returned, digging deep in the wells of memory for her name and coming up with a palmful of oldies lyrics. The wind was picking up, twisting fiery wings from ancient boughs. Like monarchs, they danced in concert before swaying to a stop, layering the sidewalk, street, and stonework walls in their crisp blaze. The ground crunched beneath rapid footfalls.

Muna's Cafe was owned by a Catalonian woman, who was its namesake. Neither Hugo nor Esteban were one hundred percent clear on where Catalan was, knowing only that it was somewhere in Europe, and that its language was a blend of French, Spanish, and some other Middle Eastern tongue. As the cafe cemented itself as the go-to pastry supplier of the banking district, Muna herself worked the counter less and less frequently. A spritely teenager with blue close-cropped hair, thick glasses, and a filthy apron greeted them from behind the register. "Good afternoon! I'll be right with you," she called over the sound of steaming lattes, her high-pitched voice younger than her face. She capped and handed those off before taking the men's orders.

With hot paper cups burning flesh, cardboard cozies failed to shield, they claimed a table by the front window, resuming their usual debate. When would the next round of promotions be announced and who would be moving up? Esteban hadn't been with Northfield Citizens Bank as long as Hugo, but they'd both been around for longer than Veronica. However, while Hugo was immodestly the hardest working loan officer on their team, and Esteban was the most efficient—Veronica was the best connected. Hugo insisted she'd be offered the next spot on the commercial loan team, where openings were anticipated as several members were past the age of retirement.

"Look man, I've seen how things work. Veronica goes to the same church as Nate, and she's in a running group with his wife. Even if she wasn't dating a Walton—she knows too many people. She's tied herself to the decision-makers."

Esteban, naively in Hugo's opinion, remained convinced Hugo was a shoo-in.

"Nobody cares who she's friends with. You do a better job than her. Hell, I do a better job than her. It's gonna be one of us."

Hugo shook his head, taking a sip of the mint-citrus tea he'd reluctantly ordered, complying with Meyers' instructions.

"If she was bad at her job, you're right. They'd—"
Cutting the link between his brain and mouth, a poised, voluptuous figure in a marigold sweater dress cut across the street, gliding purposefully towards him, her feet never touching the ground. *It couldn't be.* Those wide slanted eyes, that straight round nose, black upper and scarlet lower lip, her features enunciated without any hair to distract. *It's her!* Reaching the sidewalk, she turned, striding from view.

Hugo jumped up, primed to run. Two times in two days? This was no daydream, but fate. Unless, he was hallucinating. The lifeguard hadn't seen her.

"Hugh? Hugo?"

Summoned back to his place by the window across from Esteban, Hugo shook his head, settling back into his seat. His throat remained raw after the incident at Pebble Beach.

"Sorry, man. Didn't mean to go off like that. What was I saying?"

"Something about me being right. What happened?"

As much as Hugo wanted to tell someone, anyone, about the beauty who'd waltzed from the pages of a library book, he swallowed the truth. Insanity was not the ideal trait in an employee, especially in a public-dealing loan officer who'd been vying for a promotion since day one.

"I thought I recognized someone. Did you happen to see a black woman just now? Shaved head, orange dress?" he whispered, hoping he didn't sound as desperate as he felt.

It was Esteban's turn to shake his head.

"Nope. Sorry. She's probably a bank teller or staying at one of the hotels. There isn't much else here, and if the dress looked clean, we can assume she's not working for one of those mom and pop shops down the road," he replied, in like volume. "Clothes don't stay nice in food service," he added.

Hugo's attention caught on the word "hotel," and he trembled. If she didn't live nearby, he might never see her again.

"Oh, shit! It's already five after. We're late," Esteban announced, rising from his seat.

"Fuck!" Hugo exclaimed, nearly following suit. His hands were shaking and he pocketed them on reflex. "Go without me. I need a minute."

Esteban tilted his head quizzically but shrugged. "Alright. See you in a few."

Hugo waited until his friend was gone before approaching the counter, where he ordered a blondie and another tea, draining his first.

The barista had just passed him his drink when *she* entered, pausing on the welcome mat as the glass door swung softly shut. Looking for him? No, that couldn't be. He didn't know her, and she couldn't know him. Except he did know her, had memorized her figure from her toes to her crown. And knowing her, why wouldn't she know him? A lump rose in his throat, but no, she sought another, found none, and approached the counter to order. He had to say something. Anything. *Try.*

The barista was handing her a to-go cup and his dream was giving thanks, turning away. She couldn't leave! Not before he'd had his chance.

"Hi," Hugo said, planting both feet before her, blocking her path.

He felt more than saw a myriad of intrigued eyes swiveling their way, patrons' ears pricking up.

"Hello?" Anaïs responded, visibly irritated, frowning.

Hugo should have flinched at the coming dismissal, but instead he was in awe of the sound, a trait that had escaped his visions, imaginings, dreams. Her voice was low, firm, with all the doubt of a queen.

"Sorry. You look like you're in a hurry, but I—can I get a moment?"

Her lips thinned and he could see the refusal in her eyes before the words left her mouth.

"You're wasting your time. I'm not from here and I won't be staying long."

"But—"

"No. Good day."

Hugo frowned but stepped out of her way. This wasn't over.

"I'm sorry to have bothered you. Take care."

She took a breath and nodded, shoulders set and chin high as she strode past, dropping a dollar in the tip jar on her way out the door. Hugo looked around. The barista kept her eyes glued to the pristine glass surface she insisted on wiping.

If she was staying at a hotel, if Anaïs was only in town for the night, then there was no chance he'd have convinced her to stay, no matter how persistent his appeals. Not even had he dressed with the sophistication of Esteban, been likewise suave, impressive. Regardless,

Hugo would see her again and convince her of his significance. He had no choice, believing them destined to cross paths again and again until they accepted their roles in the universe. Hugo was ready and willing, knew he loved her body, the fierceness of her gaze, her confidence. He knew too that fate wouldn't have gifted him to her were he unworthy.

If he told her everything he thought and felt in that instant, not only would he have returned from lunch exceedingly tardy, he'd also have terrified her into avoiding him from that noon on. So, without further ado, Hugo tossed his pastry wrapper and slipped out the door, to-go cup in hand.

The afternoon passed in a haze. Much as he tried to focus on the task at hand, Hugo kept circling back to the moment their eyes met. Yes, she'd been looking for another, or was that only what she thought? Mightn't she have been summoned by the sense that he was near, without knowing who he was? The hours dragged, and all he wanted was to race from his cubicle, the bank, into every lobby, restaurant, bar on that street and those surrounding, in search of her. But he'd fallen behind during his time off, and he couldn't justify stepping away without handling everything overdue. Between his consultations with new customers and the annual sexual harassment seminar that afternoon, it was a miracle he got any work done during office hours at all. Nate checked in to see how he was progressing as the day was winding down.

"Thursday and Friday's requests are about done. I want to give them another once-over before I finalize rejections and whatnot. Then I'll head out."

"Alright. And you think you'll be back on track by Thursday?"

"Uh, yeah. Sure."

"Glad to hear it. Well, g'night. Beth's at her book club, so I'm gonna go pick up the kids from soccer."

Thursday? He'd hoped to be fully caught up by Friday. Instead of running after Anaïs, Hugo slouched under a fort of request forms and their corresponding tax returns, W2's, credit checks, gift letters, scans of photo IDs, and rent-history printouts. He analyzed each in turn, slamming "accepted" and "rejected" stamps like gavels.

It was after eight when he headed out, exhausted and famished. The sky was dark, street lamps lit, horizon empty of stragglers as he located his car. He dreaded eating leftovers for dinner, but it was late for grocery shopping, and he was too hungry to wait for delivery.

"It's okay that I didn't look," Hugo told himself before taking the melatonin a few hours later. "Everything was closed anyway, and even if she was staying at one of those hotels—what are the odds I would have caught her in the lobby?"

Nobody hung out in lobbies on purpose. Those seated were waiting for the lines to clear, taxis to arrive, for their room to be cleaned. Then again, why would she be visiting Burlington in the middle of the week? And alone. Though he may simply have missed her traveling companions. Was she in town for business?

Before bed, Hugo stepped into his closet to ask why she'd rejected him, but the frame was empty. Swearing, he took it down, peering first at the void on the wall where two nails protruded, ready to resume their duty, then at the frame itself, inspecting the back, and the interior, as if she might be hiding within. Placing the frame on the floor, he looked at the closet. Was anything out of place? No. Well, what about the bedroom? The kitchen? Livingroom, or bathroom maybe? Retracing his steps, Hugo recalled the key in his grip, was certain he'd twisted it, felt the tumblers give way before he'd pushed the door in. He checked the windows. They held fast.

He looked through his filing cabinet. The checkbooks, his passport, were in place. Hugo wracked his brain for anything else of value. The TV, DVD player, his over-priced watch with its drained battery remained where he'd left them. Who else had a key? The landlord? Why would he have stolen a painting? Yes, it was precious to Hugo, worth every penny, absolutely. But what would it sell for in a gallery, or on the black market? An American passport would go for more. Could Claire be in town? Had she stopped in, expecting to find him home, bypassed his other belongings, but taken offense at the nude woman in his closet?

And when had he last seen the painting? The morning was a blur and he may well have dressed in the dark. As for yesterday, he'd crawled into bed after coming home from the beach, not even bothering to change.

Stumped, he called his ex, unsurprised when a stranger picked up. Apologizing for interrupting their dinner, he didn't bother with the inquiry before concluding with well wishes. Chris too didn't answer, and Hugo hung up, leaving no message. The artist wouldn't have known his address, had he the inclination to reclaim his creation.

"Our creation," Hugo amended. It wasn't the artist she'd haunted, taunting from the in-betweens. The painting would never have been considered, let alone articulated, without Hugo's passionate input.

That night he did not dream.

Though he lunched at Muna's for the remainder of the week, Anaïs never showed. Drowning in disappointment, he was forced to return to his desk, no closer to his ultimate goal. As per Nate's suggestion, Hugo spent Wednesday night working, making up for the hours spent lazing while ill. First thing Thursday, Nate was pleased to see Hugo's cubicle cleared of the stacks that had sunk their team's productivity ratings. Friday nearly passed in a blur of mundanity, except for a familiar silhouette catching Hugo's eye as the light turned green and he was ambling forward. Tempted to hit the brake, leave his Alliance running just beyond the intersection, and charge after the fleeting figure, he cursed the limitations cast by society, the law. Expletives loosed in a deluge of spittle, Hugo took the upcoming right, pulling onto a narrow side street and parking behind a dumpster. Struggling to maintain his composure, Hugo turned the car off and, having exited, locked it.

Returning to the main boulevard, he picked up speed, his shoes pounding against the pavement. He looked left, then right. Which way had she gone? Left. Definitely left, he thought, running in pursuit. Were people staring? Who cared? They would have run too, had their dream lover just disappeared around a corner. Was that where she'd gone? Swinging around to an emptier street, perhaps returning to her vehicle? Or had she ducked under neon signage, into one of the few open establishments? Hugo called out, begged her to wait, to hold up, but if Anaïs heard, she ignored him.

If she'd claimed her car and was even then turning away, he had no hope of catching up. If however, she'd wandered in search of food, entertainment, booze, then he had hope yet. So it was that Hugo poked his head into Mao Su's Dumplings, Veggie Heads, EZ Laundry, and Muna's Cafe. Fourth time's the charm, he thought, but they were no-go's, all. Backtracking, he peered through hotel lobbies, in search of an angular face. The longer he paced, the deeper the nighttime chill, and the fewer lights beckoned from behind more frequently locked doors. Two hours after he'd left work, Hugo finally admitted a fresh truce with destiny, found his car, and sidled home.

Too frustrated to eat, Hugo went to sleep, planning to hit the banking district anew come morning, but was ripped from a dreamless slumber by the shrill cry of his landline. Rubbing his eyes awake, Hugo rose, lifting the receiver on the third ring.

"Hey."

"Hey, Hugh. It's Esteban. I'm glad to catch you at home. I half expected you to still be at the office."

"Oh, no. I only stayed a half-hour late today."

"That's an improvement. Veronica said you were there 'til a quarter to ten on Wednesday."

Hugo shrugged, then remembered how phones work.

"Eh, I had a lot to get done."

"Because Nate was rushing you, right? That guy. Ugh. Anyway, do you have plans tonight?"

"Nah. I was thinking of catching up on sleep, though."

"You can sleep in tomorrow. Meet me at The Rock. It's that bar underneath the Hampton Inn. I'm already a few deep, but I'll be here awhile and it'd be good for you to get out."

Hugo had half a mind to say no but realized he was already too awake to get back to bed with any ease.

"I'll be right there. See you in ten."

Ten minutes was an underestimate, but barely. Deafened by the blare and whine of music booming onto the street, Hugo dropped the entry fee with the doorman, wished he'd brought earplugs, and entered the fray. Bodies roved in clumps, dancing, too densely packed for comfort. In the event of a fire, someone wasn't getting out alive. Hugo glanced above for exit signs and max occupancy posters, finding neither. Ah well. What were the odds of a catastrophe on the one night he'd ventured out in ages? Knocking three times on the nearest piece of wood, a table, he strolled on, ignoring the confused looks of those seated there.

Tailing a zigzagging trio bearing empty glasses, he meandered towards the bar. The better to cut through crowds, he thought, keeping his eyes peeled for Esteban. The bartender, a petit and heavily tattooed man, took his card, starting a tab. Sipping whiskey, Hugo followed another wandering troupe before spotting his friend, still in his work clothes. He'd claimed a corner table and was talking to a couple of bottle blondes. One was familiar. Nicole, Hugo thought her name was. Esteban had taken her out before.

When the spotlights swiveled to illuminate their straw halos, revealing laboriously painted faces, their cleavage sparkled. What was it with women and boob glitter? He shook his head, shrugged off the absurd trend, and beelined for them.

"Hey! Glad you could make it!" Esteban shouted over the music.

"Me too!" Hugo hollered, unsure if he spoke true.

Was the stranger, a friend of Esteban's "friend," intended for him? Ideally not. He hoped Esteban had called his roommate. Mike, he thought his name was.

"They work at Illustrious, down on Central."

Assuming he'd caught that correctly over the mind-numbing blast perforating his eardrums, the blondes were masseuses. That was great, and had Esteban introduced the duo to Hugo two weeks prior, he'd have been elated to make their acquaintance. Or at least intrigued. The times, they had a-changed, though.

"Cool. Nice to meet you guys," he said, looking from the women to the current of searching eyes, licking lips, grasping limbs, the prey and preyed upon. Closing his eyes against a blooming migraine, he shook away those pencil brows, drawn lips, and listless hair. They were falsehoods all, temporary, and wanting.

Esteban shared how he'd met the ladies, a short story, given he'd been Nicole's client. The topic shifted and soon they were laughing over workplace mishaps. Apparently, masseuses were not held to the confidentiality standard of psychiatrists and hairdressers. Hugo nodded along, taking small sips until he'd drained his glass. Esteban draped his arm across Nicole's shoulder, and her friend inquired as to what the guys did for work. Leaving his pal to regale her with the tedium of a loan officer's routine, Hugo excused himself, leaving for the restroom.

He was returning with a vodka shot in hand, prepped to endure more prattling, when through a break in a sea of faces dripping sweat from beaded foreheads and slick bangs, mascara writing a plea no one needed to read to understand, he saw her. She was seated alone at a high table against the wall, nestled in a corner. Tinted by the multi-hued strobes, unevenly lit by the mounted logos flashing neon, and shrouded in the general dimness, it was her. No less lovely than when she'd emerged from the wave, she was bent over a notebook, pen racing across a page, intent on her efforts. Her crown shone, and her jacket was of pale leather over a light blouse and jeans, any make-up so subtle as to not exist. In a room of sex, she was the Virgin Mary.

Without a word, he abandoned any notion of returning to his group. Weaving through the sloppy crowd, chest aquiver, he approached her table, arriving significantly more beer-scented than when his trip began.

"Hi. Can I sit down?"

He could barely hear himself over the music, and she didn't so much as glance up. It was a miracle that the stool opposite her wasn't occupied already, filled with a more intelligent, more attractive, funnier guy, or pulled away to an overflowing table. At a glance, there were plenty of younger, fitter men milling nearby, pecs protruding through too-tight shirts. Had there been a wet t-shirt contest and he'd missed it?

Taking a deep breath, Hugo squeezed by a swaying obstacle, the guy—or girl, he couldn't tell—oblivious to the miracle at their back. Claiming the seat across from her, he awaited notice, but not for long. At this conspicuous overture, she looked to him, and he took the opportunity to offer his hand.

"Hi! I'm Hugo."

Her brow crinkled, mouth thinning in a manner that did not indicate pleasure at making his acquaintance. No matter. Fate wouldn't be thwarted. As if to confirm the universe was on their side, a buffoon with frosted tips slipped back, knocking her forward, the tip of her pen scarring the lined page. Hugo was swept up in the foolhardy temptation to challenge the imbecile, but Anaïs rolled her eyes, shrugged, and moved on. With a slight shake of her head, she accepted and shook his hand, her grip firm. Yelling, she shared her name over the music.

"Hi again. I'm Anna."

Anna? What a nice name, *Anna,* or nickname rather, he suspected. It was as modest as her attire. Unassuming, yet dignified. Well, he'd gotten this far. Now, how to be interesting, worth her time? What could he offer?

"I'm so glad you're here! Can I buy you a drink?"

She shook her head, lifting her full glass.

"No thanks. I'm working, if you don't mind."

He glanced at the notebook, and sure enough, there lay a bulleted outline on one page and a paragraph littered with cross-outs on the other. In between were sketches of faces, bodies posed, dancing. People moved too quickly for him to compare direct likenesses to her quick studies, but they looked skillfully articulated to his untrained eye.

"Of course! I'm sorry to have bothered you. Would it be okay if I asked for your number?! Or gave you mine?"

The grimace twisting her bold visage was not inspiring, but Hugo knew he could win her over. Then she smiled as one with a secret, and he wondered if she might hear him out this very night.

"I have legs but no feet, a beak but no wings, and I grip without hands. What am I?"

"What?"

"If you can answer my riddle, I will give you my number."

"Okay! Cool! Give me a sec."

Hugo looked from her face, to her notes, to the table, with its sharpied scrawl, dents, and cigarette burns. There were no hints there hidden. Feet but no legs? Various fauna, furniture, and musical instruments passed through his mind. Could it be a letter? He remembered the words "ligature" and "X-line," from one of Evelyn's college art shows, but not what they meant. Drat! Could he phone a friend? Except those in the know were his exes, and he didn't have Evelyn's number. Nor Riga's, for that matter. And Claire was no artist.

He told himself to focus, that the answer would be something simple, something everybody was familiar with. Riddles were about subverted expectations, not trivia know-how.

Animals, then. Or bugs? A caterpillar, perhaps? Did they have beaks, though?

"Are you a caterpillar?"

"Is that your final answer?"

Shit! Did he only get one? Well, he didn't have another, better answer, and her expression was unreadable.

"Yes."

"That is incorrect! Thanks for playing the Anna Petro dating game! I hope you've enjoyed your time as a contestant. Now, I don't want you to leave empty-handed so, without further ado, here's your very own *sword*!"

Smirking, she pulled the plastic toy from the olive in her drink, passing it to him. Hugo reached forward to accept his loser's trophy, but pulled his hand back before it made contact.

"How about a second round? I'm sorry I'm being so forward. You're beautiful and I'd like some of your time when you're available. Not working, I mean. What if I flip a coin?"

It'd worked before. That quarter had convinced a senior to cast a bid for him when he'd rushed to join

Delta Eta Nu. He knew the guy hadn't especially liked him. Hugo hadn't been uniquely memorable, fun, or funny at those introductory parties. He didn't have any famous relatives, didn't come from obscene wealth, nor had he pulled himself up from the clutches of woeful poverty. He hadn't been adventurous enough in high school to impress a soul in *Never Have I Ever*—but everybody liked a good gamble. Sure, the frat life hadn't been all he'd anticipated. The connections hadn't held up, and even had they, not one was worth the strife to get in, to stay. Without his lucky coin however, Hugo would've been wondering what might have been, regretting his lack of charisma, charm, forever. This way, he knew the cost of inclusion, of success, and rejected it.

He could see rather than hear her sigh.

"Look," she said, obviously struggling to maintain an even tone over the rumble and boom of a lilting pop ballad, "I don't even live in this state. This is pointless."

"What if we got together next time you were in town? I live here, I work here, and I'll be around when you're ready. When you come back."

He wasn't sure that she'd heard all he'd said. It was a minute before she responded.

"Okay. Flip a coin."

Hugo smiled. "Tails, I give you my number, and you call when you're around."

"And heads, you go back to your friends and let me work in peace?"

"Deal," he announced, flipping the quarter up, catching it, and revealing the winning side without bothering to glance down.

"And that's the game! Alright, let's have it," she replied, and to his relief, didn't appear mad.

His ears rang above and beyond the music. Was that the chime of angels welcoming him into heaven in that very bar? Chuckling at his guileless enthusiasm, she turned her notebook to the backside, passing it and the pen along. In his clearest, neatest handwriting, Hugo wrote his name, phone number, and city, in case eager men approached her everywhere she went. She smiled, reading what he'd written, and his heart danced, drumming against his ribs.

"Alright Hugo Atmen the fourth. I'll call you on my next trip to Burlington, but now, I need to get back to work."

"Of course. Thank you for your time. Good luck with your project, Anna," he said, aware he hadn't the foggiest idea as to where she was from, and may well have misheard her last name—but it didn't matter. She said she would call him, and were she another, he'd have doubted her word. This was the character he'd imagined made real, however—a walking, talking, dream. Anna lived, laughed, and would come to love him. Such was fate, predestination even, a concept he'd never much considered, had no reason to, until the universe saw fit to guide his hand and his heart.

Happier than he'd been in as long as he could remember, Hugo took a moment to himself to order, then finish his lager, before grabbing a celebratory cider and returning to Esteban and crew. Nicole's friend was persistent, but he waved off every coquettish brush against his arm, up-down glance, and twist of conversation towards the physical.

"No, I'm not stressed."

"Nope. Not tense at all."

"Never been a fan of massages. Yup, weird. I get that a lot."

Nicole's friend was attractive, but she was no Anna.

Chapter 4
House Party Hardy

Saturday night, Esteban called. He and his roommate were throwing a last-minute get-together. Now that Hugo was up and swinging, maybe he'd like to meet their friend, Sonya?

"Uh, thanks, but I'm not looking to meet anyone right now."

"Buddy, you moped over a girl you didn't even know for like a week."

"What are you talking about?"

"Cafe girl, Hugh. You want me to believe you just started hitting up Muna's every day for no reason? Or are those cupcakes liquor-frosted and nobody told me?"

"Oh. Her."

"Yeah, her. Look, man, you struck out. It happens. But Sonya's real cool. You'll like her."

"I didn't strike out. She took my number."

"And didn't give you hers. That's a strikeout. Come on over, at least chat with my friend. She's smart as hell, and she does standup every Thursday, so you know she's funny."

"So I know she thinks she's funny. Look, I appreciate you inviting me out. And I'm down to come over, but I didn't strike out. Anna said she'll call, and she will, when she's back in town."

"Hugh, man, you're nuts."

He almost explained, but then Esteban would've been convinced he really was losing it.

"Don't worry about me. What should I bring?"

Esteban sighed, dropped a list, gave a time, and hung up. Hugo arrived on cue, passed the supplies to Esteban's roommate, and admiring the fresh additions to their collection of life-sized football star cutouts, joined his friend in the kitchen, where Esteban was making drinks. He was accompanied by Nicole and her friend, who stalked off. Hugo pretended not to notice, complimenting the cardboard athletes that Esteban absolutely did not pick out, and would've preferred anywhere but the communal spaces of his flat. As for the exiting masseuse, Hugo must have strayed into cold-shoulder territory at The Rock, but that wasn't his problem. Had Esteban warned he was bringing a playmate along, Hugo would've told him not to, as he had with Sonya, whom he met minutes later.

While blessed with a flawless porcelain complexion and a chestnut braid that trailed to her waist, at first glance, Hugo found her plain. With heavy-lidded eyes, high round brows, a long wide nose, and a slight overbite, her features were indelicate, androgynous. Yet she exuded a sense of confidence from her minimal make-up, cream jumpsuit, and straight posture that drew the eye. Hers wasn't a face for the stage, but a presence that demanded one. Rather than waiting for Esteban to announce her, she offered her name, requesting Hugo's in turn, though he sensed the question was for show. Esteban wasn't subtle.

A commercial shouted from a big-screen TV nobody was watching. "Jack Attack is back and more violent than ever!" This time, the criminals wouldn't be hunting him. After what they did to his brother, he was coming for them! "Now in Theatres," the narrator concluded, as a man was shown fleeing an explosion. Esteban tilted his head, rubbed the bristles of his chin, and listed big-name films soon to be released. Were they looking forward to any of them? Nicole couldn't wait to see *Ro-*

mani Romance, which likely offered little more than the title implied. Esteban, his arm around her waist, shared displeasure that they had to wait until February—while winking to Hugo, who hadn't for a minute pegged his friend as a Rom-Com aficionado.

Sonya, just toeing the line into the entertainment industry, happened to be friends with a couple of C-list actors. To be supportive, she'd be in the opening audiences for *Thirteenth Son* and *Step on the Crack*, horror films both, though gore didn't appeal to her.

"I see blood enough every month that I sure as fuck wouldn't pay to see more otherwise."

Oh, Hugo thought. She's *that* kind of comedian.

Nicole laughed, and he assumed that Sonya assumed Nicole was the only one to get the joke. To her credit, the comedian didn't elaborate, other than to say her preferred genre involved aliens, jetpacks, and space kabooms. Some drinks later, Esteban and Nicole excused themselves for faux obligations. Neither returned. Alone together, Hugo found Sonya's humor less crass when she wasn't engaging several people at once.

Chuckling at the clash between the surrounding mismatched furniture and Esteban's good sense, they came to the topic of roommates and she mentioned her dog, a senior mutt she'd adopted last year. His pastimes included barking at other dogs, squirrels, deer, and planes, catcalling—"Or is it dogcalling?"—the mail-lady, and snorting fire ants.

"Where do you even find fire ants in Vermont?!" Hugo exclaimed.

She shrugged. "Every-goddamned-where. You'd think the winters would kill them, but I think they burrow into hell until the frosts recede. Mushroom Butt loves his spicy dirt, and so far, I haven't caught him carrying any home. The first time I find fire ants in the house though, Shroomy's getting a muzzle. Or I'm laying cement over the yard." She raised her hands, miming the weighing of options.

"You named your dog Mushroom Butt?"

She grinned. "Oh yeah, I was taking night classes while living in Buffalo, uh, in New York."

He figured that she figured he wasn't familiar with the non-Manhattan parts of the state and opted not to correct her. In truth, he'd been all over New York, visiting friends, or friends of his girlfriends, before moving to Vermont.

"They had loads of art in the library, and this one painting, Mushroom Butt, cracked me up. I wouldn't have named him for that jawn, except his name was Moxie when I got him. That didn't suit, and my boy has the poofiest butt you ever did see. I figured it wouldn't be tough transitioning from one to the other, but as he's going deaf, it's not like he's coming when called anyway."

Hugo laughed. "Do you have a picture of him?"

"Hm. Maybe one or two," she replied. Shuffling through her purse, she dumped it onto the sofa, hand fast forming a wall, blocking chapsticks and a jawbreaker from rolling off the cushion.

"I don't think I've seen a jawbreaker that size since I was a kid."

"What? Oh, yeah—" she said, shoveling junk back into her bag. "It comes in handy when I need to shut it. I don't think before I speak. I mean—who does, right? But sometimes, I've got to. Can't be calling my boss a hypocrite. That'd get me demoted, maybe fired. Can't tell my cubicle mate he chews like a cow and smells like a pig. That'd be a trip to HR, and a fun-*fun* sensitivity meeting, probably cutting into my lunch break."

"So you work in an office then?"

"Yup. Stand up's a moonlight gig, barely covering the taxi to and from. As for my day job, I work at a bursar's office."

"Huh. I guess I have no idea how much comedians make. But go on, you can't tell off people at work?"

"Oh, yeah. And I shouldn't tell my landlord his wife is either cheating with a lifelong smoker or taking death growl lessons while he's out. Their divorce could mean the end of my lease. And while everybody says making a cop laugh gets you out of a ticket, I'm living proof *that's not the case.* So, when I'm about to piss off the powers that be, I pop a jawbreaker. Safer option, all around."

"That's a huge jawbreaker, though."

She shrugged. "I've got a big mouth."

At this, he examined her face. She was right. Her mouth shared a length with Julia Roberts, and her smile was just as pretty. Had he met her before the dream, Esteban's instincts were on point. Hugo would have been besotted.

"Fair."

She laughed and he had no idea why.

"Oh—here it is!"

So saying, she pulled an aluminum binder from her coin purse. Within the magnetic album was an accordion of photographs featuring a dirty wig in different outfits, posed before seasonal backdrops. Pointing to one such image, holding it close to his face so he could make out the eyes, nose, and ears that differentiated it from a hairpiece, Sonya gestured to where a tail should've been.

"See how it poofs out?"

And so the butt did, he agreed, chuckling.

Several pale ales later Sonya admitted Esteban invited her in hopes of setting them up, but she'd also been warned Hugo's head was in the clouds, that he wouldn't notice a woman hitting on him, short of by a truck.

"He did mention he thought you and I might get on," Hugo admitted. "And don't get me wrong—you're cool. But I'm kind of, oh I don't know how to put it—"

"Stalking a stranger?"

"Is that what Esteban said?"

"Not said, so much as implied."

"Well, I'm not stalking Anna. Although, I don't think anyone could blame me if I was."

Her brows wouldn't go any higher, but she flashed open palms. "Alright, I'll bite. Why do you think *your stalking* is justified?"

The Heady Toppers he'd drunk were fog to a car with broken headlights. Hugo knew he wasn't supposed to talk about the dream, but he couldn't grasp why, and without the why, his rule was powerless.

Beginning slowly, unused to explaining himself, he detailed his past couple of weeks—how she'd danced at the edge of view, glancing away, in no way demurely, from the moment he put down *Storm of Souls,* as if it wasn't yet time they met. Or perhaps, it wasn't time for her to know him. He described the sleepless week, Anna's imprint on his eyelids, every wall, page, shadow. He described the mirrored beach, swimming in pursuit of her only to end up where he'd started, of the fluke sighting of her in real life, real time, eviscerating his belief that she was a figment of his subconscious. He talked of revisiting where they'd met, and finally, of giving her his number just one night past, though it seemed weeks prior. Time moved slowest while waiting, he babbled, leaving out the painting, still unsettled by its disappearance. Chris never did call him back, though in the artist's defense, he may not have had caller ID.

Sonya had her finger on her chin, considering him more soberly than he, her.

"And Esteban doesn't know about your—I don't want to call them hallucinations—visions? I guess."

Hugo shook his head. "Nope, just you." And the artist who may have stolen her portrait, he silently amended.

Slowly, she nodded. "You're sure you guys have never met before?"

"I'm sure."

"Well, I can see why you're set on getting to know her. And I hope she does call, that it all works out."

"Thanks. Me too," he replied, slurring the last. "You're really pretty and fun to talk to. But I've got to see this Anna thing through."

"Well, I'm invested. Look, I'm gonna give you my number. This isn't a pass at you. Obviously, you're into somebody else—but if you ever want to get together *as friends,* or even just to let me know how the Anna thing is going, get in touch."

"Okay, I'm down for friendship."

They exchanged their contact information, with him typing his number into her phone, and her writing hers on a receipt from her purse. Handing the slip over, Sonya asked if he planned on telling Anna the truth.

"I don't want to start things off on a lie. I can't mess this up."

"But you're worried you'll scare her off."

He nodded.

She paused, regarded him thoughtfully, mulling over his predicament. Carson Palmer was staring at him, too, beaming with encouragement.

"If you really did read of her, see her, before you knew she existed—it's weird. And it puts a lot on her. But if she's *the one*, and you want to make this work, then you're right. She has to go in knowing where you're coming from."

"I just don't know how to say it without sounding like I should be locked up."

Sonya looked him over and shrugged. "Everybody's crazy. We've all got *some weird thing*, something diagnosable, worth medicating over. Only some of us hide it better. Maybe she'll appreciate knowing your brand of bananas from the get-go."

"I hope you're right," Hugo said.

Sonya switched to water and he followed suit. The roommate started kicking people out around three a.m., so they split a taxi with the blonde masseuse whose name Hugo never did learn. He was the first one out and wishing the girls goodnight. He paid, tipped, and come dawn, couldn't recall entering his apartment. He awoke cozy in bed, where he may well have been teleported by a passing witch, or one of Sonya's UFOs.

***

Pouncing first thing Monday, Esteban was waiting in Hugo's cubicle, where he commented that Hugo and Sonya appeared to have hit it off. With thanks for looking out, Hugo let on how they'd concluded the night, much to Esteban's confoundment. The remainder of their day was interrupted by meetings that served no purpose beyond making management feel important, and the entire mortgage loan team stayed an hour late to catch up. Couldn't let those productivity ratings fall.

Muna's Cafe tempted from across the street every lunch, but Anna said she'd call, so she would. Instead, Hugo followed Esteban to wherever whimsy led, grateful to be out, proud of his improved social life. He didn't need Claire's circle. Esteban was fast evolving from work friend to friend-friend, and Sonya wanted to meet up. Look at him go! From most meals alone to lunching with a friend every day—this wasn't mere recovery, but growth.

Work kept him busy, and Esteban did when work didn't. Friday, he met with him and Sonya both, for Chinese food. Then during football Sunday, Nicole invited Hugo to join her book club. Had he not caught the look her friend shot him, he'd have accepted.

The following week passed in similar fashion, although Esteban got the message that pawning girls off onto Hugo was a lost cause. Sonya confessed that she was casually dating a librarian, a woman Esteban knew and liked. They hadn't been ready for labels nor monogamy before, but were headed that way. Nicole's friend gradually forgave Hugo's earlier rudeness, though given her fresh penchant for drawing him into talks on skincare, hygiene, and reality TV shows, he guessed she'd decided he was gay as opposed to straight and unattracted to her.

Two weeks to the day he'd given his number, the phone rang, catching Hugo just as he was coming in from tuning the engine. Assuming the caller to be either Esteban or Sonya, he scrubbed the oil from his hands, dried them on a paper towel, and picked up on the fourth ring.

"Hello. Hugo here."

"Hi, Hugo. It's Anna."

His breath caught, snagged on his heart, no doubt. He coughed, cleared his throat, wishing he could clear his nerves.

"Oh, wow! Hi! You sounded so busy—I figured I wouldn't be hearing from you for a while!"

"You requested I let you know when next I'd be in town. Work has me in Burlington this weekend. Will you be free for lunch tomorrow?"

"Yes! I'm definitely free tomorrow," he said, whipping out his datebook and crossing out the notes there listed without a glance as to what they said. "Any place you had in mind?"

"How about The Gilded Mule next door to the Windjammer Inn, on Williston Road, at noon?"

"That sounds great! I'll see you there, then!"

"Okay. I'm glad that works out. See you tomorrow."

He continued to hold the phone to his ear for some minutes after the click marked the end of their talk. She'd called him. Anna had actually called him, just as she'd said, and he'd believed she would.

Tomorrow, he would convince her they belonged together. Or begin convincing her. However long it took, she was bound to recognize and succumb to fate. Who was to say she hadn't dreamed of him as well, and forgotten?

Hugo could be her deja vu.

Chapter 5
With Destiny

Hugo called ahead, setting a reservation. Having dressed himself for thirty-five odd years, it irked that fashion wasn't instinctive. Claire, Riga, Evelyn—his three big exes had styled him in turns, reminding him when his hair needed trimming, making sure he never looked the fool for important occasions. Now, when he needed their guidance most, they were gone.

It used to drive him crazy. He'd be all set to go, the Alliance running, when one of the trio would demand he run in and change. Were slacks such an improvement over jeans? Who put actual thought into matching shoes to their jacket? And sneakers were more practical for a wedding he was expected to dance at than those pointy-toed oxfords. Just this once though, Hugo tailored his outfit to the standards the big three had set.

He arrived at The Gilded Mule a half-hour early and was asked to wait on the front bench while the hostess prepared his table. The counter displayed cakes and pastries, while a blackboard above the register listed specialties du jour. Fifteen minutes before his scheduled reservation, the table was ready. Seated with his back to the wall, he sipped water, watching the door.

Anna swept in at noon, wearing a white sweater, belted at the waist over a tan skirt, and brown flats. Her purse was so slender, the strap invisible from afar, that it blended with her attire. For a moment she appeared bagless, and he believed her the only woman he'd courted who could go without. Recognizing his mistake, Hugo took the scale of her purse as an omen. Anna's handbag couldn't be confused with luggage, and he judged her less materialistic for it, less shallow than many of her sex. This was a woman who didn't have to carry her half of the medicine cabinet around. Spotting his wave, she approached and he stood, offering his hand.

"So formal?" she asked, taking it.

Hugo smiled. "I try to make a positive first impression." Really, he hoped she'd forgiven those prior.

"That's a good habit."

She relaxed into her chair and he settled into his. The waitress came by, taking their drink orders and detailing the lunch specials. Hugo was on the verge of ordering the seasonal mimosa, with apple rather than orange juice. But ordering after Anna, he followed her nonalcoholic lead. When the waitress returned with their teas, lavender for both, they knew what they'd be having.

"So that's one order of the creme brulee french toast, with a blueberry scone side, and a steak and eggs meal with refried hash browns. Anything else? No? That'll be right up," said the waitress, collecting the menus and waltzing away.

Anna excused herself to freshen up, and upon returning, cut to the punch.

"I should have asked over the phone, but—why'd you ask me out? It's lucky I'm even here this weekend."

"Well, this is going to sound like a line, and it's not."

"Okay."

Hugo sat up straight, looked her in the eye, and jumped in feet first.

"Not too long ago, I was reading this book, *Storm of Souls.*" There was no sign of recognition in her expression. "It's historical fiction with a hint of fantasy, far as I could tell. Plot revolves around the revolution of Saint-Domingue, a French colony. No clue about the author, though—the cover's half faded and I didn't see a name inside. Now the book describes a woman, the daughter of one of those leading the charge. Reading about her, imagining how she'd look, I found that when I put the story down, I could see her. She was nestled in the shadows, on the edge of focus. For a week, I couldn't sleep. If I caught a wink, I dreamed only of her. My, uh, dream woman," he admitted, sheepishly.

Hugo waited for signs of disgust, for her eyes to narrow, mouth to shrink linear, brows to scrunch, drop low. He waited for a gavel to slam, and some judge yet unseen to announce their verdict, "Not guilty, by reason of insanity!" He waited a moment for Anna to back her chair away, to stand, flee, to show up fate once and for all, but she stayed, ushering his tale forward with the casual sway of her wrist.

"Go on."

Exhaling a shaky breath, Hugo continued. "I thought I was losing it. It wasn't safe for me to drive, and I was botching projects at work. Things couldn't go on as they were. I was just so tired. Finally, I called out and saw my doctor. He had me cut caffeine, start taking melatonin. It worked. I was sleeping again, but I still dreamed of—of—well, of you. Except I didn't know the woman I saw was real, until the wave receded, leaving you on the other Pebble Beach." He paused, about to explain the mirage, but didn't know where to begin, so he muddled on without. "Though given I fainted right after, I carried doubts that night as well. But then

I spotted you again at Muna's Cafe a few weeks back. I couldn't miss my chance then, but I must've said the wrong thing. Afterward, I kept an eye out. Finally, I found you at The Rock, and now, well, here we are."

"Well, I don't know about a line—but that is quite the story," Anna said, before blowing on her tea and taking a sip.

"I was afraid to tell it. I know how it sounds."

"Outlandish, for sure."

"I can prove it."

"How?"

"You have a birthmark on your chest. Or perhaps a scar. It's shaped like a heart."

"You could've been spying on me. Or talking to my exes."

Hugo didn't have any better evidence to offer so he sat tensed, ready for the gavel to fall, before recalling that bizarre dream he'd had of the large woman in the fog-veiled swamp.

"In my dream," he said slowly, pulling the flashes in order, "the last dream I remember having, you led me to your mother. She was, forgive me, a rather imposing figure. The war was won and she'd just given me orders, a message I was to deliver. Then a man, I thought he was your father, swept up from behind with these massive shears. And, well, I didn't see what happened next."

Anna was quiet. Her pupils were fixed in place, and he daren't guess what she saw, but he imagined it wasn't the rainbow of frozen margaritas lining the short menu insert.

"Let's say you didn't just make all of that up to get in my pants—what do you think it means, your dreaming of me?"

"I think it means we should give us a chance," he replied, slowly.

"What of the women you were with at The Rock?" she asked evenly, raising her chin and meeting his eyes.

"Those were friends of Esteban, a buddy from work. Or, one is a friend. I think he's seeing the other."

"And you don't want either of them?"

"I didn't dream about them."

"They were very pretty."

"You're beautiful," he responded.

"Well, thank you. Look"—she tilted her head, running her thumb along her full lips—"you seem genuine, I think. I just don't want you believing this is more than it is. How about we have a nice lunch. Maybe get to know each other a bit, and see where things go. Cool?"

"Of course. No pressure intended," Hugo said, a little too quickly.

"Great. What are your interests? What do you do for fun?"

"Fun? Lately, I haven't, but generally I like to read. Mostly fantasy. On the weekends, I'm either home in a book, or out with friends. I jog, but I'm not crazy about it. When I lived in Boston, I gave their annual marathon a shot and even finished, but I won't be doing that again."

He smiled, remembering slipping, falling in the freezing rain, and the scrape that spanned half his leg, taking weeks to heal. The scar itched in response, but he resisted the urge to scratch at it.

"You?"

"Well, I like reading. Mostly, I stick with biographies. I enjoy learning about heroes and provocateurs, people who shaped events, rather than being led by forces beyond their control."

The waitress reappeared with their meals, the interruption knocking his next compliment aside. When she departed, Anna resumed her thought process, cutting into her french toast as she spoke.

"As for my other hobbies, I travel a lot. Depending on the destination, I'm usually hiking or checking out museums. Once or twice a week, I go to kompa, though sometimes I'll do bachata, or bomba instead. I like to try new things."

"What's kompa?"

"It's a style of dance, sort of a new age méringue. Lots of gyms offer it now, like zumba."

Not for the first time, Hugo wished he could dance. He'd tried—oh boy, had he tried—throwing his beanpole limbs into line dancing as a teen, nearly breaking his date's foot in an attempt at the sprinkler during prom, and stepping through months of ballroom lessons leading up to his wedding—the instructor shaking his head all the while, ultimately forgoing the ceremony, choosing not to witness the failings of his pupil. Most of a thousand dollars spent, all for Hugo to misstep and turn the wrong way about four seconds into their first dance as husband and wife. Riga had not been happy.

"You did mention that you're in town on business," he recalled, changing the subject. "What do you do?" he asked before taking a bite of his steak.

Anna tilted her head, appraising him, making a decision he hoped she would share.

"Normally I wouldn't volunteer this, but saying what you did took bravery." She paused. "I'm a matchmaker. All services rendered are kept strictly confidential, so if I'm seen with a client, it's better nobody knows what I do. Clients tend to be ashamed that they require professional assistance with something that's supposed to come naturally," she explained, piercing whipped cream-laden toast and bringing it to her mouth.

Hugo looked around as if to see these mystery clients. "Are they all—I don't say this insultingly—geeks who flourished during the dot com boom but forgot to learn how to date?"

"Many, yes. Not most, though. While, frankly, the majority lack social grace to an extent, the greater issue is they feel they missed out. These individuals see their peers wed, having children, and they assume they missed their chance. That they should have been fraternizing with the opposite—or sometimes same—sex, instead of focusing on getting their degrees, landing jobs in their field, networking, and overworking from one promotion to the next. In short, they feel they prioritized wrong and now they need my help catching up."

He shook his head wonderingly. "Are they mostly men then?"

"Yes. There's also a subset who only recently came to terms with their gender or sexuality, but again, they have that sense of making up for lost time. It's not that these people can't find anyone they're compatible with. It's that they're in a hurry to do so *now*."

Hugo nodded, his mouth full. Swallowing, he asked if she was only able to hook clients up with other clients, or if she had a means of finding partners who hadn't paid to enlist her services.

"It's helpful when I have a pair of clients I suspect are compatible, but unfortunately, that's rare. Thankfully, with all of these dating and social networking websites, I've been able to examine more potential partners for my clients, for free or at a low cost."

"So when you said you were working the other night—"

"I was reviewing my consultation with a new client, and considering whether The Rock would be an acceptable location for their dates."

"And you're in town now to meet with that same client, check this place out, and"—he paused, glancing outside—"to test the restaurant inside the Windjammer Inn."

"It's important both my client and their date are comfortable. Not everyone knows what they like. Part of my job is knowing people, their wants and needs, better than they do. Maitresse Matchmaking, my employer, expects us to be experts not just on arranging the who, but also the how, when, and where. I haven't let them down yet."

He nodded. "So you're working right now?"

She tilted her head left, then right, noncommittally.

"Sort of. My meal is paid for by my employer, and I will be writing up my review after I leave, but I expect it'll be less thorough than my usual ruthless standard."

"Because I'm distracting?"

"Yes. I'm paying attention to service, ambiance, and the quality of the food, but I'm sure there's stuff I'm missing."

Distracting, huh? He'd take what he could get.

"Do you have territories that are strictly yours, or does your job take you all over?"

"There aren't any limits, as long as the client can pay. I've been to forty-three states, Europe, Asia, and I've spent a single weekend in South America so far. Though I haven't checked out Central America. I've stopped over in parts of Africa, but haven't left an airport. Hoping to change that next year."

"Always being on the road for work, do you have a home base?"

"Of course. Right now I'm splitting rent with four flatmates in White Plains, New York. Three of them are still in school and the fourth works at the New York Times. He does something with their printing presses, working nights and sleeping during the day."

"Wow! How's living with that many roommates?"

"Not too bad. I'm only home four nights a week, and the kids are usually on campus. I used to live in the city, just because that's where Maitresse's headquarters is, but the rent was too high considering how rarely I went to the office. The less I pay for rent, the more I can splurge while abroad, or put away for later. How do you like being a loan officer?"

Hugo didn't recall mentioning his employer, but didn't comment on the oddity.

"It's not as exciting as being a super-secret matchmaker. Mostly I pour through loan requests, corresponding credit checks, employment verifications, and rent histories all day—to see who my bank's going to charge an arm and a leg in interest, and who they're gonna reject outright. The winners are indebted until they die, and the losers don't get a fancy new home. It's not what I pictured for myself as a kid, but it pays the bills and I like most of my coworkers."

She nodded. "Growing up is prioritizing obligations over wants. What did you think you'd be now, when you were little?"

Hugo paused, remembering, then grinned. "I used to read book reviews in the Sunday paper. It wasn't a big column, and I'm sure it didn't get much notice, but I figured if there was a job I was best suited for, that was it. No part of me wanted to be an editor. Nitpicking grammar all day still sounds like the fastest way to kill a love of reading. But being the guy who points out what works and what doesn't, plot-wise? Style-wise? That would've been perfect."

"Did you go to school for anything like that?"

He shook his head, grin giving way to a wistful smile, eyes shifting to the tablecloth.

"No. By high school, I'd figured out *money matters*. If I wanted to be successful, I needed to be a money expert, you know? One of those wall street bigwigs, somebody who knew how much to invest and on what. English was my favorite class, but pursuing a literary career wouldn't have provided the financial stability I was after."

"Most people would say you made the right choice. Too many have graduated with a ton of debt and only low-paying jobs to show for it."

"That's what I tell myself. Everybody knows that one art major who works at a coffee shop, or that music major, selling CDs out of an FYE. Shame. You're living the dream, though! Do your parents mind that you're never in town?"

"Ah, well, that's not an issue. They're both gone now."

"Oh, I'm so sorry to hear that!"

Shrugging, she replied, "Every relationship is at the mercy of time. Nothing and nobody stands still." She brushed his sympathy aside. "How about your folks? Do they live nearby?"

"My folks live in Massachusetts, about an hour from Boston. We see each other every Thanksgiving, Christmas, and I swing by when someone gets married or has a baby."

"Your siblings stayed close to home then?"

Hugo chuckled. "You have no idea. My folks helped my little sister buy the place next door to theirs and my older brother lives almost directly across the street. Dad worked for the fire department until he retired, my brother followed in his footsteps, and my sister is a cop."

"If your brother is older, how come he didn't get your name? You're the fourth Hugo Atmen, right? Or was that a joke?"

"I wish it was me being funny, but no. That's my actual name. When ma found out she was having my brother, she didn't want to continue the naming tradition. Said it was impractical, would cause confusion—that it would be annoying whenever either one of them had to file an official document. Just like it was for my dad, living under my granddad's roof. He *still* gets calls for his dad, and he moved out decades ago."

Backtracking from his tangent, Hugo continued, "So, anyway, when my dad lost a bet to his buddy Brendan, ma insisted he abide by the terms since it meant she wouldn't have to name her firstborn after our dad. Matter of honor. Once I came along, she was hoping I'd be a girl. Two kids and done, no naming confusion under her roof."

"Your dad bet the name of his firstborn?"

Hugo laughed. "Well, for background, he and his friend were a couple of barely twenty-year-olds, their wives were newly pregnant, and from what I've been told, they—*the dads*—spent the entirety of their respective partner's pregnancies drunk off their rockers. Doing nonstop dumb shit, getting all the fun out of their systems before settling down. Nobody would've enforced the bet had ma not put her foot down."

"What was the bet over?"

Hugo paused, recalling what triggered their bravado.

"In typical idiot fashion, after finding a few tubs of paint, my dad and Brendan decided to use it. Couldn't just get wild and make a wall pretty. Nope. These fools got it into their heads that it'd be fun to jump off the roof of my granddad's barn. Whoever landed the farthest out won. They each painted the soles of their shoes a different color, to mark their distance. As per their stipulations, breaking a bone was an automatic forfeit.

Drunk logic, I guess. If dad won, Brendan's kid would've been named Garfield. The joke was that he hates cats. Instead, my dad went first, breaking his leg in two places on the landing. Then Brendan went, and not only did he land unharmed, but also way past my dad, who was—I mean, you can imagine. At that point, he was distraught, lying on the ground, clutching his mangled leg."

"So this guy, Brendan, jumped after he saw your dad butcher the landing?"

"Yup. And the way he tells it, my dad was screaming bloody murder. Could have been worse, though. Ma was nearby to help, and she was so grateful her kid wouldn't be stuck with my name that she didn't get mad at my dad for being a good-for-nothing dumbass."

"What's your mom do?"

"She used to be a nurse, but she retired a few years back."

"Did your dad and his buddy stay friends?"

Hugo shook his head. "Nope. My dad cleaned up his act the day my brother was born. His namesake did not. They got on well enough for a while, but dad had a job, responsibilities, and the original Brendan—he just wanted to kick back, relax, let his wife handle every-thing. There was a falling out when I was in my teens. Ma and dad were close with his wife, and they couldn't abide how she was being treated. Her, they're still in touch with. Her kids were like bonus cousins growing up."

"Are they also living across the street from your parents?"

Hugo laughed. "Close enough. None of her kids left our hometown. In fact, her daughter teaches where I went to high school."

"Wow. I guess you're the only one to leave the nest!"

"You could say that, but I see the convenience of it. My folks watch the grandkids while everyone's at work. That's got to be better than daycare. Cheaper, anyway."

"Oh, certainly. I know couples where one parent's paycheck goes entirely to childcare. They justify it, claiming they're not working for now, but for later, for the experience, building a career."

Hugo nodded, though all those hours spent working for mere experience sounded wasted. At that point, why not raise the kids, then go back to work later, when they were of schooling age? Thinking of children reminded him of his near brush with fatherhood, and warily, Hugo led their chat down a bumpy turn.

"Oh, ah, and speaking of family, I suppose I should tell you I was married," he began, unsure if the miscarriage was too heavy for a first date. "My ex and I, we weren't together long, and ultimately, weren't compatible." Riga was exhausting, unflinchingly dramatic, with expensive taste. And while her own salary was nothing to scoff at, she'd anticipated a higher income than Hugo could hope to make. "No hard feelings, of course." Yes, she'd taken the house, furniture, everything really, in the divorce. But to be entirely fair, her father'd paid for the majority, and really, the loss of property was a pittance, so glad was he to be rid of her. "I won't say we've stayed friends, as honestly, we're not in touch. But I bear her no ill will and assume she feels likewise, if she thinks of me at all."

Anna didn't blink at the news he'd been married before. At their age, he supposed divorcees made up much of the dating pool.

"Well, that's nice. Too often you hear about unpleasant divorces. Sometimes a clean break is best. Better to move on, never looking back, than to dwell on who hurt who more, who was more in the wrong. Leave that to the lawyers, right?"

"Right. Thankfully, we had a prenuptial agreement. With that, the legalities of our separation went smoothly, didn't drag on for months."

She nodded, turning to face the blackboard above the display counter. He realized they'd finished their meals. He wasn't ready to conclude their date, not on that note, and searched for a way to prolong their conversation. Luckily, she took the initiative, moving right along.

"Want to get dessert? I know it's early, but it's difficult to argue with the belly, as it has no ears, and The Gilded Mule's known for their pies."

Hugo was grateful not to have to suggest it himself. "Who can say no to pie?"

When the waitress returned for their plates, she left a fresh kettle and stepped away with their orders. Anna excused herself to wash her hands. "I think I got syrup on them," she remarked, tucking in her chair.

Hugo people watched during the brief interim while she was gone, and wasn't sure what to talk about as she reclaimed her seat. Then it dawned on him that he knew very little about her past, so he asked—did she have any ex-husbands or kids he might want to know about?

"Not at all. My mom would say I'm a free spirit. No marriages, kids, roots, but I have friends all over. When I see them, I try not to talk about work, because I have to lie then, given most work in hospitality, at hotels and the like."

"What do you say you do, when they ask?"

"A little of this, a little of that. Odd jobs like house sitting, nannying, teaching crafts at seasonal resorts. Stuff that's hard to check up on, mostly. It's hard to make friends with co-workers since there are few occasions for us to meet, and only ever for conferences at headquarters."

Their waitress laid out their pie slices, which did indeed live up to the hype, while they shared stories of riding the subways in Manhattan, or "the city," as she called it. The fewer people on board, the crazier their fellow passengers. They'd both witnessed nudity, overdoses, and exotic animals, in and out of carriers. Reports of cars on the tracks seemed a regular occurrence.

"And I didn't even come through very often! Just for the occasional art show!" Hugo exclaimed.

"Was there any other first date stuff we forgot to talk about?" Anna asked as dessert was wrapping up.

He considered, appreciating her directness. "Nothing that can't wait for a second date, I think. Can I have your number?" he asked, hoping he exuded more confidence than he felt.

"Sure," she said. "This is my cell number." In cheerful round lettering, she wrote on a napkin, adding her name underneath. He noticed that she'd written Anna, not Anaïs, and wondered if Anna was her full first name or merely the Anglicized version thereof?

"Anna Petro," he read out loud, looking the scrap over as if to etch every digit into his bones. Then, Hugo lost his balance as he reread the familiar.

"This is going to sound odd, but were you by chance looking for someone named Jacques a few weeks back?

She gasped. "What? Yeah. I was. We were supposed to grab coffee, but he never showed."

"Huh. The number he gave you then, the wrong number—that was mine."

"Small world," she breathed.

Hugo anticipated that he'd be pondering the implications of that coincidence for quite some time, but those hypotheticals could wait. He had her number. She had his. All he could do was be ready for whenever she came back around.

"Do you know when next you'll be in Burlington?"
She did not, but promised to keep in touch.

Chapter 6
So Far, So Good

Hugo got home, picked up his book, and read next to the phone, just in case. Esteban rang and it was an effort not to swear in disappointment. Did Hugo want to meet up and watch Sonya on Saturday? It was the best slot of the week, and she'd kissed a lot of ass to snag it. Would her efforts be in vain?!

Rationalizing that Anna wouldn't call so soon after their date and wouldn't hold it against him that he occasionally went out, and therefore might not always pick up—concessions any rational person would make—he agreed to leave the house. However, he swore to buy a cellphone *soon*.

There was no need, prior. When he was out, he was out. He wasn't the type to make plans while in the middle of socializing and didn't have so many friends that overbooking was an option, let alone an issue. However, the thought that she might call and suffer the rejection of a phone unanswered sparked such a wave of nauseous anxiety, he resolved not to allow for that possibility in the future.

Sonya was the third act of five, stepping up in a billowy amber blouse over green pleated slacks and gold heels to raucous applause. Hugo wasn't sure if she'd built a local following or if the largely male audience was pleased to see a fit, trim woman perform. She introduced herself as the emotional support mom of Mushroom Butt and began her routine by picking the mickey out of his telltale snort.

"My boy doesn't bark inside, but I always hear him coming!"

The audience cackled at his namesake, spicy dirt addiction, and fear of stuffed animals. She segued into accusing outdoor-cat owners of struggling to commit.

"Why else would any self-proclaimed cat lover leave their babies outside? For the same reason I adopted Mushroom Butt—they won't live long!"

Results were mixed. Boos droned beneath gales of laughter, and unflinchingly, Sonya called hecklers out, listing dangers to cats in the wild, namely traffic and unloved little boys.

"To be fair though, at least my short-lived burden loves me. What do you get, wanna-be cat parents? *Barely concealed disdain?!* I get it. If you're gonna be a dick to your pets, at least cats will be a dick back, right? You die, and guess how long your cat will wait to eat you? Well, go on now, guess!"

Shouted responses varied from a couple of hours to a month.

"Trick question! Cats won't wait! Better not be a heavy sleeper! Might wake up to Puss-N-Boots fang-deep in your eyeballs. Hope you didn't need those. You know, I dated a guy with a cat for three years. Dude had a history of violent psychosis. Had been hospitalized and everything! But guess who wasn't allowed to sleep in my bed? Him, or the *cat*?"

Those offended earlier were won back by her long-winded hyperboles. Sonya moved on to mocking those pathetic souls whose entire personalities revolved around their pets before launching into a diatribe against horse girls, "whose grip on reality is tenuous at best, living off of their fathers until they get a husband—bleeding him dry, meanwhile only ever riding the horse! I see you shaking your head, Goldie in the crop top. What's his name?! *Black Beauty*?!"

Esteban and Nicole were beside themselves, offering a standing ovation as she concluded her final bit, waving goodnight to a room of drunkards, and making way for comedian number four to take their place on the stage.

Sonya joined their table and the gang offered quiet congratulations as her replacement diagnosed Vermonters as cider addicts in dire need of rehabilitation. This evoked laughter at their table, as their lot had switched to non-alcoholic ciders and just ordered one for Sonya. Her librarian was out of town for the weekend, or Esteban was sure she'd have been there.

Sonya stayed behind to talk shop after the show. The gang congratulated her again and went their separate ways, Hugo in his car, Esteban and Nicole in a shared taxi.

Hugo was seated on the mall's front steps when a security guard in a wide-brimmed black hat, that could have passed for a UFO with enough wind, unlocked the vast row of glass doors. Not having realized that the mall, like every other God-fearing establishment, opened late on Sundays, Hugo had been waiting since nine. Not remotely discouraged, he headed inside, taking off his gloves and unzipping his coat.

Past a row of coin-release firetruck-shaped strollers was a large map. Luckily, his landline provider had a store in the mall. Hugo had exactly zero desire to order a cell phone through some overworked customer service representative operating out of a call center in the midwest, trying to meet a quota for customers helped per hour. He wanted to walk in, talk to a real live person, buy the damned thing, and go home with it that same day. No sitting on hold for an hour. No waiting for the mail. No finding out from his bill, a month later, that there were hidden fees for texting out of staters or some such nonsense. The salesperson was going to have far more difficulty rushing him out than an agent over the phone.

Still early, his steps rang loud against faint seasonal tunes playing from distant speakers. Monsters this, howling that—oblivious to the commonalities, Hugo was surprised to see the salesperson in a gecko jumpsuit, assuming he'd walked into a promotional event at the wrong franchise.

"Happy Halloween! How can I help you?"

Doy! How could he have forgotten? Esteban mentioned he and Nicole were dressing as Marilyn Manson and Rose McGowan, but Hugo'd figured his friend was being a classic oversharer. Welps. That meant Esteban would be inviting him out later.

"Hi. I'm looking to get a cell phone."

The gecko laughed. "Well, we've got plenty of those. Can you be more specific?"

Hugo spelled out what he needed, which wasn't much, and made inquiries as to the fees that would come sneaking, pouncing when least expected. The gecko clarified service fees that could have caused confusion, assisted Hugo in making an educated purchase, and moved on to the next customer. Hugo left a couple hundred dollars poorer, but with a functional mobile phone in his shopping bag, content that he hadn't been ripped off.

He set it up as soon as he got home. His first call was to his landline, assuring he hadn't botched the process, and his first text was to Anna, notifying her that he'd gotten one of those new-fangled cell phones and this was his number. Spelling was a drag, hitting a button four times just to type the letter "S," and he hoped Anna wasn't a big texter. How much more expensive would a phone with a real keyboard have been? He wondered, ill-motivated to backtrack and make that swap.

Anna did not respond.

As predicted, or rather remembered, as Esteban forewarned only for Hugo to have forgotten, he invited Hugo out to a party at Nicole's.

"I think I'm heading over around four, but I'll be leaving early. Work tomorrow, you know?"

Hugo did know. "Sure. Who all is coming?"

"Nicole's friend. Sonya and Holy Joe might show."

"Holy Joe?"

"That librarian she's been seeing."

He figured there was a story behind the nickname, but it could wait.

"Okay. Cool. What am I bringing? And where is this place?"

Esteban told him, and Hugo wrote everything down. Before hanging up, Hugo gave his new cell number.

"It's about time you got with this century! You'll be on Myspace next!"

"I don't know about that," Hugo responded. Claire quit trying to sell him on AIM during their first year together. He'd seen how she had to respond to every ping, then later, with Myspace, every comment, and he couldn't justify the added obligations. Who needed the hassle?

Before he left to pick up bulk McDonald's nuggets and Burger King fries for the party, Hugo rummaged through his closet for old costumes. There was his Van Gogh get up, and he had plenty of tape to cover his ear, but who would recognize him without Evelyn in her Starry Night dress? The piñata llama was a two-person ordeal, and it had shed a ton of streamers since he and Claire wore it. He should've tossed it in the interim. Oh—that puffy white hat! That went with the chef's jacket and those black pants—leftovers from his engagement to Riga. She'd dressed as a wedding cake, pulling cupcakes from muffin tin pockets and handing them out to guests. Not especially crafty herself, she'd purchased an antique crinoline steel cage and had the pockets inserted by a hired seamstress, who'd had to enlist the services of a welder to complete the project.

Riga's costume was so ostentatious that there were those present who, until they wondered to the hosts out loud, weren't clear on whether they'd misread their invitations. Was this a wedding shower or a Halloween party?

It had fallen to Hugo to wave off the apologies of those sheepish, giftless guests, explaining they'd done nothing wrong. "I mean," he'd said again and again, "you've met my fiancé. She'd wear an evening gown to a hike if the mood suited her." The more cameras, the crazier her get-up. He'd feigned bemusement, affection, after wasting days trying to talk her out of that overpriced cake dress—arguing that it was too much, would give off the wrong impression.

So what if she wanted to celebrate their engagement and Halloween at the same time? So what if their actual engagement party was a few months away, and they'd just sent out the invitations? She was excited! Why wasn't he? He hadn't a kind answer to that and so had said nothing at all.

Hugo sighed, reflecting on his failed romances. Were all of his costumes half of a pair? Searching, he wiped the dust off a ketchup, missing its mustard, Mulder's suit, missing Scully, and the long-stranded Chuck Noland's shorts, sans Evelyn's homemade Wilson, before giving up. *Fine*, he thought. "I'm bringing McDonald's? I'll be ketchup. Someone will think that's funny."

And he was right. Esteban cackled at the sight of a 5'9" ketchup bottle arriving under a smorgasbord of fast food bags. Incense had been lit in the living room and bathroom, but sandalwood couldn't compete with the Eau de McDonald's.

Nicole introduced Hugo to more coworkers, all tan, blonde, and leggy with shimmering bosoms. He foresaw difficulties telling them apart and tried to memorize each face-name combo to no avail. Tattoos made for better identifiers, but he realized too late, after the introductions. Her friend from The Rock was there with a new guy, their costumes from Grease, and Esteban kept tripping, struggling to walk in his platforms.

"Just take them off. No one will care," Nicole suggested, but he refused.

"I bought them to wear for one day so that's what I'm going to do."

"Men," Nicole breathed, rolling her eyes, and Sandy's doppelganger nodded, teased waves swaying up and down.

Hugo could smell the hairspray from where he stood. Snacking, he leaned over his friends' corner of the couch. He couldn't bend in his suit, but he didn't intend to stay long, and didn't mind. When Sonya joined them, she'd already filled her plate and was being trailed by a sun-kissed woman in a shoulder-length salt and pepper wig, with a faux beard to match. Her ears were dotted with studs, lining the edge like the path on a pirate's map. Her nose was pierced, the stud clear, likely not to distract from her costume, and she bore a bar through one brow, a scar having split the other. So, she wasn't "Holy" then, Hugo clarified. She was "Holey." Well, that explained *that* moniker. Sacred geometry poked from beneath her apricot collared button-down, beaded necklaces trailing to the waist of her pants. In one hand, she held a wooden pipe, doubtless in character. In her other was a plate of fries, carrot sticks, and chips. A vegetarian then, but probably not a vegan, risking anything fried by a corporation, Hugo observed.

"Hey guys, this is Joanna."

Hugo offered his hand, introducing himself. Nicole followed suit, Sandy having wandered off.

"Who are you supposed to be?" Esteban asked.

"Alan Watts."

The men had never heard of the guy, and Sonya admitted to only having learned of him through Joe, but Nicole was familiar with his philosophies.

"Not that I've read any of his books, yet," she confessed, though she had a few in her possession.

In proof, she disappeared before returning with a modest stack of volumes. Hugo scanned the titles, dismissing the lot. Self-help books, by the looks. Esteban, however, being more familiar with Joe, said that was just like her, "Dressing up as a hippie philosopher most people have never heard of."

"So how do you all know each other?" Hugo asked.

"Oh, Esteban and I went to high school together."

"Yeah, before you went off and joined a goddamned seminary, ya nut," was Esteban's affectionate response.

Hugo wasn't especially religious, but he was pretty sure seminaries were colleges for wannabe priests. This woman didn't look like any of the deacons he'd grown up tuning out.

"You went to seminary school?" he asked, skeptical.

"Oh yeah. Left the church the second I received my degree, though."

"Alright then." Not wanting to pry into how an up-and-coming nun experienced a loss of faith, Hugo was ready to drop his inquiry, but Esteban wasn't one to let a funny story go untold.

"See, my pal here discovered a power stronger than that of our Lord and Savior, the Sweet Baby Jeezum Crow."

"And what was that?" Hugo wondered out loud.

Esteban exclaimed, "Drugs!" as Joe replied, "People."

Shaking her head with a laugh, Joe turned back to Hugo. "Esteban's kind of right. I didn't do any drinking or drugs while I was in high school."

"Yup. I called her chicken shit all the time."

"Come now. You mean to tell me peer pressure doesn't work?!" Sonya interjected, her remark earning smirks from Joe and Esteban both.

"My folks were super strict. Christian fundamentalists, so you can imagine. The Lord's word was *the word.* Now, in the seminary, I got to know, not just that word pretty well, but also its history. Learning that the word had undergone revisions abiding to the arbitrary cultural norms of the very fallable people of the time, diminished its hold. Nancy said weed is a gateway drug, and yeah, that's ridiculous most of the time, but in my case, I guess she was right."

Hugo could understand that. If smoking pot hadn't sent Joe careening off a roof or on a killing spree after all of D.A.R.E.'s fear-mongering, who was to say other psychedelics hadn't been misrepresented as well?

"So you moved on to harder stuff?"

"Yup. Not right away, but eventually, on one trip or another, I came to see that we, *people*, are gods. We create. We are the power—our bodies, our temples."

"And how better to worship than with ornamentation?" Nicole suggested, eyeing what body art Joe's costume failed to conceal.

"Exactly."

"So," Hugo mulled, "When Esteban calls you Holey Joe. He's using the religious holy? *And* the holes, holey?"

"You're still calling me that?!" she yelled, hands closing into fists as she turned to face the accused.

Esteban's face fell, and he opened his mouth to explain, but his longtime friend doubled over with laughter.

"I'm just fucking with you!"

What could have been an awkward moment dissolved into chuckles, and Nicole excused herself to greet incoming guests. The living room had become so crowded with pop culture icons and sexified princesses, animals, and inanimate objects that Hugo could barely see the furniture beyond the rattan couch where the gang sat and the folk-patterned carpet on which he stood. Chattering drowned out the mellow tunes drifting from the boombox, and the musk of a towering scarecrow's authentic dreadlocks overwhelmed both incense and whatever fried goodies hadn't yet been consumed.

Sonya had just finished explaining how she and Joe met when Hugo's pocket vibrated. He looked to see who'd texted, as if he hadn't only given his number to two people—one of them standing before him. Anna wished Hugo a "Happy Halloween" and confirmed she'd added his cell number to her contacts. Unsure how best to reply, he put his phone away.

"Anybody want anything to drink?"

"Who was that?" Esteban asked, not letting Hugo escape that easily.

"Anna."

"Cafe girl?"

"Uh, yeah. We got lunch together yesterday. She was in town for work."

"You said you were going to keep me updated!" Sonya exclaimed, but she was beaming.

"Sorry. She called Friday. There isn't much to tell. Anna lives in New York, but she travels a lot. Sometimes she travels here, and now that we've exchanged numbers, we can get to know each other."

"I just don't see it," Esteban said. "You've been acting—what's the word?—betrothed, since you gave her your number. Hell, since the cafe! Now you're set on dating long distance? What's so special about her?"

Sonya gave Hugo a searching look before offering a distraction.

"Oh, there goes Michael Jackson. Think he can moonwalk?"

Esteban looked where she pointed, and assuming he'd lost Michael in the crowd, wandered off to ask.

"Thanks," Hugo said.

"Anytime. Now about those drinks—do you mind grabbing us a couple of IPAs on your way back from texting your girl?"

Hugo laughed. "Sure thing."

Hiding by the drink table, all he could think to text was, "Happy Halloween! I hope you're having a spooktacular night!" Hugo pecked it out, one painstaking letter at a time, checked the message twice for typos, and hit send. Then, hoping he didn't sound lame, he returned to the gang with their drinks.

He got the hang of texting, though witnessing the ease with which Esteban utilized the keyboard on his phone—hitting one button one time per letter—Hugo regretted buying the bargain model. When he went to vote, a poll worker instructed him to turn off his phone. Being his first time attempting to do so, they had to show him what button to hold.

Before, Hugo appreciated focusing wholly on the present, without being nagged by the notifications disrupting his peers. Now, unless he was on the clock, he had no excuse for not responding. When Esteban rang him at the grocery store, he was forced to balance what he'd trusted to two hands with one. At the library, he muttered apologies, silencing his ringer and texting the caller back. Worse, once word got around that he had a cellphone, he couldn't politely keep from tying himself more tightly to every friend of a friend, relative, and workplace acquaintance that asked for his number. Suddenly his mom wasn't reduced to voice-mails, but texts, heedless of the hour and confounded by delays. His dad preferred the cordless, and his other children, else wise Hugo would have lied, pretending he was relegated to his landline until the old man died. Esteban helped Hugo download "She's a Rainbow" by The Rolling Stones as his ringtone and alarm, but by the end of the first week, he flinched violently at the sound. Soon, anxiety became aggression, and finally, hate. After his third round of heart palpitations one afternoon, Hugo set it to vibrate.

Still, it was worth it, he told himself, when after work, he asked Anna how her day was going, and she shared the history of Joan of Arc, whom she was reading about, and when she described her day off, the calluses lining her palms after an afternoon spent laying tiles with Habitat for Humanity. It was worth it when she commended the artful towel origami of The Haathee Majal, the folded elephants greeting her from beside two chocolates and a brochure, and when she basked in the coziness of another day off and in, the steaming chocolate in her mug, saying how it was dog weather in New York.

It was worth it when he learned she didn't drink caffeine either, as it messed with her internal clock, nor greasy foods, as she prioritized her health. The human body is a temple, after all, she quoted, unable to cite whom from. Hugo told her about Holy Joe, the similarities of their stances. It was worth it when he learned she didn't partake in alcohol, tobacco, nor any illicits, and when he asked if she'd decorated her temple, learning she had not.

"It's a matter of committing, nothing at all to do with religion. What's genius today may prove foolish tomorrow."

Hugo nodded along. Having seen her naked, he'd anticipated her response, but allowed for the possibility of a hidden tattoo, or studs gone unnoticed.

"Do you have any piercings? Tattoos?" she inquired.

He'd been wearing long sleeves when they met, so of course, she hadn't seen the scale on his arm.

"Why?" she asked when he emailed her the picture. "You're not a libra."

"What do you mean?" he asked, certain they hadn't discussed birthdays.

"Your sun's in Taurus, and your moon's in Cancer. I'm sure of it."

Curious, Hugo googled for a zodiac website. Finding many, he selected the top non-ad, wherein he logged his birthday. The page requested his time of birth as well, so he deferred to the official certificate before hitting submit. Taking a moment to load, a graphic of a circle with horns and another of a "69" rotated ninety degrees appeared, long before the text. When the cursor stopped spinning, there it was in black and white.

"That's right," he responded, impressed. "How could you tell?"

As if explaining addition to a child, Anna matter-of-factly listed personality traits he'd expressed, and while some were accurate, he wasn't sure he agreed that he was dependent, nor prone to hiding his feelings. Eventually, she circled back to her question. Why the scale? Obviously, it bore significance, being his only tattoo.

Surprising himself, Hugo told Anna the truth. He detailed how he'd been with Evelyn for five years, matured alongside her during college and after, how she was his first love. He told her how, upon meeting her coworker, he'd experienced a crisis of passion. Hugo admitted that he'd never faced the temptation to cheat before meeting Riga, and never since. It wasn't love, it didn't last, and his mistake not only cost him the comfort of a long-term relationship, it destroyed Evelyn, a really nice girl, for a long time. Between long sighs and longer pauses wherein he sought the right words, Hugo described what he'd learned of her since she left.

"It got bad. After walking in on us, she stopped showing up at work, took up drinking—drunk dialed a mutual friend. Scared them, how different she sounded, so they called me, wanting to know what the hell happened. She wasn't leaving the house much, and I guess she started painting again. I'm glad for that, about the painting I mean. She made a bit of a name for herself with her art, but she was very *unwell.* By now, I've lost ties with most everyone in New Haven. Most were friends of Riga, but they said enough. Evelyn became a recluse, and she scared the crap out of people, talking to things that weren't there when she wasn't hiding."

"There are always victims in love and war. Is she still struggling? How is she now?"

"I don't know. She moved south, is keeping up with her art, but refuses to make public appearances. Another friend let on that she wrote a spiritualist manifesto, that she's a guru teaching runaways about the afterlife now. It's possible, I guess. How many cult leaders were just crazy, right? But I can't see it, can't see her playing life coach to gullible kids. The Evelyn I knew had a lot going for her, but confidence? Barely enough to share an idea, let alone defend it."

"So how does your tattoo relate to hurting your ex-girlfriend's feelings?"

"Well, when everything fell apart with Riga, after I wrecked Evelyn, I hated me. My whole self was tainted, tarnished with mistakes, pain I caused. The bad outweighed the good and I made a conscious decision to be better. In commemoration, and to serve as a daily reminder of who I aspire to be, I got a tattoo of the weighing of souls. Are you familiar with the concept?"

Anna admitted she was not.

"No problem. It's not too far off from most popular views of the afterlife. In ancient Egypt, folks believed that the soul was in the heart. When a person died, their soul was weighed against a feather. Hearts heavy with sin were devoured by the god Ammat."

"And if the heart was lighter than a feather, they went to heaven?"

"Their idea of heaven, yeah. I'm not too keen on their mythos as a whole, but I want my soul light, sinless. Uneaten, preferably."

It was worth it when she told him her Diwali plans, how there would be a celebration down by the docks, not far from the resort she'd be working from that weekend. Hugo asked if she was Hindu, surprised.

"No, but I like holidays. They're the best part of every culture," she explained. "Not too many Haitian festivals in the states, unfortunately. Gotta make do."

It was worth it when she called him on a Thursday night, eleven-o-clock his time, because she wasn't tired. Did he mind? No, not at all. Didn't he have work early the next day? Not to worry! He'd napped that afternoon, came the easy lie. What did she want to talk about?

"Do you like Burlington?" she asked over what may have been her roommates quarreling. Her lease was ending soon, and more and more of her coworkers were checking in over their phones, or webcams. Her boss was willing to make concessions if she didn't want to keep coming in. Maitresse knew her commute was expensive, and not to mention, long. It didn't make sense, dictating she come in person, with meetings so infrequent.

"Well, I haven't visited as many cities as you, but yeah. In spring, you can tour the farms, see the baby animals. Summer's mild, and there are hot air balloon festivals. Autumn is especially beautiful, what with the foliage turning red and gold. Tourists come from all over to watch. Loads of places offer apple picking, pumpkin picking—and winter looks like a scene out of a Thomas Kinkade calendar. We've got carriage rides, everything's lit, and not a house goes undecorated. There are parks nearby, trails for hiking, and campsites not an hour away."

"That sounds more picturesque than what I saw, but I mostly stuck to the city center."

"I can see how you'd get a different impression then. Burlington has balance. It's urban enough where there are jobs, events, a nightlife, but not so populated as to be dirty, concrete. Plus, the rent's fair. I've lived in and around Boston, New Haven, and I've been to New Orleans, Seattle, all over New York. Of the lot, Burlington's my favorite."

Most importantly, he wanted to say, "I'm here." Instead, he rambled on.

"In fact, the tabloids say we're the next hot spot. A handful of celebrities have moved here in recent years. Lynnette Lewis from the Lamentation Song trilogy just bought a mansion on the outskirts."

"I've heard of her. She's the spokesperson for my favorite perfume, Bousquet's Chamonix. Or she was. They don't make it anymore."

Hugo made a quick note of the perfume in case he might be able to find an unopened bottle online.

"Well, that's a shame. Hopefully, popular demand will change the company's mind. Let's see, we've also got that guy with the pie show, Haddock something. He's been here for a few years now. He's rumored to be funding next year's Saint Patrick's Day parade. His boyfriend's a model, supposed to be moving here soon. Who else—"

"I get it. Burlington is up and coming, a buyer's market. Do you know of anybody looking for a roommate, someone to sublet?"

"Me!" he wanted to shout, wanted to crawl through the phone, wrap his arms around her, sing it into her ear. "Me! Come live with me!" But he knew that could only be construed as too much, too fast.

"I don't, but I can check with some friends," he said coolly, mind racing over who might have a lead.

"If you wouldn't mind, I'd appreciate it."

Chapter 7
Warm Welcome

"I'll ask around. Nicole didn't get on so well with her last roommate. She'd rather pay more than share space. Only child, you know. But she's friends with everybody. You should shoot Sonya and Joe texts too. I bet they'll have a suggestion," Esteban said, over lunch.

"IDK Will look," Sonya texted back.

"Budget?" Joe asked. Hugo forwarded the question to Anna and sent her answer to Joe.

"OK good. Got 2 talk 2 sum ppl."

It took Hugo over a minute to translate each abbreviation, but he commiserated with the hindrance of re-tapping every letter and forgave the shorthands. Anna's phone had a keyboard, he gathered, while striving to match the standard she set for spelling and grammar.

Pulling store brand hot pockets from the microwave and a tonic from the fridge, Hugo rang Anna for their dinner date. Before taking his first bite, he pierced the pocket with a fork, shoving the meat thermometer inside.

"Hey! Just a minute," she responded over background babbling.

He heard a thud and the muffled kerfuffle cut away.

"Sorry. Donna's boyfriend is over and they're having a spat. How was work?"

His dinner was too hot, he decided upon reading the temperature, opting to wait.

"It was fine. Nate was out, so a couple of meetings were canceled. That was nice. I could get my work done without wasting half the morning listening to a monologue that could've been an email nobody'd've gained from reading."

"Is Nate a micromanager?"

"Mostly he's reactionary. A customer complains and he makes sweeping changes across the board to be accommodating, but how often are customers actually right? The new policies don't last, because they don't work—or they're only relevant in ultra-specific situations that happen so rarely as to be better handled on a case-by-case basis."

"I guess he hasn't learned he can't please everyone."

"Maybe. I think it makes him feel important, bending our team to suit that one customer, telling us how we've done wrong." Hugo sighed, shaking his head. "Anyway, what's for dinner? How's your day going?"

"Dinner's a salad, and my day's going fine. The roommates have been home more, so things are louder than I like, but I knew what I signed up for subletting with college kids."

"When are you flying out?"

Anna spoke, but he couldn't catch what she said over the alarm that erupted on her end.

"Be right back!" she shouted, hanging up.

Hugo was pecking a text, asking what happened, when his phone vibrated.

"Hey! What was that?"

The alarm continued but was fading.

"They set off the smoke detector, so I'm taking a walk."

"Is there a fire?"

"Nope. I can smell the weed from here. Our landlord lives next door so he'll be over in a minute to see what the fuss is about."

"Don't want to be there when he shows?"

She chuckled. "Not in the slightest."

Hugo asked how the weather was, watching flurries from his window. She admitted the air was icy, the wind abrasive, but she'd thought to grab her jacket, hat, and gloves. Not to worry, she said. She didn't mind the chill. He wished he was there to keep her company, or better yet, that she was in his bed, warming him.

To distract from any discomfort, he asked what she was reading that week. Without delay, she launched into a history lesson, teaching Hugo about the Mongolian warrior woman Khutulun.

"None of the men succeeded at beating her in a wrestling match, and she was getting on in years, so finally she agreed to marry one of her father's men." She paused at a commotion beyond. "Excuse me a moment. Wap pale avèm?! Yeah, I thought so! Al konyen! Ugh. Sorry, some guy was being an idiot. What were we talking about?"

"Hold on. What language was that?"

"Haitian Creole. There's a Haitian community here and I speak more than enough to put jerks in their place. Oh! Right. The warrior princess. There isn't much to tell after she was married. The book focuses on Marco Polo's record of her life leading up to the wedding."

He asked about her neighborhood. Was it safe? Was she sure she wasn't being followed? Should he call someone?

"It's fine. People are fools no matter where you go. I'm going to hang up for a second. Just found a place with a bathroom."

When she rang, he could hear the honking and rush of traffic.

"I'm going to start walking back. The landlord must've left by now."

"Good. Go get warm. Maybe finish your dinner."

"Assuming they didn't burn the place down," she joked.

They hadn't, and she was able to eat her salad in peace, cozy in bed. Between bites, she described her room to Hugo, at his request. He wanted to know how she lived.

"Not much to tell. The bed's queen-sized, and I've got enough blankets to switch them out every day of the week."

"I thought you didn't mind the cold?"

"Heat and cold both have their pros, but these are quilts my auntie and I made together."

"Do you still quilt?"

"Not anymore. I'm just one person, and I can only justify having so many blankets. If a block is looking a little faded though, or there's a tear, I repair it."

"Cheaper than going to a seamstress."

"Yeah, and I like sewing. Uh, what else—I've got a nightstand. Library books, my tarot deck, and flower albums go in there. My desk is tidy for once, with just my laptop, notebooks, sketchbooks, and pencil box. There's a world map over it, where I pin the places I've visited. My clothes hang in the closet, by color. Makes tops easy to find."

With every detail, his view gained definition, color, replacing his kitchen, framing a void in the shape of a lounging silhouette. Badly, he wished to ask what she was wearing, to complete the image, but he daren't be so bold.

Days passed before Sonya got back to him. If Anna was looking to get a feel for Burlington without committing, Sonya's neighbor would be in the Netherlands for a few months and had been looking for a subletter to cover rent while he was away. Hugo forwarded the details to Anna, suggesting she stay over if she wanted to swing by and check the place out. She took him up on his offer.

Esteban called later, inviting Hugo to join him for a charity bar crawl the following night. "It's a great cause. Remember hearing about that motorcycle accident in Colchester a few weeks back?" Hugo said he did. "Well, the guy survived, which is great, except now he's paralyzed. The money from the crawl's to buy him a motorized wheelchair."

He wasn't thrilled when Hugo declined, instead asking how big of a check to pass along.

"I dunno. Whatever you can give? I'm not going for the cause! It's a fun night out. Helping the guy is just a plus. But fine. I get it. See you at work."

Hugo was never one for spring cleaning. When he moved, however infrequently, he donated or tossed what he didn't need. Otherwise he spared little thought for how his home looked. Aside from the fridge of expired ingredients he'd planned, yet failed to cook with, he wasn't ashamed to showcase his generally cluttered flat to friends, family. Were his folks to visit, he'd have given the bathroom a quick wipe-down, cleaned the fridge, and called his home *welcoming*. But this was Anna, and ultimately, he was convincing her not just of Burlington's hospitality, but his own.

So Hugo dusted the ceiling fans, wiped the molding along the walls and over the fireplace. He spritzed every window, mirror, and picture frame, wiping the smears with coffee filters, bringing him back to his days as a teenage barista saving for a car. His dad refused to chaperone after their first driving session. Young Hugo'd made the mistake of letting loose an effeminate squeak upon accidentally veering into the wrong lane and nearly hitting a passing vehicle. For weeks, he'd assumed the stony silence of his father was over perceived recklessness, until his brother teasingly brought up the yelp.

Wincing at memories best forgotten, Hugo washed and dried the dishes, then put them away. He cleaned the counters, sink, and stovetop. The wall behind the oven was sticky with grease, and he wasted eons scrubbing it, but the stain persisted. He swiffered and swept the tiled floors, vacuumed the carpets, and washed both sets of bedding. They hadn't discussed where she would be sleeping.

Grocery shopping, he restocked the necessities. Watching his figure, the cart was largely fruits and vegetables, though he included sweets in case those were more to her liking.

Saturday afternoon, he heard his pocket buzz. His mom wanted to know if he was coming for Thanksgiving.

"When's Thanksgiving?" he wondered out loud, checking the calendar. Then he called Anna, who didn't pick up. Probably busy with work, he self-soothed.

"Do you want to stay for Thanksgiving? It's this week," he texted, holding off on responding to his folks until she answered.

"Sure," she said, hours later. Hugo called his mom, letting her know he was sorry but had to decline. He had work. She understood, but would've loved to give his boss a stern talking to, keeping his loan officers chained to their desks on a national holiday. "He oughta be ashamed!" she exclaimed, but accepted Hugo's apology, so long as he made it to Christmas.

"I will, Ma. I promise!" He just hoped he wouldn't arrive alone.

An antique convertible buggy came crawling up the street before inching to the curb, and Hugo wondered at its age and value. Anna had arrived a half-hour earlier than expected. She was stunning, the sunrise highlighting her brows and cheeks, lending a shimmer to her eyes. She wore a grey winter coat that did nothing to dull her vibrance. Her gaze found his door, and her feet followed. Not wanting to admit he'd been watching, he waited until she knocked before letting her in.

They exchanged greetings. He ushered her past his thriving pomegranate tree into the warmth of the living room, taking her jacket and hanging it on the coat rack. She left her flats by the mat, putting her suitcase down beside the couch. What was the make and model of her vehicle? She shrugged, explaining it was a gift from a client. She knew only that the chassis was a C.R. Patterson & Sons Company original. Hugo confessed to never having heard of them and she replied that they didn't exist in this day and age. Regardless, the buggy ran fine, though she had to go to a specialized mechanic twice a year for regular maintenance, and the roof wouldn't fold down anymore. He asked about the traffic, and she said there'd been little. The weatherman warned of snow later, and what with it being so early in the week, she assumed most holiday travelers would wait until Tuesday to head out, when visibility improved.

Hugo offered tea, hot chocolate, cider, and orange juice. Had she requested another beverage, he'd happily have gone to pick it up, but Anna was content with a hand-warming mug of ginger tea. As they settled in, Hugo asked when she'd be meeting the potential sublessor, offering a key so she could come and go as she pleased while he was at work. He'd hoped they could grab lunch, but unfortunately, his free half-hour corresponded with the meeting time. Brushing disappointment aside, Hugo inquired whether she had any Thanksgiving traditions? Side dishes she looked forward to?

"Most years I whip up some baked joumou and an avocado salad. I stick with my auntie's recipes, but they're flexible."

"I'm not familiar with those, but I have a ton of ingredients, and we can always run out and grab whatever we need."

"Well, joumou is traditionally a soup, though not how I make it. It's sliced potatoes, pumpkin, turnips, shallots, and sprinkled with salt, pepper, thyme, and olive oil. I usually add garlic, but the recipe doesn't need it. Avocado salad is exactly how it sounds. I lightly mix the avocados with onions, sliced limes, salt, and pepper."

"Yeah. I don't have most of that. There are potatoes in the pantry, and probably some canned pumpkin. Feel free to double-check the expiration date if you want to use that. It's probably left over from last fall. I'll be hitting the store tomorrow, either way, so we can make a list. Oh—speaking of food, what would you like for dinner?"

She shrugged. Hugo offered what meals he had the means to make, suggesting as well, food they could order in if that was more to her liking. Anna decided to make creole shakshuka. "It's similar to eggs in purgatory." He hadn't heard of either, but admired the precision with which she sliced tomatoes, peppers, and onions, mixing them, the oil, and more than a handful of spices in the skillet. She let the vegetables cook on low heat for a while before poaching the eggs therein. Anna asked what bread he had, cutting off some chunks of the Italian loaf and toasting them in a pan with a smidge of butter. "You'll want to dip these in," she explained. "Normally I make mine spicier, but I'm getting too old for the heartburn."

Hugo wasn't sure if telling her she didn't look a day over twenty-two would be endearing or patronizing, so he only said that she was beautiful, and she was. There was a maturity to the subtle lines of her eyes, her mannerisms, and the quiet confidence with which she strode—back straight, head high—that someone in their early twenties couldn't have hoped to match. Hugo didn't understand his peers who chased after college girls, daydreamed about eighteen-year-olds. They appeared to him like the children they were, with their insecure inflections, looking to others for approval.

After laying out the saucy eggs and toast, she made to scrub the pan, but Hugo waved her off. "Oh no. I'll handle the dishes later. You did all the cooking!" So too, he set the table, and in no time at all it seemed, dinner was served.

"Was this another favorite of your auntie's?" Hugo inquired, dipping the toast and taking a bite.

"Yeah, but she would've mixed in habaneros. Stomach like a rock, that one," Anna said, with a wistful smile, snipping cilantro over her plate before offering him the stalk. "She wouldn't have teared up at a ghost pepper."

Being a fan of eggs, tomato sauce, and bread, shakshuka seemed to Hugo a natural culmination of many good things, but far more pleasant was Anna.

He asked where she loved most, what holiday was her favorite, and where she generally went for Thanksgiving. Unable to pinpoint a single best place, Anna proclaimed an equal love for Barcelona and Rome. The art, museums, clash of contemporary and ancient architecture—the walkability, not to mention variety of affordable and delicious cuisines—she could have lived in either city, had she a reliable income abroad. Likewise, any holiday with ample food and people gathered, celebrating, was a great day to her. It didn't matter who or what the cause.

He intuited that the seeking of strange company could only result from loneliness.

"Where are your parents, or your grandparents from?"

"Haiti, though if you asked them, they'd say the Kingdom of Dahomey. I believe the area's called Benin now, West Africa." Anna paused, collecting her thoughts. "And as for Thanksgiving, I usually just order in. Thursdays and Fridays take turns as my Monday, so it's nice to have that off, even if I spend it at home. The last several years, I've focused on participating in communal holidays rather than familial. If it's got a parade, I'm there."

She volleyed those questions to Hugo, whose answers were more concise. He loved New Orleans, although the crime rates made him nervous. Like her, he had a preference for any holiday that encouraged binge eating. Thanksgiving was often spent back home with his folks and siblings, but this year he planned on seeing them in December instead.

Anna asked if his family had any holiday traditions, and Hugo confessed he couldn't think of many.

"The Atmens have been in the states so long, we trace back to the colonies, so we don't abide by old world traditions. Ah—my dad begins every Fourth of July by watching Independence Day with my brother. It's their favorite movie."

"Can't say that I've seen it."

Hugo was flabbergasted. That movie was a huge deal when it came out. It had Will Smith in his prime. Anna admitted she had no clue who that was, and Hugo had to take a step back.

"Do you not watch TV?"

She shook her head. "Barely. We have a set in the living room, and I'm sure the flatmates each have their own, but I've never seen the point. I'm barely home, and when I am, I'm reading or getting work done."

"Or repairing your quilts."

She smiled. "Or repairing my quilts."

After dinner, Anna stepped away to freshen up. When she returned, he offered ice cream, muffins, and cake, but she declined. He cleared the table and washed the remaining dishes, quizzing her about pop culture all the while. Essentially, if she hadn't seen it with friends, she hadn't seen it. The only actor she could name off the top of her head was Tom Cruise, and only because she'd briefly lived with his self-declared biggest fan.

Hugo's first instinct was to share this world with her, all of these stories and scenes she hadn't witnessed, references she'd never get—but then he thought better of it. Anna would have bought a TV and a DVD player if she was afraid of missing out. When he finished in the kitchen and they moved to the living room, he invited her to choose an album. She did so, listing bands she'd seen that year as she located a familiar artist and turned the stereo on.

Natalie Merchant serenaded the duo with *Wonder* as Anna settled beside Hugo, her leg against his. If only it had been warmer out, that leg would've been bare. He slung an arm around her shoulder, painfully aware that this was the most physical contact they'd shared. Had he reverted to a pubescent, leg shaking and stomach rollercoasting at every near touch?

They compared musical tastes, critiquing the evolution of bands that had found their audience, only to then alter the sound that made them beloved.

"I don't blame musicians for being happy when they're famous, or for growing as artists, but that's when I stop listening to them," she admitted, resting her hand on his leg.

He hadn't observed the career paths of his favorite bands to know which albums correlated with what grand success, but having first heard every group on the radio, Hugo could only assume he was catching them at the beginning of their tailspins if Anna's theory held.

As they spoke, they shifted, turned, facing one another, and Hugo leaned in at the first long pause. Part of him wanted to ask permission. He moved slowly, watching her eyes flicker to his mouth, meeting his gaze—then coming forward, her mouth on his, lips parting, tongues searching. They withdrew, smiled, and kissed anew, entangling. He wrapped his arms around her and she, him, his fingers reaching beneath, then up, caressing her breasts as she massaged his groin over his pants.

"Bedroom?" he asked when they broke for air, and she nodded.

He undressed en route, half tripping over his trailing pants, ducking by the front door, past the wreath of red petals drifting from his little tree. Anna closed the door behind them, shutting the light away before undressing. Like a cat, emeralds shone from behind her retinas. Two orbs in a sea of shadow, her eyes floated toward him as she climbed into bed and they resumed their exertions.

Chapter 8
No Fowl Play

"The meeting went well. He's friendly and I like the apartment. He's going to clear out the closet and store his bedding so I can organize my things. I'm welcome to whatever food he leaves, and the internet is hooked up. The landline is fair game, too, but why would I need it?"

"So you're going to do it? Come live in Burlington, I mean."

Anna blew steam from her tea and took a sip.

"At least for a few months. If I like it here, I've got time to find a place and put down roots. If not, I have friends in White Plains who'd let me crash while I get back on my feet."

Hugo waved away the second half of her statement. "That's great! When do you move in?"

"Soonest would be the first week of December. He knows I work weekends and will be around to hand off the key. Then he's leaving."

"For the Netherlands?"

"He's seeing family for a day or two before flying out, but yeah."

Had the universe drawn some stranger across the pond just so Hugo and his soulmate could better bond? Why was their love so important, unique? Or was everyone being inexorably led to their one and only—he'd just remembered the broadcast? Did everyone catch glimpses likewise, but waved them off rather than heeding the message?

"That's fantastic. Want me to help you move? I can take Monday off."

Anna declined, shaking her head. She was intent on leaving her heavier belongings behind. "The apartment is already furnished, and my flatmates are looking to move another friend in. They said she'd be happy to take my bed, desk, and dresser, which saves me the trouble of getting rid of them."

Anything else, she could easily fit in her car, she assured, while peering over a picture of Hugo as a chubby toddler. She'd pulled the photo albums from his bookshelf and was paging through, asking—who was who? When was what? Hugo hadn't taken any pictures all year and hadn't developed his film rolls in far longer, so neither album had been touched in ages. She glanced over childhood birthdays, a new puppy in a floppy bow, parties crowded with exuberant little faces, then later, another of a crestfallen boy whose classmates were no longer obligated to attend every invitation. There he was older, smiling again, playing with a cuddly mass of a dog, past the weddings and funerals of relatives, dates with forgotten girlfriends, a prom he was sick for half of, a prom he couldn't recall, he'd been so hammered, five years of Evelyn, an aftermath of Riga, and a few vacation shots with Claire. The only major life event that hadn't measled its way into the Photographed Times of Hugo Atmen IV were his wedding pictures, and only because those claimed several of their own albums, all of which went to Riga in the divorce. He needed no reminders of *that* mistake.

Anna admitted she wasn't one for taking pictures either. Confessing a preference for flower clippings, pressed dry and labeled by species and location, she described many full binders. Shortly, she'd be done with the one in her backpack and start another. Hugo wondered what she'd done with her inheritances, after her folks passed, but didn't ask. Surely they'd taken pictures of their little girl, and who but Anna could those have fallen to? Not to mention all of their other earthly possessions. Perhaps she'd sold what she could to pay for college, or her travels when beginning in her field, and tossed the rest.

Flipping back to Hugo with his dog, Anna inquired as to the breed.

"No idea. Ma adopted him from the pound. He was the last of the litter to be picked up. All the shelter knew was that his mom was part lab."

"Huh. I always liked dogs, but they're such a big responsibility. Can't be flying out every weekend with a pup at home."

"You can if you've got a guy who'll stay behind to look after it," Hugo replied.

After work Wednesday, he wrote out the shopping list, double-checking what ingredients they lacked.

"Do you like turkey? I don't mind cooking one, but as it's just the two of us, if there's something you like better, we can do that instead."

"Oh. I'm vegetarian. Sorry, I thought I'd mentioned."

Hugo was one hundred percent positive that she had not, but he could accommodate vegetarianism without serious inconvenience. He was just glad she'd informed him before he bought and cooked a ten-pound bird he'd have been stuck eating alone.

"Do you like tofurkey? What's your go-to main course?"

Anna laughed. "Let's not get a tofurkey. They're flavorless. And honestly, I'm fine filling up on side dishes."

Hugo reflected on his cookbooks. Evelyn had been vegetarian, but she'd also kept most of their library.

"What if I made stuffed acorn squash? I could fill it with rice, pecans, thyme, and feta."

"Sure, stuffed squash sounds great."

He spent the drive to the supermarket pointing out quirks of the neighborhood, indicating which houses decorated for Halloween, Christmas, and Hanukkah. He bragged about the amateur firework displays shooting off every Fourth of July and named the best packies for grabbing funnel cakes, tacos, and donuts on the go.

"Not as many Dunks as Boston, but look! Drivers use their directionals."

McMart was packed. Passersby shoved on with their squeaky wheeled carts and the overhead speakers assailed the yuletide-averse with Christmas carols, jingles, and pop hits that would ping-pong around their melancholy skulls for days. The aisles were dense with shoppers, and the duo split up. Anna handled drinks, the refrigerated, and the frozen sections, while Hugo gathered dry goods and produce. Spotting Anna on the long line for the registers, Hugo joined her. He scanned magazine covers for topics worth bringing up, but saw little more than pop culture gossip. Once an employee indicated which register was open, they stepped forward, laying their finds along the conveyor belt, which churned the mound past the cashier, who forced a tired smile. Hugo asked if the squash was free when the teenager couldn't find the code for it in his system. They offered a halfhearted chuckle and Anna flinched, mid-bagging. "What did I say?" he wanted to ask, but opted not to draw attention to his mistake.

Dinner was light. For dessert, they caroused under the cover of night. Hugo imagined aiming a spotlight on her, observing her every expression, swivel, and turn, but refrained from asking her to leave the lights on. Thus far she'd only undressed in the dark, and he assumed she was self-conscious of her body, cursed to see nonexistent imperfections.

Had she grown insecure listening to the jealous jeers of youths who craved the distinction of her delicately embellished chest? Internalized the belittlements of the small-minded?

To communicate her loveliness wordlessly, Hugo kissed her, beginning with the soles of her feet and working his way along her taut calves, soft thighs, up to her waist, arms, breasts, paying extra attention to her nipples, before moving on to her neck, ear lobes, mouth. When the pressure became too much and she pulled him this way or that, he joyously complied before taking up where he'd left off, nuzzling where she shied him from. He couldn't abide that his soulmate, perfection incarnate, might feel shame.

Hugo was resolved that when Anna inevitably came to live with him, he would tell her how beautiful she was every day. She'd wake up and he'd remark at the sparkle of her eyes in the changing light as she passed beneath fluorescents, incandescent, sunlit panes. When she'd smile, he'd compliment the subtle curve of her lips, her porcelain teeth, the cute crinkle of her nose. He dreamed of waltzing home from the bank, spirit lifting upon meeting her in their foyer, on the couch, in the kitchen. He'd commend her grace, her poise, her voice. She'd love him, love being loved by him, and come to love herself as he did.

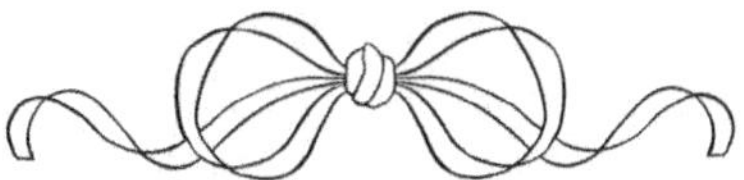

Thanksgiving day, Hugo crept from bed to the chorus of pecking and clucking. A flock of unfamiliar black birds had surrounded his apartment days back and apparently ceased their southward migration. They were chubby, with white cheeks reminiscent of the telescope goldfish's protruding eyes, bright red crowns, and neck flaps. They were bundled as tightly together as was physically possible last he'd checked. He didn't need an alarm during their stay. Not that he trusted them to stick around. Heck, he half expected, and frankly hoped, they'd have moved on overnight, while the snow was coming down. Surely there were warmer nesting spots than his roof. The birds were bound to leave a layer of guano up top, down the siding, over his car, and hers. He dreaded the task of cleaning after them.

Tiptoeing to the kitchen, past fresh pomegranate petals, Hugo set the kettle to boiling, careful to raise it from the burner before the hiss became a whistle. Dunking a ginger tea bag into each mug, he let them steep before returning his attention to the stovetop. Dropping a handful of chopped spinach into the hot skillet, he sprinkled salt and pepper, capping it with a lid. The eggs, he cracked into a cup, stirred, and poured into a nonstick pan. Adding crushed garlic and a pinch of basil, he set their burner to medium heat. One side solidified, Hugo poured the sautéed spinach into the eggs, followed by a generous portion of shredded parmesan cheese, folded the omelet over, and let that cook.

Eggs then divided onto their plates, he added toast, catching the pieces as they leapt. First, he carried her meal in, using the cutting board as a platform and leaving the plate to cool on the nightstand before returning with each mug of tea. Then he carried in his meal/cutting board combo. The bed trays had been missing for months, and he assumed Claire'd co-opted them for Seattle.

"Breakfast is served," he announced, seeing Anna sitting up, stretching, as he claimed the cool space at her side.

"Oh, wow. Breakfast in bed! That's so fancy!" she laughed, wiping the sleep from her eyes. "What time is it?"

"Almost seven. The sun's only just coming up."

They spoke little, enjoying the meal, the warmth of the comforter, and each other. As breakfast came to a close, it was Hugo who rose first, collecting dishes and returning to the kitchen to plan his cooking. Anna detoured to the bathroom, adding a hint of color to her mouth and a glimmer of gold to her eyelids, he observed when she reappeared.

Truth be told, Hugo preferred Thanksgiving at home, with his kitchen accessible. While he adored his mom and didn't hate his dad, cooking was easier with fewer obstacles. It was nice, setting a microwave timer without needing to ask if he was clearing someone else's. He didn't have to make alterations to his recipes to account for the temperature of an oven shared by other dishes, other chefs. Anna's salad wouldn't require the oven nor timer, and her baked joumou wouldn't take long.

They lunched on hors d'oeuvres. Instead of the mini hotdogs in Pillsbury croissant buns that were his holiday staple, Hugo substituted the filling with mozzarella, putting out marinara for dipping. Rather than Swedish meatballs, which he'd have preferred the Italian variety to regardless, and therefore barely missed, he made bruschetta, chopped up some veggies, and put that out alongside crackers, dips, and a bowl of olives. They took to cleaning dishes in turns, whenever they broke from eating.

Hugo inquired more about Anna's family, and she, his. She'd been incredibly close with her mother while growing up, then more so with her auntie as she matured, dreamed of leaving the nest. She knew her dad, but he was barely involved in her upbringing, and she didn't resent his absence.

"Not everyone is meant to be a parent," she explained when Hugo grimaced at the failings of another lackluster father.

From a big family, she had relatives in New Orleans, Haiti, and some had returned to Africa. None up North, but she didn't miss seeing them.

"My mother and auntie have never gotten on well, and given my auntie was close with everyone else, the majority sided with her. As you can imagine, we weren't invited to much. Still, we'd visit for holidays, and I got to know my cousins, aunts, and uncles. I like everyone fine. Just didn't connect with anyone enough to miss them now. What's your family like?"

Hugo described his folks, siblings, aunts and uncles, cousins, and their kids. God, he was getting old. The eldest of his niblings had just entered his teens. Having listed too many names for a non-savant to recall, he focused on those of note, relaying their idiosyncrasies. Hugo brought up the time an uncle "accidentally" shot his wife's singing coach while on a hunting trip, how no charges were pressed, as the philanderer was also a prominent member of the local church. For years, the congregation admired how the singing coach upheld the Christian standard of forgiveness, never suspecting he'd earned that bullet.

"Did your uncle leave your aunt?"

"Not yet. They're waiting until after the kids go off to college."

She shook her head, exasperated. "I'll never understand people choosing to waste years of their lives in unhappy relationships. Do they think the constant bickering is better for the kids? What kind of lesson does that teach?"

"Hopefully nothing they can't unlearn," he agreed.

Hugo told her about the time his brother took LSD to impress a girl he'd just met.

"Brendan ran outside during a Colorado winter, in just a t-Shirt and boxers, screaming *'We are stars!'* at the top of his lungs until the police showed up to talk sense into him."

"Oh no! Did they give him a hard time?"

"Luckily the girl hadn't bailed, so she calmed his ass down and pulled him back inside. Thanks to her, he didn't end up in a cell or a hospital that night."

"What the hell did he mix his acid with?"

"No idea," Hugo admitted, curious as to how familiar she was with hallucinogens, "but I doubt he's experimented since. Oh! There was also the time my nephew got caught with a mouse in his mouth."

"Alive or dead?"

"Alive. It ran away when my sister made him open up. She raced him to the family doctor and tried to make him administer those crazy-long rabies shots. Can't say if the doc went through with it. I wasn't around, but my brother said she was in hysterics for a week—had an exterminator come and everything, but they didn't find signs of any mice in her house. As far as they could tell, the kid must've brought the mouse in from outside, and he'd been in for hours by that point."

"So he was walking around with a mouse in his mouth *for a while*?"

"That's the idea."

"Kids are wild," she breathed, shaking her head in horrified disbelief while arranging the finishing touches of her salad. The baked joumou, looking to him like ratatouille, sat on a burner set to low heat.

Lunch rolled into dinner, and thanks to their small portions, neither had trouble squeezing in more food. Hugo pulled the stuffed acorn squash from the oven, setting it in the center of the kitchen table. Around the headliner, Hugo set salad, roasted vegetables, mashed potatoes, vegetable broth gravy, stir-fried balsamic ginger carrots, a mound of croissants, and warmed butter. Anna poured them each a cider, offering to grab him a beer if he wanted.

"Just because I don't drink doesn't mean nobody else can."

"That's okay, thanks, but I don't mind taking a break."

What he missed was the traditional entree. Hugo loved a good warm turkey, moist in the middle and flavored with lemon and rosemary, but the acorn squash wasn't bad. He couldn't get past the texture to have more than a bite of the avocado salad, but the joumou was tasty. There wasn't much that went with radishes, but he suggested they shred some over the dish next time, and Anna was amenable to trying that, making a note. She ate a bit of everything and was particularly impressed by the gravy.

"You're sure this doesn't contain any meat broth? I won't be offended. I just have to know so I can take something to settle my stomach, or I'll be sick later."

"Oh no. You should be fine. It's vegetable broth, vegetable oil, soy sauce, spices, and flour."

She grinned. "Well, it's fantastic. You could market this as a beverage."

They put out the desserts—cheesecake, pumpkin pie, and a platter of cookies, but neither of them had more than a few bites of any one snack, with Anna joking she'd eaten far more than her share. On they chatted, and on the hours wore, until they had room for a cookie here, a sliver of a slice there. When time came for bed, both of them were far too full and exhausted for any kind of rolling, let alone in the sack. About a quarter of each dessert had been consumed.

Hugo didn't want the night to end, for Anna to leave, but time doesn't care what people want.

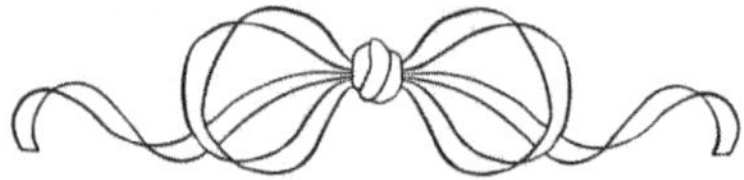

He saw Anna off, kissing her beneath a winged canopy of clucking and flapping in the freezing wind. Then she climbed into the front seat of her surprisingly pristine antique, inserted the key in the ignition, and set the engine to rumbling. He watched as she ambled away, turned, and was gone. After a moment, he headed down the walkway at a jog, burning some of that holiday mass in a loop around the block, before showering and watering his fiery tree. Hugo could put off sweeping the petals for later. The boss expected everyone in on time.

"Here's the man! I would've called out today, but I wanted to know how everything went with the girl," Esteban said by way of greeting.

He would have remained in Hugo's cubicle to pry, but Nate poked his head in, summoning them for an impromptu meeting. Once the mortgage loan team was gathered around Nate's desk—sans the hungover absentees—they were assigned partners for Secret Santa and encouraged to pick out the office holiday tree.

"It can't be taller than four feet because of where it's got to fit, but what do you think of these?" Nate asked, pulling out a Home Depot catalog.

There was a single vote for glistening white, but classic green was the victor, and Nate promised to have it on-site Monday morning when they could expect to take a half-hour from their morning for a little seasonal cheer. A cup of names went around. Hugo drew Veronica's. A date was announced for the upcoming office party, and the team was reminded it would be a "dry" shindig.

Hugo spent the morning making up for that lost hour, fully aware he hadn't been the employee of the month since September. His productivity was slipping and Nate needed to see results. When Esteban knocked on his cubicle for lunch, Hugo waved him away, gesturing helplessly to the papers on his desk. Nibbling at leftovers, he was careful not to leave crumbs on the forms as he persisted in dismantling the stack. Esteban returned promptly at five, pointing to his watch in emphasis.

"Come on. The first beer's on me."

Sighing, Hugo resolved to spend Saturday at his desk, and followed his friend. Over foaming glasses, Esteban begged details, as Hugo hadn't sent nor so much as checked his texts while *she* was in town.

"Anna's great. I mean, I told you she travels for work, so she's been everywhere. We spent the visit getting to know each other better. I learned more about where she comes from, about her family. It's intimate, talking in person, after being restricted to phone calls, you know?"

Esteban did, indeed. He'd tried long distance in college and planned never to do so again.

"Thankfully, it's only for another week."

"So, she's gonna stay?"

"Yup. For the winter, to check the city out. Plenty of time to convince her to move in with me."

"You're sure that's the best idea? You've only been talking to this girl for what? A month? You don't know her friends, what she's like when she's PMSing, drunk, or her team's just lost the Superbowl. She's still basically a stranger."

"She'll make new friends, here. I've lived with women before, and couldn't even tell when they were...on their cycle, until they announced it. That's never been a big deal. And Anna doesn't drink. She doesn't watch TV. What she does is *live her life*. She works with people from all over, joining in on their festivals, taking in their music, art."

"And you're cool with that? Her taking off to meet people, all the time?"

"I mean, it's her job. I don't have a choice."

"Hugh, you're being dense. The choice is *do you wanna date some chick who's never there*? You guys haven't known each other long enough to be committed. End things now, nobody gets hurt. She comes, she leaves, you see other women—women who live here, and aren't going anywhere."

"I appreciate the concern, but I know what I'm doing. Choosing. I pick Anna. If dating long distance is the price, so be it. We've been connecting. I can't say she's got both feet on the ground," he admitted, thinking of the tarot deck she'd mentioned, "but she's got a cool head. The only time I've heard her raise her voice was when some punk was messing with her."

"Because it's been a month, and you live in different states."

"I guess, but everybody fights. We will too, once we live together," Hugo said to be agreeable, though he didn't believe it. "But I can tell she's special," he insisted, pausing to find the right words. "And fighting—it's just another kind of communicating. As long as we listen when the other speaks, and I mean *really* listen, maybe we won't have to be like everybody else."

Esteban took a long sip. He stared into his glass before peering at Hugo, then spoke plainly. "I just don't get it, I guess. Acting like you love this girl you can't know. Have you considered that you're just rebounding after Claire? She left you high and dry, no notice, I get that. It had to suck. But rushing into it with this new girl—I mean, you regret your marriage, right?"

"I do, yeah, but that was different. I didn't propose because Riga was the one. She was pregnant, man. I didn't have a choice."

"Well, now you do. Take your time. If you think Anna is the one for you—act like it. Trust her not to up and run. Don't cling. Let things progress naturally."

"You really think I'm moving too fast?"

"Hugh, your master plan is to move in with a stranger. That's nuts. If she's any kind of sane, she'll agree with me. You both need to get to know each other. Date her like you would any other pretty girl who expressed an interest. Don't worry about the future. Have fun now."

"What if she wants to move in, though? What if she wants to move fast?"

"Then give her a chance to say so. You're putting too much pressure on her. You're in the honeymoon phase, right? So have a lot of crazy kinky sex, do whatever nondrinkers do to forget the world, and be merry. Let her come to you."

"Maybe," Hugo sighed.

They heard their names and turned to see their coworker, Rick, waltzing over.

"Hey, guys! What are we drinking this fine young evening?" he asked, before ordering the same, claiming a stool, and asking about their Thanksgivings.

Esteban had gone to his abuela's, spent the day watching football, and feasting on the best tamales this side of the border. Rick spent his at the in-laws, mourning a turkey destined to be overcooked and dry.

"Every year I offer to cook and every year her mom insists. God, I can't wait 'til they retire. Two years and they're heading to Florida. Then we'll only see them for Christmas."

Hugo replied that he'd stayed home before changing the subject. Would their sick coworkers get stuck putting in overtime to get their numbers up?

"Probably. Fuck man, I'm hungover and I still came in," Esteban laughed.

In moments, they were commiserating over the unpaid overtime trend, when Rick mentioned how another coworker was looking rather nippily all day.

"If women want to go braless, I'm not gonna complain," Esteban commented.

"Sure, but at work?" Hugo said. "How's that make the bank look? She should be glad Nate's the boss. He's too scared of being called sexist, getting written up by HR, sued or some shit, to say anything."

Rick laughed, but Esteban disagreed.

"Nate could report her to HR, let them handle it, but I don't see how she's in the wrong. There's no way our contracts state female employees *must* wear bras. A policy like that would've already landed the bank in hot water," he said, thinking out loud.

The others considered his point, conceding that he was right.

"I can see it offending elderly customers and prudish moms. If they make a complaint, Nate will handle it. Doubt it'll be a regular thing though. Day after Thanksgiving? She definitely just forgot," Esteban continued, and Hugo shrugged.

"It's just a shame it wasn't Veronica," Rick sighed.

"I'm pretty sure her back would give out," Hugo replied.

The trio exchanged glances before cheering to "Veronica's back giving out!"

When he got home, trees, bushes, and roof alike were bereft of loiterers, but graffitied grey and fuzzy as if to say, "We were here." Entering the foyer, the aroma of blooms gave welcome before giving way to mustiness. Already the homey scent of roasted vegetables had dissipated.

Chapter 9
Claus-trophobic

The week had been consumed, eaten away by work, friendly outings, and the phone calls around which time truly revolved—until finally, Anna invited him over. Rolling to a stop, she set the vehicle in park. She'd just gotten back from applying for her library card, and peering through the passenger's side window, Hugo could see a stack of books on the seat, though he didn't recognize the figure of note featured on the topmost cover. Stepping out and coming around to meet him, she introduced Hugo to her gnome-lined walkway, miraculously bare of droppings despite the fat black birds circling the yard, gathering scraps for their nests. She walked him past the wicker chair-laden stoop, accented fiberglass front door, earth-tone living room, marble countered kitchen, Mediterranean themed bathroom, and a bedroom featuring a king size bed covered in quilts.

"Want to test it out?" he asked with a wink.

Afterward, Anna toasted cabbage, carrot, and butternut squash sandwiches. It was sour for his taste, but hardly the worst sandwich he'd ever eaten, he thought, recalling some of Evelyn's culinary experiments. For dessert, they had baked bananas sprinkled with raisins, powdered sugar, and a splash of rum from the pantry.

"He left a lot of food. At this rate, I won't need to grocery shop for a couple of weeks."

Overall, Hugo was enjoying her oddball recipes. They provided a wonderful break from his stale routine of fast food, takeout, off-brand Hot Pockets, and cereal. Even when he didn't like it, he could say he'd tried something new. Eating Anna's cooking was an adventure, and given he was not a professional globetrotter, Hugo was happy to claim what flings with excitement he could.

To his surprise, she insisted he sleep at home that first night.

"I like my space, and this is all new for me. I want to be comfortable before I start letting people sleep over," she'd stated, not unkindly, though his chest buckled at the implications.

People? Was Anna sleeping with other men? Sure, they hadn't had *that* talk yet, regarding labels, denoting where they stood, were heading, what was and wasn't okay. But he'd been forthright, he thought, sharing his dream, his bed, his home.

Was that who Jacques had been, the other man? When he'd laid eyes on her at Muna's, seen her turning, searching for another, was that who she'd sought?

Sunken into his couch, Hugo read and reread the same paragraph, failing to distract himself from the turmoil within. He was not to Anna what she was to him. "*But the visions!*" he cried out. Except there was no one to listen, to care, to debate in favor of one or the other—fate or serendipity. He hadn't made it all up. It was her he'd followed, Anna the haunting, until they met beyond the veil of his mind.

She hadn't seen what he had, or else hadn't retained the sight. Anna needed him as he did her, only she lacked his foreknowledge, faith.

Was it a coincidence he hadn't dreamed since meeting her? Not once that he could recall. Could it be chalked up to mere happenstance that he'd imagined a lover, visualized the figure on the page, and barely a week later, she'd walked from the waves into a cafe he hardly frequented? Okay, that was an exaggeration. He went there regularly enough, but still! She didn't even live in this city! State?! It was destiny, goddamnit! They were soulmates, meant to wed and grow old together. What they had—okay, would have—was special. Anna was incredible. Anyone could tell, and he couldn't blame those who hadn't seen as he had for their pursuit. Hell, not having foreseen him—for she would have said so, had she—could Anna be blamed for allotting another their chance?

They, Hugo and Anna, hadn't communicated their expectations, and they needed to. He could forgive any transgressions thus far, or so he told himself. Without labels, set boundaries, there could be no betrayal. He refused to believe that a higher power who'd save him for her, save him from making the mistake of chasing after Nicole's immemorial friend, or Sonya, who could only be wrong for him, not being Anna—would tie him to one unfaithful. That defied all logic. Why intervene, if not to bless?

Hugo calmed. All was well. He would talk to her and they'd reach a consensus. The sooner she lived under his roof, however, the better. He told himself he trusted her, that he only wanted for her company, her warmth in their bed, that delaying the inevitable was senseless—but why was she not shown?

Aside from the interruption of her weekly kompa session, she spent her afternoons with him, in whichever bed. They'd share a meal, then one would leave. Anna remained insistent she sleep alone.

"It takes time to bond with a home."

Then she spent the weekend in Montreal, texting little, calling not at all. Aside from work, she had friends in the city who craved a little girl time. She'd warned him she would be busy, but the silence irked, nonetheless. Not knowing these strange women, who were so intimidated by her man, a country away, as to limit their communication, burned. Wasn't that just the way? The newly single would advise breaking up, moving on, playing with the hearts and cocks of men. Doubtless, her friends were pressuring her to flirt with Canadian randos for free drinks, rounds for the girls. If she wasn't slutty, they couldn't comfortably be, and he could see Anna in a mini skirt, crop top, smudged with too much mascara, sporting the lip shine of a teenager—or a stripper.

"She's done nothing wrong," he whispered. "Nothing yet," he amended.

She couldn't cross a line that hadn't been marked. So he sat, tried and failed to read, bearing the wait, the image of her leaning on a burly man in flannel, brushing her fingers along his sinewy arm, her eyes on his, asking about his work in broken French. Ugh, with his luck she spoke great French! Hugo told himself to be patient, that it wasn't her fault she couldn't text back, call, as the scene of her kissing a lumberjack became a migraine. By noon Sunday, Hugo called the weekend a wash and slept his anxieties away.

Upon her return, he was relieved to finally hear that she and the flat were getting on so well he was welcome to sleep over. Hugo assured her vice versa was also encouraged, as if she'd been in doubt. He wanted to ask what she'd meant when she said "people" in her bed, wanted to have their first serious talk as a couple, but wasn't sure how to broach the subject without seeming pushy. Instead, he asked after her Canadian friends, how they'd celebrated their girl time, but she responded with one-word non-answers, her vagueness exacerbating his concern.

Days later, as she was telling Hugo her assignments for the week, which included reviewing a Chippendales for a recently uncloseted client and their date, he finally suggested a heart-to-heart.

"Okay," she said. "What about?"

What about, indeed? Hugo didn't recall this part being difficult with any of his exes. Though looking back, they'd each taken the initiative, calling for labels, behavioral standards, and he'd gone along with their reasonable requests. Mostly.

"I was wondering where we are as a couple. Are you my girlfriend? If not, would you like to be? I'm not sure what to call us—what we have. I just know I don't want to be seeing anybody else, and I'd prefer if you weren't either."

"Do you think I'm seeing other people?"

Hugo paused, quoted her decision to sleep alone, specifying her wording.

"Sorry, I wasn't thinking. No, I'm not seeing anybody. If you want to call me your girlfriend, that's fine. But 'boyfriend,' 'girlfriend,' they just sound—oh, I don't know...infantile?—to me. If I've seemed hesitant over giving our relationship the validation of a title, that's why."

"I can see what you mean. What about partner? Or lover? Paramour? Significant other?"

She laughed. "Paramour sounds very dramatic. I'm gonna have to pose and wink for invisible cameras every time I call you that."

"I should buy a nicer lens."

Anna grinned, tossed her hands into the air, and chuckled. "Drama can be fun. Paramours it is—we are."

And just like that, they were a monogamous couple. Hugo had her word she was committed. To celebrate the occasion, he pulled out his Canon camera, tripod, and set the timer. Standing beside her, inhaling her coconut perfume—or was it shampoo?—he couldn't see if she winked. He snapped a few candid shots more, catching her in the kitchen, then on the couch, flaunting the careless seduction of Marilyn Monroe. It stunned him how women could look so incredibly different from one another, yet equally glamorous, and he wondered if she thought the same of men, and where he stood on the totem of handsomeness—who she compared him to?

Before she left for work, Hugo admitted he wasn't thrilled about her watching sweaty, fit men gyrating for her amusement, but she reminded him that this was her job. She didn't plan on quitting until she was old and had saved enough to retire to the nation of her choosing, or to tour the globe until she dropped dead of exhaustion. Besides, she'd said she was with him. Did he think a bunch of dancers would change how she felt? "No," he sighed, consoling himself with the knowledge that one day, if he worked hard enough, she wouldn't have to. Anna loved her job because it was the most affordable way to border hop. That wouldn't be the case if he paid her way.

Just a couple of promotions would do it.

Esteban asked about her absence at the office holiday party and Hugo explained she was away for work. He reiterated that she'd be away a lot, but it was okay. Esteban shook his head and flashed his palms in confusion, but let the subject drop. Hugo didn't share his consternation. They'd rapidly gone from being fully long distance to her living in Burlington half the time, a definitive improvement. Veronica thanked him for the "Survived Another Meeting That Could've Been An Email" thermos. Rick found it so funny he asked if he could take her picture with it, and she acquiesced. Their interaction left Hugo wondering if *she'd* forgotten her bra that day, but she'd turned away, and he couldn't see to tell. From Esteban, Hugo received a dreamcatcher. He'd bought it off an Abenaki woman who'd been selling wares at the Holiday Artisan Market downstreet, by the Town Hall.

"I had no idea what to get. Sonya helped me pick it out."

"Sure she wasn't shopping for Joe? Nah, I'm kidding. It's cool. Thanks, man," Hugo said, wondering if while drunkenly oversharing he'd told Sonya that Anna had been the last of his dreams. Did she think to lead them back, guiding pleasant maybes with the feathered net, or was she offering protection from a nightmare made real? It stood to reason that if Anna could step from his storytime imaginings, the boogie man might as well. Or, more like, it was a joke, and she was the one laughing.

Either way, he had a hunch Anna would like it, and hung the hoop in her room on his next visit. That night, when Anna climbed into bed, he heard a twang. Looking up, he spotted a snapped thread at the center, the frayed ends curling away.

"Damn. Guess they wound it too tight," he commented, rising to take it down.

"Oh, leave it up. It was already pretty. Now it just has a little more personality."

Not a week before Christmas, he invited Anna to celebrate with his family. He wasn't surprised when she palmed her forehead, shocked.

"That's this Saturday?!"

"Yup. My folks aren't vegetarian, but I always make a few dishes. They're just three hours away and it's a scenic drive. The guest room's set up if we want to spend the night. If not, we can head out after dessert."

"You want me to come?"

"Yeah. I'm not going to force it if you're not ready, but I think you'd enjoy yourself."

Inwardly, he admitted that while he was grateful for what time they shared, he resented their conflicting schedules. The only full day they'd spent together, uninterrupted by other obligations, was Thanksgiving. He'd rather have spent Christmas spoiling her than seeing any one of his relatives. Unfortunately, he'd given his word. Now he had no choice but to show up with or without Anna, or his mom would be upset.

Envisioning Anna alone in that borrowed apartment on a day when everyone else would be surrounded by loved ones pricked behind closed eyes. Hugo prayed in silence she'd make do with him and his.

Anna had mulled long enough.

"Alright. I'll come."

Intending to wake his paramour to another omelet in bed, Hugo found that she was up, earlier even than the tumult sounding through the roof, walls, windows. Clucking, pecking, and stamping chorused at odds with the din within, yet the sun slept on. Heaving the coconut-scented blanket aside, he too rose from the bed and, yawning, located Anna in the kitchen.

"Did the birds wake you?" he asked.

When she stared at him uncomprehendingly, leaning her head to the side, he motioned above.

"Oh! No, the hens never bother me. They let us know it's day."

"Hens? Like chickens?" Come to think of it, he'd seen black chickens before—he just hadn't guessed they could fly, which they must've, to be up so high.

"Minorca chickens. They've been leaving eggs. Have you not been collecting those?"

He shook his head, flabbergasted. Was he supposed to have been?

"Don't worry about it. The weather's been plenty cold, so there's no danger of them spoiling. I'll go around, grabbing them before we go."

Oblivious to his confusion, Anna gave him a peck on the cheek and served tea, lavender for them both.

Wondering at her sour breath, he hoped she was feeling alright, but he didn't ask, as to not embarrass her. He'd observed a similar odor the last time she'd slept over, but it'd been replaced by toothpaste when she'd seen him off to work. Hugo resolved to pick up Tums and Pepto, to keep them stocked just in case. It was a mistake not to have better packed the cabinet already, given her history of heartburn.

They wished each other a "Merry Christmas," and she popped a holiday hits album in the stereo. Hugo retrieved a pack of cinnamon buns from the fridge, preheated the oven, and left them to bake. Over a platter of cheeses, jams, crackers, and easy-baked sweets, the duo exchanged gifts. Anna had gotten in touch with a colleague based in New Orleans, and through him, had an authentic poppet made for Hugo. The effigy was stitched and consecrated by a voodoo priest. A destiny spell had been cast on Hugo's behalf.

"Keep it near and the poppet will protect you from false opportunities," read the note folded into its certificate of authenticity.

While Hugo didn't hold much stock in magic, he appreciated that Anna remembered his affection for New Orleans. She really did care about him, maybe even love him, as he did her.

He held the doll out, admiring the gaudy feathers sewn into the head, their hues naturally vibrant, not dyed, as far as he could tell. Both the skull-wide eye sockets and ribbon-belted waist were lined with amethyst beads. The craftsmanship was remarkable. He'd picked up a handful of novelty poppets on his last trip, handing them out to nieces and nephews when he'd next seen them, but this doll was larger, elaborate, genuine. Thanking her, he placed his new friend atop the scant Charlie Brown tree he'd arranged beside the TV. It took some maneuvering, but the branches served to hold it up.

For Anna, Hugo'd hit the mall while she was away, picking up loose leaf tea, a variety pack of incense, rune carved crystals, and a book on palm reading. For her "big gift," he'd looked everywhere for the discontinued perfume, but failing to find an unopened bottle for sale online, he'd picked up a travel journal from the Lake Champlain Maritime Museum's gift shop. It was hand-made, a world map seared across the removable leather book jacket. Sliding the cover aside, Hugo pointed out the French link stitch binding and explained that the pages were antique, deckle-edged.

"The sales clerk was adamant that quality paper would inspire your art."

Anna smiled, thanking him, tracing the map with her finger before opening the cover and feeling the paper itself. "It's a little rough. This will be good for watercolors. In fact, I know just what to do with your old coffee." With a pot brewing, she pulled a paintbrush from her purse. Then, seated on the mat in the foyer, she faintly sketched, then painted, a pomegranate bloom.

True to her word, fifteen minutes before they were set to go she disappeared outside, returning with a mixing bowl full of eggs, which she then set on the counter.

Hugo made an exception regarding caffeine for the drive, chugging his third cup of Folgers as they merged onto the highway. He'd brought CD's, but Anna was content with the rumble of the Alliance, the horns and hollers of trucks flying past, the whisper of the wind. Her window was down, a bare hand surfing the chilled breeze as wet and shimmering flakes gained in mass, density, and visibility grew poor. There was a close call when the sedan parallel to them slid into their lane, and Hugo, cursing, swerved off-road to not crash—but the ground barely sloped down. Once the sedan righted itself, he followed suit, heart racing.

"Nice save," Anna said, but a moment later her head was between her knees. He asked if she wanted to pull over, but she assured him she'd be fine. It was just motion sickness. A few controlled breaths later and she resumed her previous posture.

A half-hour passed and they were pulling into his parent's driveway, staining the snow muddy. Not bothering to knock, Hugo led Anna in, where they were acknowledged first by passing children and the only teenager as he and Anna hung their coats by the door. The kids called out greetings, and he made introductions, aware they stayed put out of politeness, that they wouldn't retain new information when they had toys to play with, snacks to eat, and a cat to find, to chase.

His mom answered to two cats for the longest time, Mr. President and Your Majesty. Nobody was quite sure what became of Your Majesty. He'd vanished while Hugo's folks were at work, when they still worked. There was a search, every door and window inspected for signs of tampering. His mom went so far as to make a police report. "He's a purebred! He could've been stolen, sold!" The way his dad told it, she'd insisted it didn't matter that Your Majesty was fixed. He was an asset, *a prize*. The police were incredulous at her assertion of theft when nothing else was amiss, not so much as a picture frame knocked askew in the whole house. Not to mention the hypothetical cat burglars hadn't taken Mr. President, who was also a Siberian purebred. An exterminator was called in case Your Majesty was trapped in the walls. His mom wasn't thrilled to learn they'd only know if the cat was loud. A chunk of the laundry room beside the washer and dryer was pulled away, apparently over a family of rats Hugo's mom hoped was Your Majesty being shy. Then his mom, dad, the siblings, and niblings all hung fliers around the neighborhood, and while they'd received many calls, nobody ever did locate the fluffy overlord.

The only lasting effect of their failed search was that the children had such great fun looking for their fuzzy friend, Mr. President never enjoyed another moment's peace around them. While Hugo's folks adored visits from the grandkids, Mr. President was displeased at being placed in cabinets, toy boxes, closets, the bread box, or whatever other nook caught the kiddos' fancy before they counted down and spread out, competing to locate the floof.

This Hugo rushed to sum up as his niece opened the microwave and a giant mass of orange fur flew out, taking off across the kitchen, into the living room, and out of sight.

"Poor little guy!" Anna exclaimed, staring where he'd fled.

"Not to worry. He loves it!" chimed a pudgy bespectacled blonde woman in a poinsettia patterned apron stained with flour. Her tree light earrings twinkled as she turned from the oven. "Hello. Merry Christmas! I'm Barbara, Hugh's mom. And who might you be?"

As Anna introduced herself, Hugo's sister appeared, claiming a seat at the table. She was trailed by her husband, dripping blood from his hand. Hugo was relieved of introduction duty by Erin, who listed their names, and those of their kids, as she wrapped the wound. It was lucky she had, as Hugo could never remember if her husband's name was Harry or Henry. This visit was no exception. Forgetting that he'd forgotten his brother-in-law's name, Hugo paid no heed to his sister's retelling, and was forced to continue avoiding naming the man at all.

"What happened to your hand?" inquired Anna unnecessarily, the answer made apparent as a shuriken flew past the seated couple, wedging itself into a mounted cabinet door.

"Language!" chastised Barbara as Hugo and Harry-Henry swore, and Anna jumped backward, nearly onto a cat-seeking middle schooler who wasn't aware Mr. President had relocated the oval office to an undisclosed location upstairs.

"I'm going to kill your brother," Erin spat, pulling the star from the wall and shoving it into her bulging purse. The seams were already split, threads hanging loose. Ruddy, she stormed off from whence the blade came, Harry-Henry following swiftly after, crying out, "He couldn't have known they were sharp!"

Erin's clipped tone carried on from the living room, syllables muffled by an intervening wall, laughter from whichever kids weren't being berated, and *A Christmas Story* playing on the TV. Escaping the hubbub, a man with grey hair and the shoulders of an ex-football player ducked into the kitchen, his sweatshirt featuring a buck racked atop Santa's sleigh.

"Oh, hey Huey-boy. Long time no see. And who might you be?"

Anna offered first her name, then her hand, the latter of which he accepted.

"Well, merry Christmas, Anne. Always lovely to meet one of Huey's girlfriends. I'm Hugo, Huey's dad."

Hugo IV asked Hugo III where his brother was, assuming him nearby as it was one of his girls who'd freed Mr. President from the microwave, when that very same niece snuck up from behind, taking Anna's hand. "Come with me," Robin said. Anna asked where they were going but was shushed by the pigtailed four-year-old. Leaving his paramour to her fate, he placed the gift bags on a shelf for pulling from as he located each recipient.

"Brendan's out back, laying down concrete for a path to the pool. That's his gift to your ma and I," Hugo III answered, puffing out his chest with pride. "And I think I saw Molly heading upstairs. She wanted to settle Jilly-Bean down for a nap."

"Dad, it's snowing. You can't pour concrete over the ground when it's frozen. It'll expand when it gets warmer, and crack."

"Since when do you know about concrete? When have you ever built anything?!"

Massaging his forehead, Hugo refrained from reminding his dad that he'd helped build the shed out back just as much as Brendan had, and ditto for the treehouse. Yes, it had collapsed, but only a few years back, and a structure built by children couldn't be expected to survive Massachusetts winters forever, now could they? Likewise, he did not drag his dad to the Alliance that would've been relegated to a junk heap a decade prior if not for Hugo's mechanical know-how and willingness to get his hands dirty.

"I'm just gonna go talk to him."

"Fine, but go around the side. He was running the path to the back door."

Sighing, Hugo pulled on his gloves, jacket, boots, and headed out into the elements, circling to the gate, unlatching it, and letting himself into the yard. There was Brendan, his back to Hugo, the concrete scraper rubbing onto his greyscale camo jacket. Nearing, Hugo spotted Robin and Anna just beyond.

"But I wanted her to see the yellow brick road, daddy!" Robin was saying, holding tight to Anna's leg.

"It's my fault. I didn't realize the concrete was wet, but I shouldn't have let her outside anyway. It's snowing and neither of us are wearing jackets. Would you like help smoothing it over?"

Brendan was shaking his head, explaining that of course, it wasn't her fault, she couldn't possibly have known, and *what a force of nature* his little Robin was.

Then Hugo stopped listening, because trailing from the back door to Brendan was a single set of footprints, and they did not belong to a grown woman in flats.

"Anna, Robin walked you down the path?"

"Oh, hey Hugo. Yeah, we didn't realize it was wet."

"How did—how did you not leave any footprints?" he asked.

Brendan too stared from the indents tarnishing his work to her feet and back.

"Huh. Well, how about that? There aren't any tracks in the snow, either."

"I have a light step," Anna replied before casually lifting the child, promising Brendan a beer, and carrying Robin to the side of the house. Hugo called out to let her know where the gift bags were located, to hand Robin hers. Watching as she swung the fence door shut, he examined her path, and sure enough, Anna hadn't left a mark.

Shaking his head, he recalled his purpose. Hugo explained to Brendan the flaw in his plan, but his brother only reiterated what their dad said.

"Hugh, I know what I'm doing. I do this sort of thing at my own house all the time. Who do you think weatherproofs my driveway every year? Not dad. Cleans the gutters? He ain't climbing no ladders anymore. *I've got this.* Why don't you help ma in the kitchen?"

Anna passed him as he stomped his boots clean on the welcome mat. Then he did ask Barbara if she needed any help, and when he could pop his dishes in the oven. She scooted two slender pans to either side, letting Hugo fit the pyrex of sweet potato bread and another of cheese-and-vegetable-stuffed onions in between. He adjusted his recipes for the higher temperature, taking them out sooner than he would have at home, letting them sit for longer. Anna cut her avocados carefully, as they'd forgotten to bring the proper knife. She sliced, mixed, and spiced her salad at the kitchen table, popping on a lid and leaving it in the fridge.

Dinner was announced a little after four. Barbara led her husband and guests in filling their plates, claiming seats where they could. The kitchen table was circled by a set of four chairs, plus an additional two from the basement, which left a couple of adults and all of the children to fend for themselves. Brendan wanted to watch TV, and his wife Molly was missing in action, so Hugo and Anna spent dinner with his folks, Erin, and Harry-Henry.

Neither Anna nor Hugo IV felt the need to mention she was a vegetarian, but Hugo III noticed.

"Not one for meat, Anne?" he asked.

"No, not for a long time now."

"That's fine," interjected Barbara. "Better for you, Dr. Orion says. Have you seen his show? It's on CBS. He swears meat's why Americans have such high rates of obesity."

"And not because we're a bunch of lazy asses, living on the couch with remotes glued to our hands?" Hugo III argued, laughing.

"Speaking of going outside, when was the last time you went out, Hugh?" Erin asked.

"Your sister's right. You've got to get some sun. Just look how dark your hair is! Ugh. If only you'd taken after my side. You would've been so handsome, blond."

Barbara reached affectionately for his waves, brushing a lock from his face. "This red just doesn't suit you. Have you thought about dying it? Men do that now, you know. They dye their hair."

"Don't you put that idea into the boy's head. No, Hugo. Men do not *dye their hair*," his dad scoffed.

Anna swallowed a bite of her salad, which was admittedly more of a spread, that not one of Hugo's relatives was brave enough to try.

"I prefer the red, actually," she said, looking at him appraisingly before glancing at his mother's, sister's, and father's faces in turn. Harry-Henry was staring at his finger, the bandage turning crimson. Funny they should call him pale, he thought, when Harry-Henry's complexion had taken on a greenish quality and geishas were tanner than Molly.

"Well, there's no accounting for taste!" bellowed Hugo III.

Hugo IV, partially out of genuine concern but mostly to shift the subject from himself, asked after the finger. "Do you think you're going to need stitches?"

"No. It should be fine. I'll elevate it after dinner, see if that stops the bleeding."

Then came the sound of running water followed by yelling from the living room. One of Erin's kids had gotten it into their heads to bring the hose inside while Brendan was in the restroom and the other adults were distracted. Hugo III sputtered a creative torrent of expletives, but Barbara exclaimed only shock that the hose wasn't frozen solid. Erin left the table to shout at, and then to dry, the sopping and shivering children before attempting to dry the couch, tree, and a mound of toys with towels and a blow dryer roaring from her white-knuckled grip. Harry-Henry offered to help, but he wasn't much use one-handed, the other held aloft as if he were Lady Liberty and his butchered finger, her torch, enlightening the masses huddling under his missus' towels. Barbara upped the central heating until it was on blast, but the living room remained damp when dessert was laid out to melt in the kitchen.

Molly finally reappeared, admitting she'd been asleep. Her hair was up, revealing the jolly rancher tattoo behind her ear, which had provoked Barbara's immediate disapproval when Brendan first brought the girl home. Mouth full of pie, Brendan updated Hugo III on how the guys were doing at the firehouse, who was getting married, divorced, having a kid, and talking about retirement. Hugo III twisted the topic back to "Huey-Boy" and his career. He'd been with that no-name bank for what, three years? When was he going to march into his boss' office and demand a promotion?

"I mean what was the point of getting that degree if you're not going to use it?"

Hugo sighed but refrained from rolling his eyes, which would've driven his folks mad. "Dad, I'm using it.

I wouldn't have my job without a degree. As for moving up, I'm happy with my current position. I like my boss, my team, and I have a good rapport with our customers. If a commercial loan officer position becomes available, I'll apply for it, but there are only so many moves I can make that wouldn't be lateral. Unless a manager decides to retire—or, you know, dies—I can't move much farther up."

Hugo III shook his head. "Leader of men, my son."

The old man swallowed a bite, then opened his mouth to say something more, perhaps to argue on behalf of the joys of giving demands and being obeyed, but Brendan spoke up.

"What about your fraternity? Can't you find a better job through them? Some of those guys must work for bigger banks. Or on Wall Street. Couldn't they get you in?"

Anna turned to Hugo in surprise. "You were in a fraternity?"

"Yeah," he said dully, looking not to her, but at Brendan, and wishing he had Superman's laser vision. Not to kill his brother exactly, but maybe he didn't need two eyebrows, or hair. Maybe he could've used another scar on the side of his face, to balance out the cauliflower ear of the other.

"I don't talk to those guys anymore. We've moved on."

"Then what were all those sleepless nights for? I recall you scrubbing dorm room after dorm room. Those dues we paid?" gasped Hugo III.

"It went to waste," was Hugo IV's unapologetic response.

"Well, the wrestling must've toughened you up some. Those guys taught you not to be a pushover," Brendan commented, amending for Anna's benefit, "Don't get me wrong. My brother wasn't a wimp, exactly. He did track, swam, played basketball sometimes. He just wasn't as jacked as some guys, you know? Didn't do well when we fought."

Anna placed her hand on the fist Hugo IV hadn't realized he'd curled.

"It's a good thing adults handle arguments without resorting to violence. I don't think wrestling would do any good at a bank."

"That's right," Barbara said, smiling at the other peacekeeper. "And what do you do, Anna?"

"Oh. A little of this. A little of that. I'm a travel temp. Resort needs a last-minute fill-in for the craft shack this summer? I'm there. Cruise ship looking for a short-term live-in nanny? Count me in. Last month I worked as a dog walker in Montreal. The past couple of weeks I've been a personal shopper for businessmen visiting New York from Saudi Arabia."

"That's *a lot* of moving around. You must've saved up a ton of flyer miles!" exclaimed Hugo III, letting loose a cloud of carrot cake crumbs.

If not for the weather, Hugo would've insisted they drive the three hours home the second they'd cleared the dessert table. Instead, he took their overnight bags from the car and lugged them to the guest room while Robin showed Anna her volcano kit, Hotwheels cars, and Legos. When Hugo descended, he discovered half the living room had been converted into a fort, which Anna was in the process of surrounding with a lego moat.

"Is there a bridge I should cross to get to the kitchen?" he asked.

"Of course, and I can show you the way, but not without a token of payment."

Anna had usurped the antlered headband of one of the niblings and wore it with a throw blanket tied at her neck, serving as a cape.

Grinning, Hugo pulled a coin from his pocket, placing it into her open palm. "There you go—my lucky quarter." She could have all the luck in the world, so long as he had her.

She examined this most sacred of articles, grinning at the two tails, and winked. "Very well then, traveler. I bid thee passage," she announced, kicking a path through the toys and gesturing him forward.

He joined his mom in watching Anna and the kids from the kitchen.

"She'll make a great mother, this one. I like her," Barbara whispered, politely not mentioning how Riga had been curt, at best, with the children, nor how Evelyn frequently mixed up their names. One thing Hugo appreciated about his mother, and his family as a whole, was that they forgot every ex he'd ever dated the second they exited his life. Forgot their names, how long and seriously he'd been with them. All of it. As if they'd never been.

"One day, maybe," he said, not wanting to admit the extent of his affections, given Esteban's reaction. "We're still new."

"What's all this?!" Hugo III hollered, coming out of the bathroom to find the TV off and the couch on its side, tented with blankets and surrounded by legos like fairy mushrooms offering a honey pot invitation.

Chapter 10
Satellite Crossing

They'd gone to bed late, woken up later, and still found themselves downstairs before Hugo III was out of bed. Barbara was making pancakes.

"Brendan should be here in a few minutes."

No sooner had she spoken than they heard a knock, the squeaking of hinges, followed by an influx of wind and clucking before the door swung closed, shutting winter out. There was the swish of winter jackets being hung and boots being stamped dry, kicked off, placed.

Robin poked her head in first, followed by Molly carrying the burrito that was Jilly-Bean, Brendan, and a waist-height toddler lagging behind. Molly's waist, that is, her being rather petite.

"Uncle Huey, Anna, you're still here!" Robin trilled, skipping to the table and scurrying onto Anna's lap.

"Yup! Not heading out until after breakfast. You just caught us!" Hugo IV replied.

Molly coaxed Robin from Anna, but the girl refused to budge, and Anna said she didn't mind. Hugo III deigned to join the family after the last pancake had been claimed. Barbara offered to make another batch— "Erin should be swinging by and they might want some"—but Hugo IV told her to relax. He whipped up more batter. Smearing butter across the pan, he let it melt and sizzle before pouring each round.

A pancake was mid-flip when a clipped swear interrupted his concentration, and he dropped it, the half-raw patty folding over onto itself. Tuning to the sound, Hugo saw his brother and father with their heads against the back window, hands outspread as if to pry cell bars aside.

Turning the burner off and laying out what pancakes were ready, Hugo IV approached them.

"What's up?" he asked.

Brendan shook his head.

"See for yourself."

So doing, Hugo IV immediately spotted what had them shaken. Concrete and snow alike were so densely lined with small clawed footprints that Hugo was surprised not to see a row of raptors along the back wall, where the imprints ceased.

"I don't see steps leading back to the woods," he commented, tilting his head, perplexed, "or towards the fence."

Then, thinking of his own fowl infestation, he turned. Without a word more, he moved to the front of the house, investigated from the cropped window over the sink, nodded at the perimeter of upturned snow, and stepped outside in his socks and pajamas.

"What the hell?" Hugo whispered.

Scanning the drive, walkway, and surrounding yards, he gauged how far they'd crept, confirming that his parent's house was the epicenter, the destination where they'd gathered. A single set of tracks stuck out, the steps wider, of small hooved feet. Those ended at his folks' front door. Squinting upward, what he mistook for the roof was a plateau of hens packed tightly as shingles, twisting to face every gale. Directly above the welcome mat was a pig. Hugo blinked, rubbed his eyes, and the view did not change. Black, it initially blended with the flock, only its size ruining the camouflage. Squinting, Hugo could make out the golden bead of each eye, and no tusks, for which he was grateful. There was a flash of red along his muzzle that made him nervous. The wind tugged it this way and that, revealing the hue was not that of fresh gore, but rather of a flower.

Anna came to meet him, having donned her customary flats. She carried a serving bowl, leaving Robin watching from the doorway.

"What's up?"

Hugo pointed from the marked snow to the twittering roof.

"Cool. Boukman is here. Hey, Boukman!"

Hugo opened his mouth to ask first if she nicknamed every animal she saw, planning to follow up with an inquiry as to how the hell a pig got onto his parent's roof, but the swift-moving swine redirected him. It leapt, extending its legs, revealing skin flaps like wings. The part of him that was adjusting to the absurd, thought, *Oh yes. Like those flying squirrels,* as if that explained it. Gliding above Anna, it loosed the bloom before landing gracefully on the snowy ground.

Questions vied for his voice. "Did that pig just give you a flower?" was the victor.

"Oh, yeah. He's one of my mom's pets. Strong and loyal, she named him for a great hero and longtime friend. Hibiscuses are her favorite," Anna explained, accepting the offering and calling thanks.

"Your mom raised pigs?"

"Not exactly. She took on pets in the way that if you leave food out, you have cats and raccoons."

Hugo mulled that over, watching as the pig raced back to the house and jumped, reclaiming its rooftop perch. The living canopy flexed along his childhood home, making space for the bizarre creature.

"Can't blame him for wanting to get off the ground. It's frozen," she added.

Hugo was quiet a moment, what warmth he'd carried from inside having leached away, and he shivered as he spoke.

"I guess that makes sense. Heat rising and all. Why are they all together though? On one house?"

"You mean the hens? That's Boukman's posse."

"Your mom's pet pig has a *posse*? Like a rapper?"

"They like him," Anna responded in earnest. "He's big and keeps them out of trouble. Why are you making that face?"

Hugo wiped the disbelief from his expression. "No face. Here, I'll help you gather their eggs."

How hard could it be? Peering into his folks' hibernating hydrangea bush, he reached past a wary hen into the first nest he saw, before pulling his bloodied hand back.

"What the—?!" Hugo cried, looking not at his hand, but at the snarling chicken who bit him.

"I thought chickens didn't have teeth?!"

Without so much as a glance at his attacker, Anna bent to get a better look at Hugo's cut, gently pulling the flesh taut to check the depth. At the sting, Hugo bit his tongue to keep from releasing an unmanly hiss.

"Most don't. These do. I'd suggest approaching more slowly in the future, asking before you take from them. Not to worry, though. You're nearly done bleeding. Head on in, wash it out. I'll be out here a little longer."

"Alright. I should get back to making breakfast," he replied.

Barbara couldn't have cared less about some prints in the snow, or the tracks along the back path, so long as the birds kept to themselves. She wasn't the one cooking and that was novelty enough. Anna left the egg bowl on the counter, explaining the eggs were good for a month, and wouldn't require refrigerating. Given Hugo's scratch, the kids were warned away from the chickens.

"Why would we poke at them?! We're not crazy!" Robin remarked, admonishing her wayward uncle with a laugh.

At noon, Hugo and Anna departed, delving out hugs and asking Barbara to distribute those gifts they'd forgotten to deliver. Erin was running late, but Hugo wanted to get going. Traffic would only get worse as the afternoon wore on, and roads were icy.

Hugo pulled from the slick muddy drive, watching in the rearview mirror as the flock arose as a cloud, trailing after his Alliance.

"Well, they seem nice," Anna said.

Hugo gave a tired laugh. "In their own way, I guess. Dad's a curmudgeon, and ma's a saint for sticking by him all these years. I hoped she'd given up on my hair by now, but my aunts are the same way. Maybe when I go grey," he said, adjusting his shoulders. The guest bed lacked the support he was accustomed to and he could tell he'd be sore all day.

A turn later, the house was gone, but the flapping sound remained. Hugo kept the visor tucked up despite the reflective snow along the lane, the amorphous shadow shielding him from the worst of the glare.

"Why didn't they listen to you about the concrete?"

"Dad has a thing against effeminate men. Oh, what's the term now? Metrosexual?"

"Isn't that a well-dressed straight guy?"

Hugo shrugged. "I don't know, but they all bleed together to him. He's old school, you know? Likes his men tough, outdoorsy. Every time I lost a fight or turned one down, he'd take it as a personal affront. Complain Erin was tougher than me." Hugo paused, comparing himself to his sister. "Guess he was right. I'm not cut out to be an officer. Next you see him, he'll say I should've been a mechanic or a carpenter, depending on his mood. Drives him nuts I went to school for accounting instead. That's what that *swipe* was about."

"Parents," Anna breathed, her lips curled in a rueful smile. "They're never happy."

"What did your mom want for you? That didn't quite work out?"

Anna rolled down the window, letting her hand ride the breeze. Hugo turned the heat off, glad he was well bundled.

"My mom's mute, has been for ages. There was an incident. She was attacked, her tongue removed."

"Holy shit! Did they catch the guys who did it?"

Anna paused. "You mean, was her attacker locked up? No. He wasn't."

"That's insane! I'm so sorry to hear that."

"Thanks, but it was a long time ago. Initially, she struggled to communicate, but we worked out a system, she and I, until I could translate when she had guests, saw friends, or our family. No doubt due to the trauma, she's also suffered from a hand tremor since. So I was also responsible for maintaining all of her correspondence. That's what she wanted for me, and I don't blame her. She went from being a matriarch our community looked to for guidance to someone incommunicable, regardless of her experiences, her wisdom. A lesser person would have been crushed, too discouraged and impatient to train me, as I did *not* learn quickly."

"She wanted you to translate for her, forever?"

"Yes. Not just for her but for the good of our community. I cannot overstate the solemnity with which folks take her advice."

"But surely she wanted you to get married, start a family of your own one day? Isn't that what every mother wants?"

"Most, I assume. Anyway, I sat on my eggs for a long time, thought I was content handling her affairs into perpetuity. But then I started reading. I've always known how to read, or at least for as far back as I can remember, but it was limited to notes to and from my mother, keeping track of her date book, paperwork regarding her accounts, property."

"You never read in school?"

"No. I was homeschooled, and my family is a strong proponent of maintaining oral history and traditions. My father let it be known he wasn't keen on the mainstream media tainting my worldview and my mother didn't see fit to disagree—one of the few stances he took on my upbringing. It was actually my auntie who passed along some books she'd been gifted, not being much of a reader herself. I read them in secret, and well, you've read plenty. You know the magic of stepping into an adventure in an unfamiliar land, all from the safety of home."

He nodded, wondering what other miracles he took for granted.

"I let Auntie Freda know I'd appreciate any other books that came her way, and she kept on smuggling them to me. My mom found out eventually and forbade further contact between Auntie and myself, except I wasn't a child any longer and refused to submit one day more to her control."

"Didn't go over well?"

"No. I was given an ultimatum. Do as I was bid or leave."

"So you left?"

"Yeah. I hitchhiked to my auntie's place,"—Hugo flinched at the image of her climbing into the car of a stranger only for the predator to lock the doors and windows the moment hers shut—"shacked up there for a bit, worked odd jobs, saved up. Wasn't sure what I wanted to do, what I was good at, so I did what every soul-searching young person does who can afford to."

"Which was?" Hugo asked, unsure how anyone figured out what they wanted in life.

"I went on a trip. The second I had my passport in hand I booked a flight to Europe and backpacked until my funds ran out. Met loads of interesting people from every walk of life, got to see the monuments to their faith, take part in their celebrations, enjoy their music, literature, art. Filled a whole album with dried flowers, or leaves when I couldn't pick a bloom. You can't beat free souvenirs. Returning to the states, I stopped home, thought I should make peace."

"Was she understanding? Had she cooled off while you were away?"

Anna gave a bitter laugh. "Oh no. Hell hath no fury like my mother. She was as mad as the day I packed my bags, maybe madder after a year spent without her personal translator and scribe. Anyone else would've accepted my absence after word spread that I'd left the country. Maybe looked into learning American Sign Language or Black Sign Variation. Not her. Why should she abandon the language she'd created? A full year of silence wasn't enough to change her mind. Chucked a knife at me on my way out. In insult, not to injure. Mother doesn't miss."

"Does everyone in your family carry a knife?" he asked, keeping his tone level as he signaled before changing lanes.

"Mostly. Anyway, I hiked back to my auntie's, my time in Europe having wised me against climbing into stranger's trucks. I told her about my adventures. We pinpointed my passion for travel. Within the week she hooked me up with Maitresse. We don't visit each other much. It's a shame, but she can't be seen going against my mother. Bad politics, you understand. But we maintain a correspondence."

"So that was the last time you saw your mom?"

"Yeah. Pointless to go back."

"Christ. Miracle you turned out okay, after having been so secluded."

"She would debate that perception. My duty was to her, to our community, and I shirked it without so much as an apology. What's right for me was wrong for her, and many others," Anna amended, though she didn't sound regretful. "So, what's the deal with your fraternity? I thought those were forever?"

Hugo flinched, veering for the opposing lane before righting himself. If Anna noticed, she gave no sign. He took a deep breath, wondering how much to tell.

"I joined Delta Eta Nu, or DEN, as a freshman at Northeastern. Not having had friends in high school, I worried college would be more of the same, unless I was brave, and *made the change*. So I rushed, pledged, and it was hard, the—chores. The chores were hard. But I paid my dues, like a man, dad would say, powering through it until I was in. Then I had friends, and I was invited to parties, set for whatever job I wanted, or so it seemed. So we were told, I guess. I had a 'leg up,' is more accurate. Being a part of DEN made my college experience far better than high school. But uh, Delta Eta Nu, the Northeastern University branch anyway, was disbanded in 1991, and that was that. I don't talk to any of those guys anymore."

"Disbanded? Why?"

She wasn't looking at the green blur of passing firs, or her breath tracing the breeze. Anna was staring at him, but he kept his eyes on the road. They passed a deer crossing sign, another obstacle to watch for.

"There was an accident with a sophomore, this kid by the name of Harley Jacobs. He'd uh—he was supposed to help with initiating the new pledges, but he never showed up. After a few days, he was officially declared missing. There was a search." Hugo paused, swallowing. "It didn't last long. He'd killed himself, jumped off the

Mystic River Bridge. Northeastern and DEN both tried to play it off, pretending he suffered from psychosis prior to university, before he'd ever joined up, but he left a note. One of his siblings found it. There was an investigation then, well a few, really. Everyone wanted to have their own, Northeastern, DEN, the cops, his folks even hired a private team. Our entire branch was questioned, including rushes that didn't make the cut. I guess an agreement was reached. In the end, his parents got a lump sum, I think just from the school, and Northeastern formally cut ties with DEN. The consensus, at least as far as the news went, was that an initiation ritual had gotten out of hand, and he couldn't live with it."

"But he'd skipped out on the initiation."

Hugo didn't say anything, keeping his eyes on the post-holiday traffic.

"Was his note made public?"

"No. I don't think so."

Anna was quiet for some minutes before asking another question.

"When did you graduate from Northeastern?"

"May of 1990."

They didn't talk for the remainder of the drive.

Hugo hadn't been putting off introducing Anna to his friends. Inconveniently, her free time was the reverse of theirs. So when Esteban invited Hugo to bring cafe girl to his New Year's bash, Hugo was happy to oblige. She suggested it would be fun to dress up, stepping into the shoes of those they most admired to begin the new year on the right foot, later admitting her ulterior motive was making up for a Halloween spent in her day clothes, as she'd been busy commuting and hadn't time to celebrate on the appropriate date.

Unfortunately, she called Hugo the Wednesday before from Manhattan, apologizing as her posting was being extended and she wouldn't be back in Vermont until Saturday, New Year's Day. Hugo understood. She didn't choose her postings after all, and he had a manager of his own, with whom he rarely agreed.

"No worries. I'll see you then. Call you tomorrow?"

When Esteban came to greet them at the door, Hugo was dressed as John D. Rockefeller, the most successful accountant in history—decked out in his only back suit, a tie, and his pointy-toed oxfords. To drive the role home, Hugo carried an oil can, which while emptied and washed, provoked the nervous double-take of the host. Anna had planned to wear classical sailors' attire. Her hero was Jeanne Baret, a woman who'd disguised herself as a man in order to circumnavigate the globe centuries prior.

Hugo imagined introducing Anna to their host, Esteban shaking her hand, his face twisted in confusion.

"You know this isn't a costume party?" he inquired, moving aside for Hugo to pass within, alone.

"Every party is a costume party if you wear a costume," he replied with a devious grin and wink combo, exactly how he pictured Anna replying.

Esteban flashed his palms in acceptance. Hugo noticed new football star cutouts posed along the hallway between the bedrooms, as well as a bamboo stalk potted on a table beside the bathroom door. It was the only plant in the entire apartment and, being far from a window, Hugo doubted it would live long. Meeting up with a rather beer-scented Nicole, Hugo pictured her relaying how glad the gang was to finally meet cafe girl, over a hiccup and slurring.

"Cafe girl?" Anna would have parroted, her turn to be confused.

"Oh, yeah. Because we met at Muna's," Hugo would have said, staring at his feet, trying to forget how *that* interaction went.

"It's lucky he was at the Rock that night. After Hugh moped for days about you shutting him down, I called him out to cheer him up," Esteban would have explained.

"Then it's thanks to you we got together," Anna would have replied with an easy smile.

Sonya appeared with Holy Joe in tow, and Hugo wished Anna was there to make their acquaintance. They, at least, weren't inebriated to the point where Hugo had to worry they'd have embarrassed him. Anna'd heard about Sonya and her beau, so likely would have asked about the local comedy circuit.

"Given the recent election, politics is my new go-to. Just have to read the room right—I've got an act that makes fun of Republicans, and another for teasing the Dems, but it doesn't get much use in this town."

"Do you ever get to use both?" Anna would have asked.

"You know, I started with both. Figured people love to laugh at themselves. Turns out, when it comes to politics, *they do not.* Everybody just wants to see the other guy look stupid."

"I guess once someone picks a side, it's forever. Can't critique their own."

"Exactly! I wish I hadn't waited so long to try my 'dumb conservative' jokes. I would've filled the house in November."

With Joe, Anna would have asked for news in the world of literature, learned her preferences, asked for recommendations.

Hugo would have left his date amongst friends while he made himself a red-eye and filled a paper cup with caffeine-free soda for her.

Loading a plate with crackers, cheese squares, and hot gruyere to share, he scanned the room for other familiar faces. Watching Nicole's masseuse friend fall backward into a cardboard footballer, nearly knocking the Christmas tree into the decorative fireplace, it seemed he would be the only partygoer to ring in the New Year sober. Sighing, he faked a smile. Anna was working. She wanted to be with him, too.

Returning to the group, he imagined her regaling the bunch with the adventures of Jeanne Baret.

"So she was a crossdresser?" Nicole would have asked.

"Technically yes, but probably not in any way having to do with sex, so much as to keep her dream job."

There was a resounding crash as someone knocked over a lamp, pulling Hugo from his fantasy. He didn't recognize the fellow who took credit. Sighing, Esteban turned back to the group.

"Oh! I almost forgot. You guys know my roommate. See that bamboo by the bathroom?"

Looking again, Hugo nodded.

"It's from his girlfriend. They put tags next to it if you guys want to write your new year's wishes and hang them up. She said it's normally a summer tradition in Japan, supposed to make your dreams come true."

"Like Christmas in July, but the opposite," Hugo observed.

The gang promised to fill out slips and add them to the modest stalk. They discussed their hopes, resolutions for the new year. "I'm going to cut out sugar," Nicole announced. Esteban inquired as to the type before gasping in mock terror. "Or was that a euphemism?!"

She clarified that it wasn't. "I'm cutting them all out—fructose, sucrose, white sugar, brown sugar, honey, agave. They're terrible for me and I wanna live forever."

While Nicole beamed at her choice, she failed to rope Esteban into her spur-of-the-moment diet, the cream puff in his hand proving more enticing than the carnal pleasures she was drunkenly, and not in any way subtly, hinting at as rewards for his compliance.

Sonya's goal was to be able to pay a single monthly bill with money earned through her standup performances, and Joe wanted to read a hundred books by the new year's end.

"What about you?" Joe asked. "You've been quiet all night."

Anna would have tilted her head, giving the question its due attention before responding with, "Well, I've never been to Australia." Or any other place she'd yet to visit. "This could be the year."

Then she'd have looked expectantly at Hugo, who was far too self-aware to say what he was thinking—that rather than a year-long goal, he wanted Anna to move in with him at the end of her sublease in two months and a week's time. He'd marked his calendar, was counting down the days. What he needed was a grand gesture to sway her his way, a gift, an experience tying her to him, convincing her their love was unique. That he was her future.

Instead, after too long of a pause to have seemed genuine, Hugo said he wanted to be promoted at work. His goal was to be a commercial loan officer. No one called him on the delay, and they ambled, as a group, to the hallway table.

"Wonder if Mike will remember to water it," Esteban mused out loud.

The gang jotted down and looped their wish slips over the shoot. The unintroduced girlfriend watched approvingly from the living room and Hugo felt quite cultured—more so as he wasn't used to being the only sober person in the room. That, he figured, was just a Tuesday for Anna, and he wondered how old she was when she'd cast booze aside for good. Or had she never tried the stuff? Perhaps her parents were alcoholics. That would explain the violence. Then again, considering, Hugo recalled a certain ninja star whizzing past his beloved not too long ago, and while his niblings were many things, he doubted any one was yet an addict.

When next he stepped away to refill his cup, plate, Hugo returned to find Joe divining with her Tarot deck. He hadn't heard the question, but Sonya was pleased with the answer. Nicole wanted her future told, and Esteban followed after.

"Want to do me?" Hugo almost asked, beginning to feel left out, though he held no confidence in the foretelling abilities of printed cardstock. But, on second thought, he didn't want Joe to read his card in case she read wrong, in case she foretold a great leaving, an end to the epoch of Anna. Declining Joe's offer when it came, he saw Anna instead, putting aside her deck, shaking her head.

"No need for a reading. I know your future."

The others would have exchanged curious glances, but she wouldn't have elaborated. "She wouldn't need to," Hugo thought. "She knows we're meant to be together."

The countdown erupted at ten seconds to midnight, horns blew and poppers popped as the ball dropped, and having stepped outside to breathe in the chill, to shield himself from revelers expressing their love within, Hugo felt himself embrace his paramour, pulling her into a kiss. From beyond, he heard cheers of "Happy New Year!" being wished all around, received from friends and strangers alike.

Anna had plans to see a friend after landing in Vermont, so she missed dinner. It was after ten when she pulled up, the sound of her rattling ancient mobile alerting Hugo to her return. He experienced a minor pang of jealousy, but told himself he was being immature as he pulled her to bed. They made love in the darkness, wordless, her eyes flashing, before they slipped into a deep slumber—Hugo's uninterrupted by dreams.

He awoke late in the dim light as she was crawling back into bed. Soon Anna was asleep again, her breathing rhythmic, slow, undisturbed by the antics of Boukman and his pecking posse. Illuminated by a streak of sunshine where the blinds cracked, Hugo discovered a flaw in Anna's complexion. It wasn't her rippled birthmark, which reminded him of the scarification features on National Geographic, amplifying her bohemianess.

No, the blemish coursed down her legs. Running from Anna's thighs to her ankles were raisin-hued, three-dimensional veins, and after a moment's silent introspection, he told himself she was all the better for it. Wasn't that the point of the New Testament? How could a god relate to man if he'd never bled, knew no suffering? Her veins were akin to the wrinkles at his mouth, salt above his ears, scar marring his knee. To be flawed was to feel, and he didn't want an unfeeling partner.

In devotion to the human, rather than the goddess born of the story, called forth by his mind, Hugo woke

Anna with a prolonged bout of cunnilingus. Coming to slowly, she gave verbal cues indicating her pleasure, and upon climaxing, reciprocated his efforts. Then they relaxed an hour more before rising. She announced a need to freshen up, so he waited for her in the kitchen, and was ready with ginger tea and toast topped with scrambled eggs when she emerged from the bathroom.

There was no better way to begin the new year than together, he thought.

Monday passed slowly, everyone struggling to face the reality of due dates after the weekend holiday. Knocking Hugo steady came a lunchtime email headlined "Commercial Loan Officer Position Available," as if Esteban and Human Resources joined forces to prank him, but no. When interrogated, Esteban had just received that same message, and Janet, with HR, confirmed the vacancy was genuine. An unnamed member of the commercial loan team had moved on to bigger and better things, bailing with no notice.

"The sooner this position gets filled, the better," Janet proclaimed.

"What luck—that's exactly what you wished for! You have to apply!" Anna said, when he told her.

And he did. Going so far as to cancel dinner plans with her that Tuesday, with her full understanding, Hugo updated his resume to include the relevant duties of his current position and sent an email to Nate requesting a letter of recommendation. He had the entire application filled out, double and triple checked, when Nate came into his office Wednesday morning to tell him the bad news.

"Look Hugo, you're a good guy, a strong member of this team. And had you requested the letter a year ago, I'd have written it. But your productivity has been slipping, and you weren't the only person to ask. It weakens my word, vouching for more than one employee. I'm sorry. Get your numbers up, and next time, I've got your back. But right now, you're not the best fit, and it's not just my team I'm thinking of. It's Northfield as a whole. You're in the best place for you, and that's my final word."

Hugo thanked him for his honesty and feedback, biting back from asking if Nate was recommending Veronica instead.

Despite acknowledging the truth of Nate's criticism, Hugo spent the remainder of his shift, and that of the following day, dejected to the point of distraction. He used to be such a fast worker. "What changed?" he asked himself between texts to Anna, venting his frustrations.

Veronica's promotion was made official a week later, her role on the mortgage loan officers' team filled by a new hire, a recent graduate who'd interned under Nate the previous fall. Esteban admitted to Hugo that his request for a letter of recommendation had likewise been denied, but handled the snub coolly, claiming, "Business is business, and what he thinks of me ain't none of mine."

About to crawl into bed that night, Hugo asked that they keep the light on, that he might undress Anna himself, remove every layer with his teeth, but she declined on account of a headache. Would he mind if they didn't have sex tonight? she'd asked.

No. Of course, he didn't mind.

Hugo persisted with his request for over a week, but gave up his plea because when he pushed the matter, she invented excuses preventing any manner of sex, regardless of how much he complimented her smooth complexion, obsidian eyes, bountiful breasts, or dancer's legs. He blamed the magazines, the media, for promoting an anorexic waist, equating dietary deficiencies with desirability, and he hated them. So what if she was gaining weight? Did he care if her belly curved out, rather than in? No! Wasn't that healthier than living off cotton balls and laxatives?

To shield her from the influence of those paid to starve, Hugo offered to handle her shopping on the weekends while she was away, complaining errands filled what hours could be better spent relaxing together. When they went on a whim to check out an apartment complex on the water, as his lease renewal was only a few months away, Hugo was horrified to see the slew of magazines spread across the coffee table in the reception area. While Anna excused herself to the restroom, he flipped copies of Elle, People, and Cosmopolitan over, then seeing the Timberton-esque figures sprawled across their backs, stuffed them under the table altogether. When the radio blasted an ad for a juice cleanse, he changed the station and drew their conversation from fad diets to how disc jockeys and video jockeys alike should play commercials at a lower volume, to offset the intent of the advertisers to blare them. Especially for those featuring sirens, alarms, or singing out-of-tune.

He invited Anna to jog with him in the mornings. Through resilience would come self-love, that was the idea. Better than comparing herself to the paper-thin twenty-somethings dancing at the studio. She could build endurance while bonding with her paramour. However, while she was willing to join him for the occasional run, Anna refused to quit kompa, and Hugo found himself wondering more and more who was teaching these classes she couldn't bear to bail on.

He asked and she said it depended on the week—that the instructor, like a pastor, could be swapped out to a new studio or time slot without any warning, and often were. As for who was she stretching, bending, twirling, alongside? Nobody he knew.

While he'd once insisted, if only to himself, how much she'd missed in never having seen the Star Wars films, Back to the Future, or the Rush Hours, now he argued against going to the movies whenever the topic arose.

"Why watch a life when we can live our own?" Hugo quipped, buying tickets to a roller rink, where he'd observed women to be fuller-bodied, bulkier.

It hadn't occurred to him that the last time he'd worn skates, he'd been a foot shorter, twenty years younger, and regularly athletic. Less than fifteen minutes into their date, he'd only avoided serious injury through the assistance of a neon-haired goth who grabbed hold of his shoulder, bracing him against the railing when he slipped.

"Almost ripped myself a new one," he remarked later, laughing off his clumsiness while shrinking from the image of what nearly became of his balls.

His consternation over what might have been paled to what transpired after leaving the rink. They were almost to the car when Anna turned back, realizing she'd left her phone on the counter. Hugo would've gone with her, but she suggested he get the car running, defrost the windshields. She'd just be a moment. Barely five minutes later, Hugo heard a shout over the sound of his engine and, too rapidly to later recall, pulled his keys from the car, slammed the door, and raced to where he'd last seen her. Turning the corner, he spotted Anna backing from an alley, moving onto the street. Just past her was a man, half-hidden by the night, sprawled across the litter-strewn ground, darkness a wet halo circling his head. The man grunted, whimpered, howled.

"Are you alright?! What happened?"

"Oh! Hugo! Thank goodness! He grabbed me, then tripped when I pushed him away."

Hugo reached for her, looking for signs of injuries and finding none, glanced back to the moaning lump slumped against the dumpsters.

"Shit! Should we call the cops?"

"No. I think this," she said, gesturing at her assailant, "is punishment enough."

"Karma," Hugo agreed. "Ambulance then?"

"He did just try to rob me," Anna said, and then meeting Hugo's eyes, continued, "or worse."

So they left the attacker where he lay. Hugo guided Anna back to his Alliance, an arm around her waist. He peered into every nook and cranny they passed, a song of suffering trailing them over the grumble of the engine as it started up, over the wind when she rolled the window down to finger-surf the breeze, over her slight snore while she slept, and he coiled around her, wide awake.

"Why sit and stare at a screen for two hours, when there is an entire sky we've never given its due," he remarked later, before purchasing a sleeping bag for two and booking them a night at a campsite off Emerald Lake. He shivered and quaked as they lay against the frosty ground, his portable heater billowing fog that blocked the stars above. At her insistence, they slept not under the Milky Way, but in his car, with the engine off, her curled over the back seat, and he in the passenger's, until it was time to rise and drop her off, so he could head to work.

When he suggested parasailing, Anna replied that a quiet night in could also be nice. Not every date had to be an adventure, so he sprinkled chocolate chips, caramel drizzle over stovetop popcorn, and they played scrabble, which she won.

"The hell is a quire?" Hugo asked, flabbergasted, convinced she was misspelling choir.

"Twenty-five sheets of paper, I believe."

He looked it up, less because he cared about points than out of genuine curiosity.

"Damn," he said, recording her total on the notepad.

"Well, that's the game," she said.

It was time for bed. Still, she kept the lights off, the covers up, and the blinds closed even to the moon.

Chapter 11
Them Thar Hills

With Valentine's Day fast approaching, Hugo was taking Anna on a trip, preferably somewhere she'd never been. It was paramount to convince her of their potential before her sublease ended and she was forced to choose between Vermont and New York.

Before deciding on a vacation spot, or an itinerary, Hugo let Nate know which days he wanted off. Gone was the guilt at leaving his team in a lurch. Work would be there when he returned, and his one chance at a promotion in years had come and passed. He wasn't optimistic there would be another anytime soon.

Turning first to Esteban, then to the gang as a whole, Hugo asked if they knew of a scenic town, village even, without a single hotel or resort. He needed a location that was beautiful but unheard of, preferably where they had a connection to a resident whom he could pay to step out for a few days. He wasn't about to ask Anna to list every place she'd ever visited, partially to draw out the surprise, but also because he doubted she could.

He didn't care if they had to drive or fly, nor a whit about the climate. The *what* would come after the *where*. It was Joe who came through, her aunt Malee having hosted spiritual retreats out of her ranch for decades before the Dhammakaya Buddhist movement fell out of fashion in the states.

"She's not really my aunt, but she took me under her wing after we met at Berkeley, so I like to call her that."

"Berkeley has a seminary program?"

"Maybe? I dunno. I wasn't a student there. Just happened to be in the area when she swung by to give a lecture. Had to pay at the door. Anyway, I hung around while things were wrapping up. We got to chatting, one thing led to another, and we ended up exchanging numbers. I actually introduced her to the memoirist she's been working with since she stopped touring."

It turned out Malee'd retired five years prior, leaving her property in the capable hands of a follower by the name of Fred.

"No idea what his last name is, but he keeps the place from falling into disrepair. Her real niece suggested turning it into a bed and breakfast, but the area doesn't see enough tourism for that to be profitable. Anyway, it's in Windsor, Massachusetts. I'll call first, see what she says. I imagine Fred will be happy to have the company, remind him of old times."

The following morning, Joe texted Hugo the sum he was expected to pony up for the days he'd requested, as well as a rough description of the property.

"Not that I've been there in ages," Joe said later when they met for lunch.

"Not to worry. It's a place she's never been! She'll love it."

The minute Nate left the office, Hugo dialed Fred, introducing himself properly and requesting more information about the area. The location was rural, activities equally so. For an additional two hundred dollars, Fred would prepare their meals.

"That sounds great!" he agreed, satisfied his savings would more than cover the expense. "I'll call you with an ETA Monday."

As much as he'd wanted the trip to be a total surprise, Anna needed to be notified in advance. He wouldn't have minded packing for her, but doubted she'd have approved of him pawing through her things behind her back. It wasn't like she'd given him a key either, so he would've had to break into her flat.

That evening, Hugo pulled a gardenia and waxflower bouquet from behind his back, handed her the flowers, and announced, "Happy early Valentine's Day! We're going to Windsor!"

Anna smiled, accepting the bundle of off-white blooms, stood, and planted a kiss on Hugo's mouth.

"When? And also, which one?" she asked, circling the kitchen, and then the living room, in search of a vase.

"It's in Massachusetts. We're driving out Monday morning, as soon as you're back from Chicago, so I suggest sleeping on the plane, but you can rest in the car, too."

"Great! What's in Windsor?" she asked, settling on a water pitcher from the fridge, placing and arranging the bouquet within. Moving spray bottles from the window sill above the sink, she set the flowers down before reclaiming her seat at the table.

"Well, the big winter pastime is cross country skiing, but there are hiking trails, a bird watching group that meets every morning, rain or shine—"

"Blizzard or hail, you mean!" she quipped.

"Pretty much. They sound like an intense lot—the extremists of the bird-watching world. Let's see—Fred also mentioned hunting and a place where we can rent gear—"

"Pass. Also, is renting a gun even legal?" she inquired, brows raised.

"Hell if I know, but small towns make their own rules. Or maybe he meant archery?"

"Have you ever tried archery?"

He shook his head and she smirked.

"Let me guess what else they've got—ice fishing!"

"You know, I didn't ask, but I've got Fred's number so I can just text hi—you were joking."

"I was, yeah. It'll be fun. We'll figure out what to do when we get there. No worries."

"Alright. I just figured packing would go easier with a game plan. Are you excited though? Have you ever been to Windsor?"

"I am excited and no, I don't believe I have. This will be an adventure."

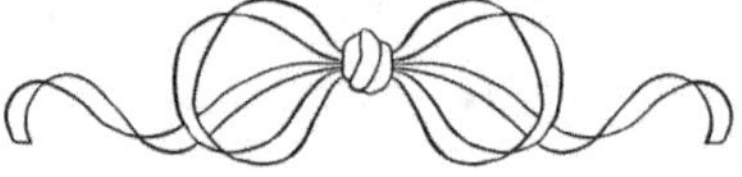

Anna fell asleep before they'd pulled from the airport parking lot. While she rested, he ran into her place and grabbed her bags. She'd set them by the door before leaving for work Thursday morning. Hugo kept the music low. At red lights, he glanced her way, admiring the shadows cast by her long eyelashes, her flawless complexion, wondering how he got to be so lucky.

Thanks to her oddball schedule, there was no traffic en route and they were making great time. During their only gas stop, Hugo reached for Anna's shoulder, gently squeezing, and she stirred, suddenly awake. He told her the time, how far they were from their destination, and encouraged her to use the bathroom. He had a hunch his GPS would struggle with the Massachusetts backroads and didn't look forward to holding his bladder in the middle of nowhere. His paramour was a lady, and ladies did not go to the bathroom outside if he could help it. Even when they'd gone stargazing, there had been a communal outhouse on the campgrounds. Filling the tank, Hugo shot Fred a vague ETA text, then followed his own advice upon Anna's return.

Trees and ground alike were white, but the sky was clear, azure. Passing gaps between woodlands and snow strained copses, the sun threatened to blind, but the shade of a solitary cloud kept the glare at bay. His cheap sunglasses remained tucked into the visor. During a gap between songs, he heard the telltale clucking above and realized the source for their shade. Boukman's hens were tailing them. "Well," he thought, "at least they're not riding on the roof," though he wondered at Boukman himself. Had the pig stowed away in his trunk? The backseat? Was he running alongside them? There was no pig in the side mirror. Would the birds fly back for him, guide him to the retreat, or did Boukman have a sense for where Anna went? The rearview mirror showed an empty backseat, though even sans foliage, the forest was sufficiently dense to conceal a charging swine. At ten to ten, they passed a simple white sign in the shape of an open book, which had been made illegible by the crisscrossing of orange spray paint.

Hugo pulled over to read the wide-lettered scrawl of the plank leaning against it. "Gageborough" proclaimed the sloppy stake.

"What's a Gageborough?" Anna mumbled, rousing from her nap.

"I don't know," Hugo said, "Maybe that's the idiot tagger?"

"Makes more sense as a town name, doesn't it?"

"Sure," Hugo replied, shrugging. "Though the GPS says we're in Windsor. Keep your eyes peeled for the 'Great Ashokan Retreat.' Fred said we'll see the name on an arch, where we turn, and again on the ranch itself."

As he'd anticipated, the GPS gave up at the first unmarked dirt road and began dictating strictly cardinal directions, assuming they traveled on foot. Anna noticed that they'd passed that same blue mailbox twice, the houses nestled in the woods, invisible from the road. Backtracking to the "city" center, they located a formidable grey-brick building, denoted the Windsor Town Hall by their, apparently recovered, navigator.

Hugo parked in the empty lot at the back, leaving Anna in the car with the heat on, aware that the instant he was out of sight, she'd be switching it off and rolling the window down. He crossed the pavement—which was neatly paved, the painted lines unweathered—tread the path around to the front door, and unsure if he should knock first, let himself in. A bell chimed, announcing his arrival.

"Can I help you?" inquired a severe-looking woman, her hair wrapped in a silver bun, drawn back from wire-rimmed glasses. She stood in the doorway of an office behind the front desk.

"Hi. I'm lost. My"—he paused, about to say paramour but guessing that title wouldn't go over well with this prim stranger— "wife and I are looking for the Great Ashokan Retreat. Have you heard of it?"

The woman's mouth thinned, and she raised her jaw, eyes narrowing. "Is Malee back to ripping off hippies then? You're wasting your time and money. She's an utter charlatan! Malee's not even her real name! It's Maribelle."

"Be that as it may, that's our destination."

"She's not going to help you and yours commune with some higher power. She doesn't have any sacred wisdom to share. There is a reason she went broke, a reason no religious authority has dignified her *retreat* with any formal recognition—she's full of shit."

Hugo took a step back, expecting an authority figure to rush out and redirect the self righteous diatribe of this woman, who Hugo assumed a mere secretary. None came.

"Maribelle didn't go to Oxford, and she wasn't welcomed into some reclusive Buddhist sect while in Thailand. Hell, I'd eat my shoe if she could prove she'd stepped foot on Everest, let alone meditated at the peak. That lady is in it for the money. Don't give her yours."

"Okay," Hugo replied, pausing to best articulate his response. "I'm sorry if I gave off the wrong impression. Malee's, I mean Maribelle's niece"—he opted against explaining how Joe and her *aunt* knew each other—"invited us to stay at the ranch for a few days. Fred, the caretaker, is expecting us. We aren't taking part in some spiritual gathering. Just planning to enjoy each other's company in a beautiful small town, surrounded by nature. Romantic getaway for Valentine's, you know? If you could point me in the right direction, I'd be grateful."

Softness returned to her face, and she nodded. "Alright then. Here, let me write it out for you. Some of the private roads don't have names, but they'll be faster for where you're going."

She turned to her desk and retrieved a pen and a sheet of paper from the printer. Hugo watched while she listed their route. Her handwriting was immaculate.

"Thank you," he said, glancing at her directions and making to leave. "You have a good day now."

"I apologize for being unwelcoming. I've seen too many kind people bled dry by that woman. Take care."

When Hugo returned to the car, it was an icebox, taking several minutes to start. He handed the sheet to Anna and turned the GPS off. Its constant *rerouting* announcements were useless. Later, he could tell his paramour about their retreat's reputation, but at that moment, he just wanted to get there and get warm.

They recognized the arch, despite how the naked wood blended in with the dappled forest light. It had been painted gold once, the lettering blue, but was so chipped that had they not been looking for an arch and been directed to its exact location, they'd have driven on. What letters remained spelled gibberish.

The road beneath was unpaved, unlined, and narrow, nature encroaching until the woods gave way to fields of knee-height grass and the gridded trees of neglected orchards. An abandoned fruit stall leaned beside the open gate of a rustic split fence that separated the once-purposeful sections of property. Pulling slowly forward over the uneven ground, they passed frozen corn stalks, a well, and what may have been stables, though they sighted no livestock.

The caretaker was waiting, dressed in a puffy jacket, wrapped in a blanket on a patio rocker, and sipping from a steaming metal thermos. He was bald, but Hugo couldn't tell whether from zealotry or genetics. With his free hand, Fred waved. They parked and exited the vehicle.

"Hi! I'm Hugo and this is Anna."

"Hello Hugo, Anna. I'm Fred. Let me help you bring in your things," he called, rising from his chair.

"Oh no, that's all right. We only brought a small bag each, but thank you," Anna replied.

"Alright then. How about I give you the grand tour? I'm the only person around so your stuff will be safe in the foyer, or we can head directly to your room to drop everything off."

Anna was amenable to seeing their room first, so they cut through the house. Passing amber wall after amber wall, each framed with patterned indigo molding, they finally turned down a hallway to a door with a welcome mat and a "Do not disturb" sign hanging from the handle. While the room didn't have a number, it was marked by a calligraphic "M" shape, the left ascender bending up and in, forming an eye at the center.

"This is the 'ta' suite. Malee labeled them with letters from the Thai alphabet. The heat works, and can be set from your room," Fred said, unlocking the door and handing Hugo the key. "Mine's a little farther down, the only other with a welcome mat. You've got my number, but if I don't pick up and you need something, give me a knock. I won't respond if I'm meditating, but I don't do that too often. Oh, and heads up. The cell reception around these parts is awful."

Fred gave them a moment to peak in and ditch their bags before turning back the way they'd come.

"Here's the lounge. The fireplace works. We've got that pile of wood there, and more outside if you need it. You're welcome to read any of the books, play the board games, and whatnot." Hugo observed that most of the titles mentioned Buddhism or hinted at general spirituality.

Fred pushed on, past the couches, rockers, love seats, and tables, through what Hugo would've called a lobby but Fred dubbed the meditation area, to a room with big windows and bigger picnic tables.

"This is the dining hall," he proclaimed once they'd stepped inside, and Hugo noticed a mural of a Buddha on one wall, and what may have been a prayer on the other, faded beyond legibility, probably from prolonged exposure to harsh sunlight.

"The side doors lead out. There are picnic tables and grills that way, but it's chilly for all that. The kitchen," he said, pushing a handleless steel door, "is through here. I'm around for cooking, but if you can't find me or you've got something really specific in mind, feel free to help yourself. You're welcome to anything in the fridge and pantry. Have you used gas stoves before?"

The couple confirmed they had.

"Great. Well, you won't have any trouble with these then. If you see tape on a knob, that burner isn't working. Best use another one. I don't mind doing the dishes. Just make sure they find their way back here, by the sink."

The couple assented, then Fred showed where he kept the fire extinguisher, just in case. Outside, he walked the couple to a shed full of skiing equipment, offering directions if they wanted to rent any hunting gear.

"Oh, no thank you. We don't hunt," Anna said, and Hugo realized with a start, he hadn't forewarned Fred she was a vegetarian.

"Well, I can also show you where the trails are if you want to hike. We've got snowshoes, but it's all slush now, and it's not supposed to snow tonight. There are ruins in the woods, parts of an old mill, and the foundations of some of the first houses built 'round these parts."

"Do you have a map? And would you by chance know where I could pick up a metal detector and a shovel?" Anna asked.

It would never have occurred to Hugo that treasure hunting was a winter activity, but Fred was right. The snow was melting, so the ground shouldn't be frozen.

"Yeah, I've got a map, and we've got shovels, so you don't need to buy one of those. As for a metal detector—there's Doug's Sporting Goods in Pittsfield, only about ten miles out. I'll bet he sells 'em."

"Great. We'll head over in a little bit, pick that up."

Fred concluded the tour by pointing out where the trails cut into the woods, and handing Anna the map.

"I suggest bringing a flashlight, in case you get lost and can't get back before sundown. You won't want to be out there after dark. And keep your phones on you. There might be some reception if you're high enough up."

Then he wished them luck and left them to it. The couple returned to Hugo's Alliance, got the antique warmed, running, and typed their destination into the GPS. Hugo remembered how to get to the highway, so he ignored its uninformed directions until they were beyond Windsor.

"Treasure hunting, huh?" he asked.

"I figured it might be a nice day out, make hiking fun. The snow isn't right for skiing. How's your leg been since the roller rink?"

"It's fine. I barely knocked it. Have you used a metal detector before?"

"Nope, but how hard can it be?"

They pulled up to Doug's Sporting Goods and Anna found the metal detectors immediately. There were only three different models, but the prices varied wildly.

"Should we each get a cheapo, or the fancy one and share it?" Hugo asked, not sure what the differences were beyond the price.

"Let's just get the one," Anna suggested, insisting she buy it, as he'd covered their room and board.

A man they took to be Doug was working the counter, and when he asked if they knew how to use it, Anna gave him the same answer she'd given Hugo. The man shrugged, swiped her card, and handed her the receipt.

In the car, she glanced at the instructions, waving the base above the zipper of her coat. It chirped and she squealed, delighted.

Twenty minutes later, they were pulling up to the retreat, double-checking what they needed for their hike. There were flashlights next to the shovels, so they borrowed one of each. Hugo emptied his bag onto their bed, filling it with granola bars from the pantry, water bottles from the kitchen, the flashlight, and a grocery bag in case they found anything, so as not to muddy the other contents. They patted their pockets for their phones, Anna double checked she had the map, and they set out.

The path was overgrown. Hugo would've assumed it was a deer trail had Fred not directed them to it. Pines leaned close, and the couple ducked to not wack their heads. Fallen branches like skeletal fingers caught at the hems of their pants as they hiked on, kicking slush. They heard the burbling before they saw the creek, and stepping over its rivulets, Hugo's sneakers sunk into the mud on the other side. Anna's assumedly faux, fur-lined boots remained spotless, but his were soaked through, pants wet to the ankle, hands chilled in their gloves, shovel quaking in his grip. The detector sounded on a trail marker, then again at nails sunken into a plank that was more mud than wood. Again it sounded and again they found dislodged nails. They passed what may have been the foundation of a house, given the multitude of rusted nails, a rusted cast iron pan, and a spoon. The floorboards, if that's what they were, had rotted away. Deeper into the woods, Hugo spotted a stone wall, sloped behind a thicket, half-hidden by a naked oak.

"Would you look at that?" he exclaimed, letting out a low whistle.

Anna glanced up and made a beeline for the crumbling structure. The mill was so far from the path that losing their way was a concern, and Hugo made a mental note as to which corner faced the route back.

Scrambling up the low hill, which was slick with snowmelt, they scurried around to investigate the ruins. Anna kept her wand to the ground, but it chimed frequently now, and she was dropping buttons, pins, and nails, into his bag as they progressed.

"Oooh! This might be a nib from a quill pen," she crooned, adding the point to their collection.

Turning, they found what remained of the corner where two walls merged, and a solitary stairwell too rusted and broken to be safe. The stairs led to a dead-end platform above the keystone of an arch, where perhaps there was once a raised walkway. A wheel, poles, and pipes leaned against the mildewed frame. Metal sheets, perhaps of the roof, lay strewn across the largely buried wooden floor, torn, bent, and rusted through. Anna waved the detector over them, eliciting a stream of beeping, before she pulled it away, taking a seat on an exposed bit of brick. Hugo took a cold seat beside her, and they admired the ruins together. He traced a crack with his finger, unspeaking.

The wind picked up, shaking dead leaves and snowmelt from overhead. After an upward glance to determine it wasn't raining, Hugo pulled out a couple of granola bars. They ate quickly, tossing the wrappers in his bag. Then he stood, wiping crumbs and debris from his pants. After a moment, she rose as well, the motion dislodging leaves from their stony perch. Beyond the crumbling structure lay another wheel, and farther out, a bucket. As they explored, and the plastic bag grew heavy with clutter, he mulled over how best to word his inquiry, which at its heart, was more of a request. They'd been exploring for hours when he finally asked how she felt about staying in Burlington, if she'd like to move in with him.

"I know it's a big step, but I'm ready if you are."

She turned to face him, tilting her head in consideration. She raised a hand but pulled back without making contact, likely to spare him what dirt caked her fingers.

"Sure. You're right—we spend every non-work minute together anyway." Not those you've spent at kompa, or with friends, he corrected in silence. "May as well halve the rent," she reasoned, smiling.

"That's great! We can even redecorate if you want! Maybe pick up a new living room set. I'm not married to the couch."

Anna chuckled, said they could talk about it later, and then yelped with excitement as her detector blipped over a half-buried eagle medallion. Hugo pulled the badge free, passing it to her.

"Looks like an award, maybe a military honor!" she exclaimed, holding it to the light, wiping away the resilient chunks of muck gravity hadn't called home with adequate force.

"That could be. We're a good two hours from Lexington and Concord, where 'The shot heard round the world' fired, but those soldiers came from all over, some of them probably from here. If so, there might be more valuables buried nearby. Most colonists didn't have access to banks. They stored their wealth underground, on their properties."

"There was a battle only two hours from here?"

"Yeah. There's a museum, the Battle Green and everything. I used to go every year on school trips."

"Awesome! Then we can go metal detecting there tomorrow," she announced, admiring their find and dropping it with the remaining food in his pack, safe from the grotty relics in the grocery bag.

"Just not on the Green or museum property itself," he cautioned. "The state claims valuables found there, and might fine us if they see the detector."

That night he ran out for grape juice. They toasted to the next stage in their relationship over grilled cheese sandwiches and mashed potatoes, Fred's specialty dish. Then they read in front of the fireplace, burning through the woodpile before heading to bed.

Tuesday Hugo awoke early, thanks to Boukman and his posse, but found that Anna was already up and dressed. She located a kettle and set it to boiling. They watched the sunrise, blanketed, rocking the rockers, quietly sipping lemongrass tea. Above, the hens pecked and hissed. Within, they heard Fred meditating, repeating his mantra, dragging out the vowels of "Samma araham." After, they returned to the kitchen where he was making scrambled eggs and bacon. Hugo joined in, toasting bread in the oven, and invited Fred to eat with them. The caretaker declined, not wanting to intrude on their vacation.

"Do many Buddhists eat meat?" Hugo asked, eyeing the sizzling strips in the pan.

"Many, yes. It depends on the sect," Fred explained. "If I can catch those chickens," he added, pointing upward, "I'll have no problem handling the skinning myself."

Hugo let the subject drop. He had no authority over the odd posse and hardly a satisfactory explanation for their trajectory. Besides, Boukman would keep them safe.

Anna had eggs on toast. Hugo had the bacon. Both were full when they set out for Lexington. The Alliance trembled with every knick in the road, every crack in the path. He left the radio off so Anna could hear the wind. A truck ahead bore construction equipment, including a ladder that didn't appear secured, so Hugo slowed, giving them more than ample space. The sky grew moody, threatening to rain, or perhaps sleet as the temperature dropped, but Anna remained optimistic.

"The museum will sell umbrellas and maybe ponchos, too. Can't let a little rain spoil our day."

Hugo agreed, grateful she wasn't the kind of woman to let minor inconveniences wreck her mood. Riga would have called their outing off the moment she saw the sky turning grey. Then again, she wouldn't have agreed to vacation anywhere *quaint*, having a strong preference for urbanity, and the tropics.

As he was looking for parking, Anna stirred, suddenly alert. He hadn't realized she'd nodded off until she awoke.

"Careful crossing the street."

"What?"

"When we get out of the car. Be careful."

"Uh—okay," Hugo said, eying an available space.

He pulled in, set the car in park, and withdrew the key. Patting his pockets for his wallet and phone, he gathered trash from the front seat as they stepped out. Spotting a garbage bin, he told her he'd be right back. Then, having tossed their wrappers, cans, and receipts, he saw a brochure rack on the opposite corner. Yelling to Anna, he gestured, indicating his intent. Not five steps later, the SUV to his right rolled from its space, and he leapt sideways, then backward to dodge it, the rear wheels just missing his feet.

Hugo yelped, expecting a chastised driver to pull forward and exit the vehicle to speak with him, or at a minimum to roll their windows down and apologize at a safe distance. Instead, the car continued to roll, crossing the narrow lane and coming to a stop when it bumped the truck across from where it had been parked. Peering in, Hugo saw the front seat was empty.

"Shit. That was close," Anna commented, her words half-a-cough as she caught her breath.

She must have run over when she saw the car pull out.

"Did you know that was going to happen?" he asked, stunned.

"Just had a feeling," she replied, holding her middle. "Are you hurt?"

"No. Shaken, not stirred," he said, attempting humor. In truth, he was more unsettled by the accuracy of her warning than the near accident.

Before hitting the attractions, they stopped by the Visitors Center and reported the incident, passing along the license plate numbers of those vehicles involved. A bespectacled clerk gave thanks, and as they were leaving, advised them to pay close attention to the weather.

"Looks like a wicked storm's blowing in."

The Battle Green was triangular and smaller than he remembered. A wrought iron fence shielded the memorial tower from grubby hands. Spotting a tour group, the couple joined in, coming to stand near the guide, who was dressed in passable colonial garb—a wide-brimmed black hat, blue vest, billowing white sleeves, pants cropped at the knee over tight white leggings, and black leather shoes. He spoke with a standard American accent, rather than denouncing "r" sounds like the British, or adding an "r" to words concluding in "a," like lifetime Bostonians. Having already covered the history of the Green itself, he was explaining the historical significance of a nearby tavern, which was a meeting place for the local militia, and later, hosted the first postal service in town. He spoke quickly, anticipating a heavenly turn for the worst, Hugo figured, weighing his own misgivings.

When the tour concluded, Anna asked Hugo if he wanted to swing by the tavern for lunch, but he explained that the property was being used as a museum and no longer served food.

"I can find us somewhere else to eat if you'd like."

"That's alright. Let's check it out, and then the National Heritage Museum. We can get lunch anywhere. By then, it should be drizzling and everyone will have gone inside," she said, with a nod towards their vehicle, where the metal detector lay.

The tavern was drafty. The exhibits at the National Heritage Museum had shifted only slightly since he was an annual visitor, but Anna enjoyed the displays, pausing to sit through the video showcases before examining collections of colonial art, tools, weaponry, and attire. On their way out, she claimed a free map, using it to find food.

"How do crepes sound?" she asked, pronouncing crepes like the French.

"They sound wonderful. Lead the way, fair lady."

"At once, good sir!" she replied, and in minutes, they were being seated at an intimate table for two by a window overlooking the street. Over lingonberry crepes and between sips of herbal tea, they watched the celestial gloom take on an angry glower, the drizzle fast turning to sleet.

"I'm down if you are," he assured, wondering at the impact of moisture on their new toy.

"I'll ask for a garbage bag before we go, to keep it dry."

Hugo nodded, dreading the wet cold to come, but glad Anna could hunt to her heart's content. There was no way a museum employee nor police officer would notice, let alone bother them, in *this*. Without asking why, the waitress provided them with a large bag when she came for the check, and Anna wrapped the detector back in his car.

The toy's screen was lit, and while they couldn't read the writing through the white plastic covering, they could make out the buttons just fine. She left the flat rod base bare to not diminish its detection ability.

"How are you never cold?" Hugo asked over the howling wind, between chattering teeth, his hand in his pocket and the other gripping a shovel he hoped wasn't suspicious to anyone peering out.

"I follow hot showers with short, cold ones," Anna hollered slowly, to be heard. "I didn't want to be limited by the climate I grew up in."

They could just make out the clicking sounding from her grip, and while they pulled forth what appeared to be a bullet casing, it didn't look ancient nor impressive, and Hugo's bag was fast filling with screws, nails, change, and the occasional earring. A few pennies featured wheat on their backs, and the Sacagawea dollar coin was a neat find, but they discovered nothing to compete with the eagle pendant of the previous day, not in interest nor value.

Before heading back, they stopped into a coffee shop, enjoyed a hot chocolate each, and hopped back on the road, where the storm was receding as quickly as it had come.

"Funny. Had it stayed sunny out, we might not have been able to hunt at all."

"Lucky it wasn't sunny," Anna agreed.

Back at the ranch, rather than searching for metals along the path, she suggested they spend their last day checking out the overgrown orchards and pens. Fred said that'd be fine, and let them know where they could find the first aid kit, as any one of those fences was likely to leave a splinter.

Before noon, they'd found more than one horseshoe, keys, a spool of copper wire, several rusted tools, and enough nails to intimidate Pinhead. They'd filled two grocery bags and Anna insisted on seeing if they could fill a third after lunch. To her delight, there were blossoms on the apple trees. Most were frozen, sealed into ice cocoons, but remarkably, there were untarnished petals on the ground. Anna selected a flower that appeared intact. She carried it to the ranch, where she let its shell melt while they washed up, snacked.

In the early spring sun, the couple walked languidly, only half listening for alerts before stopping in unison, peering at two stunted trees tied with shredded fabric atop a hill, overlooking the rest of the retreat.

"Did you hear that?" Hugo asked.

"It sounded like laughter," Anna replied. "Maybe a kid."

"Can you imagine letting your kid wander this far out into the woods?" he asked, hoping they'd misidentified a chipmunk or similar.

They crept on, eyes peeled for unsupervised little ones as they approached where they'd heard the sound. Beneath the scraps of weathered prayer flags, the detector chimed. Expecting more junk, Hugo plunged his shovel into the ground, but Anna reached for his arm.

"Gently. This might be something."

Nodding, Hugo got to his knees and pawed the earth away with frozen fingers, wondering what she'd seen on the screen. He didn't have to dig far, which was good, as his hands rapidly grew numb. Moving a section of dirt aside, Hugo saw gold and his pulse increased despite silent protestations that *it couldn't be.*

Gently, he withdrew what appeared to be a child-sized bracelet. Beaded, it was linked with tiny bells that rang in the open air, and a single pendant. Brushing dirt from the charm, it was revealed to be of fired clay that was framed by patterned gold, featuring a rudimentary bass relief of a buddha figure on the front, and lines of text in a language Hugo guessed was Thai, on the back.

He handed it to Anna, who suggested they show it to Fred. They found him in the dining area, touching up the prayer wall with fresh paint.

"Well, that's a prim—uh, an amulet, for sure, meant to be worn for luck. They're rented out by Buddhist temples. The gentleman seated on the front is almost certainly Somdej. He was a very important monk."

"Rented? Should you send this back, then?" Anna asked.

"Oh no, they're rented for life. And their being "rented" is more a matter of tradition than a binding agreement. Let's see." Fred held the tiny bracelet to the light streaming in through the dining hall windows, the bells echoing off the vaulted ceiling and walls. "I recognize this. It belonged to Kim. She was very close with Malee, essentially her right hand, and our top recruiter. A truly lovely woman."

"What happened to her?" Anna asked.

"I don't know. She left in the eighties, maybe a year after having a baby. This hung from her daughter's bassinet. Did you happen to find a golden figurine of a child where you dug this up?"

The couple shook their heads.

"We can show you where we found it if you want to check the area out," Hugo offered, but Fred declined.

"No, that's alright. Kim kept a Kumon Thong in the baby's room, swore by its protective charm, but I've always had a bad feeling about those dolls. Traditionally, they're made with—you know what, nevermind. You didn't find it. That's good. Anyway," he said, passing the prim to Anna, "this is meant for a baby, and I'm an old coot. My child-rearing days are over. You both are young enough yet. Hang it high, and keep it where it won't be knocked over or stepped on. Those bells aren't real gold, so you won't make much hocking it, but think of it as a keepsake of your time at the Great Ashokan Retreat. This place won't be around much longer. There's plans to sell, and the buyer wants to knock it down, so this is a nice little piece of history. Proof that you were here, that there was a here to remember. Not everybody has that."

Chapter 12
Friendly Fire

In a single trip, Anna moved her belongings from her place to Hugo's. The amulet she hung on a hook beside Hugo's poppet, which they'd relocated to the top of a bookshelf in the living room. They left most of the ancient junk with Fred in case they had some historical worth, but the eagle medallion they kept, and Anna took to wearing, the pin proving resilient. She waited until the final week of her sublease to save herself the effort of going back and forth, keeping the house plants watered. They christened their apartment, as if it was new to them both and not her second home for months already, downing wine glasses of grape juice and making love on any surface that wouldn't break under their combined weight. Despite Hugo's hopes that the spontaneity of their lust would best her desire for darkness, Anna flipped each light off before fully stripping, regardless of their haste. In the dark, toes were stubbed falling onto a table here, a cabinet there, and the bruises swelled, but Hugo never complained. Anna was there to stay.

They awoke together. Boukman's posse knocked at their roof with the rhythm of a drummer signaling each new dawn. Their song, the beat, preceded Hugo's alarms until he stopped setting them. Most days he jogged alone, but Anna kept up when she joined in, and Hugo suspected, easily could have passed him. He took to singing in the shower, the flock harmonizing from beyond the blurred and tiled window. After a failed attempt at showering together in which neither of them exited fully cleansed of soap, they took turns in the bathroom, sharing the sink and mirror only when he shaved his jaw, and she, her skull. Then he and his paramour would eat, struggling to hear themselves over their winged neighbors, laughing between shouts. He'd go off to work, striding past bushes and trees wrapped in nests like garland. Were the commute any less, he'd have made a habit of lunching in her company. Except for Wednesdays when she had kompa, five on the dot he was logging off his PC, saying his goodbyes, and leaving. Humming a song all his own, he raced after his heart, smiling until his cheeks grew tight.

Work would be there tomorrow, but Anna was home, where the hens would have quieted, having caught their every seed, nut, worm for the day, and were huddling to rest. He crossed the welcome mat, stepped over fallen petals, and there she was, poised, beautiful, in the kitchen with her tea and notebook, or in the living room, emailing clients, reading a biography, being. And so they'd chat.

Did he know Marie Antionette wasn't fluent in French when she married Louis XVI, or that it was unknown then that he would be king, and therefore, she, queen? Was he aware Joan Jett nearly quit learning the guitar as a teen because her instructor taught folk music? What a world. Could he imagine the folk musician Joan Jett, or more accurately, Joan Larkin?

There were times she read silently on, only rising to make or eat dinner, depending on whose turn it was to cook. After eating, the other would clean. Then, carrying thermoses of cocoa, they'd take a walk so she could enjoy the chill, the tickle of snowflakes before mud season set in and the outdoors lost their appeal. If the weather was wrong, or they were too stuffed, they'd sit and talk about their day, their week, their dreams.

When grocery shopping, Anna would fill their cart with fresh produce. The first time, he tried to stop her.

"We can't buy all of this! It'll spoil."

"Trust me. It won't," she said. He did, and it didn't.

He'd fall asleep holding her, occasionally waking in the night to the tinkling of bells, like a child's laughter, but come morning, phantom sounds faded to the annals of make-believe, with deja vu, and the near memories of familiar scents. Not that he'd have heard it anyway, over the birds.

Anna found the white walls draining. Their home pulled from her until she'd had enough, and he returned from work to find every room refreshed. The living room was blue, for comfort, the kitchen green to maintain their good health, the bedroom violet to inspire wisdom in their dreams. Hugo never did mention the last real dream he'd had was of her. Only the bathroom retained its original hue, for purity, she explained. She mounted rosemary above every window and the front door, lit incense daily, and placed a potted avocado tree in the foyer, across from the pomegranate tree. Their flat smelled like an herb garden.

She had the habit of leaving cabinets open, cups half drank, abandoned when they reached room temperature, but Hugo didn't mind closing a door here, collecting and rinsing a glass there. In turn, she handled running the washer, dryer, and the folding. As before, they split the dinner chores, cooking on alternating nights and scrubbing the dishes when they didn't.

Then came the dreaded Thursday mornings when he'd kiss her goodbye, praying time would hurry to Sunday night or Monday already, depending on when she was due back. He'd text and call while she was away, and she responded when she could, which was infrequent.

Esteban was miffed Hugo stopped coming to football Sundays and especially disappointed he'd flaked on his Super Bowl party. Hugo defended himself by pointing out weekends were his chance to prove himself at the bank. A raise was far past due, and either the next promotion was his, or he'd walk—a hard line Esteban advised against. Already, in his downtime Hugo was checking the classifieds, the hiring pages of various banking and financial groups' webpages. His dad was right, though he'd never say so. His lackluster position was his fault for settling with the first bank that said yes. Now that he had experience in the field, he could move onward and upward, even if that meant spreading out. So far he'd been interviewed twice, by different banks, but there hadn't been any follow-ups.

To pacify Esteban, and in support of Sonya, Hugo prioritized Thursday comedy nights. By that late hour, he'd have been useless behind a desk, anyway.

Sonya was constantly altering her routine, testing out what worked and what didn't, but the changes were subtle to viewers. Given the gang had been watching her regularly for months, Esteban was certain he had her entire act memorized, and to prove it, ran it through one night as they relaxed on Nicole's couch. Sonya nodded when he was done.

"I guess it's time to shake things up," she agreed as he took a bow. "Sounds like I've been in a hell of a rut."

The gang offered to put their heads together and she accepted. Nicole passed notebooks, pens, highlighters around, and they brainstormed, jotting down jokes, breaking them down into parts to see what worked, what was funny, if there was anything she could build from. They looked to societal norms that made no logical sense, how prostitution was a crime unless there was a camera involved, how men benefited more from skirts than women, and how citizens were forced to deduce what they owed in taxes though the government knew better and would fine them over mistakes. Hugo texted Anna, asking if she had suggestions, but when he checked his phone every five, ten, fifteen minutes, she hadn't answered. Would she still be working at this hour? He wondered.

Anna called the following afternoon, from the Borowitz Oceanfront Hotel on the Jersey Shore. He wanted to complain about her ignoring his texts—ask what she was doing that was so much more important than her paramour, but refrained. What if she thought him pushy, jealous? She vented over the ills of collaborating with another matchmaker, how it was always a bust. Anna didn't enjoy toeing the line between helping and overstepping. "All they have in common is their net worth and where they grew up. Their musical tastes clash—and of which, the DJ supplied neither! They abide by opposing diets and they don't even share a faith!" Meanwhile, he reverted to his less sociable self, eating cereal for every meal rather than cooking with the ingredients they'd carefully purchased, a week's worth of recipes written on the calendar and a week-end's supply ignored.

The cacophony of their upstairs neighbors exacerbated his mood. Saturday morning, after three hours of tossing and turning, trying and failing to fall asleep amidst their squawking, Hugo banged his broom against the ceiling, leaving a dent, showering his eyes with dust. The flock screamed back. Swearing, Hugo retrieved the phone book. In minutes, he was on the line with an exterminator.

"Because the infestation is on the exterior, we don't have to kill the vermin—just make your yard inhospitable. I'll be over at noon. See you then."

Hugo had just finished washing his bowl after lunch when a dingy orange truck pulled up to the curb. A man in a grey jumpsuit hopped out, and Hugo met him at the stoop.

"What in the Lord's good name?! Is that a pig?"

"Yep. Quite the jumper, that one."

"Damn. Well, I see what you were talking about. Any idea why they've gathered here? I'm not seeing a fountain, or berries, unless they're out back."

"Haven't got a clue," Hugo lied.

The exterminator bade Hugo return inside and don earplugs while he blared an air horn. Despite his protection, he felt the vibrations and heard the boom sounding at regular intervals from various points on the property. After several quiet minutes, Hugo returned to the front yard where the man was waiting.

"That did the trick. I'm going to hit the perimeter with goose repellent. It's effective against most birds. No reason it shouldn't scare swine. If they come back, pick up windchimes, or statues. I'd go with predators. There's a saw shop up in Colchester. You can find sculptures of just about any animal you can think of. Hell, get a flag, too. Birds don't like their flapping. Hypocrites, if you ask me."

Hugo thanked the man, watching as he spritzed the few trees, then bush after bush. Once the exterminator was confident the pests were properly repulsed, he handed the bill to Hugo, who paid without complaint. The second the truck was out of sight, Hugo drove to Colchester. The GPS announced his arrival a block early, but he found the saw shop regardless, where he purchased two basswood wolves. On the way home, he picked up the other supplies. It was to his shock and awe that the posse had reclaimed their perches while he was out. Beady yellow eyes traced Hugo's trajectory, Boukman's snarling betraying his ornery disposition.

Hens circled in an ominous black cloud as Hugo arranged the wolves, posting an American flag by the door and windchimes over the porch. The birds were so fat, Hugo was surprised at their grace in the air, wondering at the strength of their wings, the speed with which they flexed to propel themselves upon takeoff. The wind was picking up, flag and chimes making a ruckus, but the posse refused to disperse, growing louder, wild, apparently irate. Under a hailstorm of guano and suddenly dive-bombing chickens, Hugo rushed inside, dialed the exterminator anew, and left a message, which went unanswered.

Esteban didn't call, but Hugo didn't mind the absence. Without any distractions Monday, he spent his lunch break catching up on work. Anna was watering the pomegranate tree when he arrived home and he smiled. Here was his joy, he thought, as he listened to Anna describe her heroine of the week.

Tuesday, Esteban popped in, asking him to lunch, but Hugo declined, wanting to push ahead. Esteban rolled his eyes and left. Wednesday was a different story. Hugo was low on projects and went to Esteban, asking him to Muna's. His friend didn't need any persuading.

While they were brainstorming for Sonya's show over hot drinks and biscuits, Hugo saw a remarkably familiar blonde woman outside—gaunt, fair skinned, and as she turned to enter the bakery, he choked on his bite.

When he could speak, he whispered an explanation. "Holy shit. It's Evelyn, my ex," he said, leaving the addition, "that I cheated on with Riga" unsaid.

Evelyn spotted him before Esteban could respond, darting over without having ordered.

"Hugo? What are you doing in Vermont?!"

"Live here now. You?"

"Oh, I'm here for a show."

"Really?! I'd heard you don't make appearances anymore."

"You heard right! I don't go to *my* shows. No point, really. I don't have much to say beyond my artist statement, and hate having to bullshit the other attendees. Nah, I'm here for a friend. He's a photographer and he's having his first solo exhibition. You guys should check it out!" she said, listing where the show was being held and for how long. "Oh, and I'm Evelyn by the way," she added with a wave at Esteban, who introduced himself in turn.

Hugo declined on his friend's behalf. Having seen more than his share of art shows, he was confident that photographs didn't interest himself in the slightest, and assumed the same of Esteban. Evelyn understood, insisting instead that they meet up for coffee when he got out of work.

"Sure! See you a little after five." he replied after they'd exchanged numbers.

Evelyn was apparently familiar with Muna's. She regularly visited Burlington on her way to an artist's retreat in Maine, and the blue-haired barista greeted her by name, getting started on her usual order before asking Hugo what he wanted. She'd invited him out, and so insisted on covering their drinks and a pastry each before they set themselves at a table with a view of the street. Evelyn confessed she hadn't paid the meter, and they kept an eye out for officers in case she had to move her Ford.

"So how are you doing?" he asked after they'd eclipsed what small talk either could muster. They hadn't exactly parted on positive terms, and had only seen one another in passing since, years ago. "I've heard some wild rumors," he admitted.

She smiled that old crooked grin, and a wisp of hair fell before her eyes. He fought the urge to brush it aside.

"Lemme guess. I went off the deep end, started talking to the dead, taking in wayward youngsters and indoctrinating them into an occult faith founded on my own delusions. Close?"

"Nail on the head, really."

"And you're hoping I'll dispel such wild accusations."

"Are you not going to?"

She looked down, examined her paint-speckled fingers, before her eyes met his again.

"It's true. All of it. I mean, naysayers have their spin, but the facts line up. I see dead people. It's not a secret. And I do run a safe house for runaways down south. Thing is, my house changes people, and I warn these kids, if they like who they are, there are better places for 'em. I'll make the calls, buy the bus tickets myself. Now if change is what they need, changing from their core on out, then yeah, I welcome them in. But I'm no cult leader. Nobody is being initiated into some religious establishment. That book I wrote, it's more about the house, how and what I see, than belief."

Listening, Hugo thought he heard a tint of scorn in that last word.

Hugo chose his words with care, for while certain she'd heard far worse, he didn't want to hurt her more than he—and life—obviously had.

"But Eva, how do you know you're right? And not suffering from some psychosis? Schizophrenia?"

She shook her head, still smiling.

"Do you like who you are?" she answered without answering.

Hugo considered the inquiry, responding in earnest.

"I don't know. I didn't used to. Not after everything with you and Riga. Hoped moving here would be the fresh start I needed, help me be better. But when I arrived, I was still me. Then, some months ago I started seeing things."

He paused, scanning her face for a reaction. When she merely blinked, nodding his story forward, he acquiesced, explaining first about the book, before dallying on the fantasms, skirting by the pastel portrait, and finally described nearly drowning, trying to chase his figment down.

"That is pretty serious, for you."

"Right? Then, get this! I saw her. In real life, right here in this cafe! Asked her out, and I mean, she said no—but I was persistent and she changed her mind. Now we're living together. I love her. And having foreseen her, having some higher power tell me, point blank, this is the one, that I'm worthy of this goddess, well, I'm feeling a lot better about who I am. If I'm good enough for her, I must be good, because she's great."

"I'm glad you're happy. My therapist would suggest not tying your self-worth to somebody else, but that's easier said than done."

"That's in case she leaves. But she won't. What God or gods would show me my dream woman if she'd never feel the same?"

"I've got to ask, how do you know you're right? And not suffering from some psychosis? Schizophrenia?"

"I saw her in my head before I ever met her."

"And she looks exactly like the portrait? How did she react to that?"

"Oh, ah, that actually disappeared, come to think of it, on the day we met."

"So you have no proof?"

When he didn't respond, she reached forward, gently patting his hand.

"There are no mandatory rituals taking place under my roof. No religious services. If the kids want to pray to the deity of their choosing, so be it. But before long, they see as I do. They see the dead. You could write it off as mass hypnosis, but I've met the departed, then seen their faces on the evening news. You don't have to believe me, and that's fine, but I choose to believe you." She paused for breath, then concluded, "There is more to our world than we know."

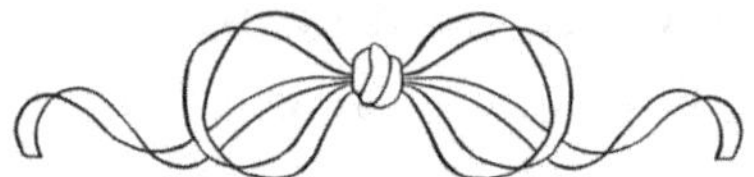

It was to an empty home that Hugo returned. He and Evelyn had talked for longer than he'd anticipated, and the stove clock read after seven. Anna should've left kompa at six. What if she was with someone else? He checked the bedroom, in case she was napping. The bed was made, empty. Her car wasn't out front, and her purse wasn't on the counter. Could she have met someone? Was she having drinks with another guy?

"Stop being crazy!" Hugo told himself.

Fate wouldn't deliver the unfaithful. Texting her, he said he was home, asked where she was.

What if she'd gotten into an accident? Was his destiny to have prevented it, kept her off the road, but he'd been too busy fraternizing with his ex and the drunk driver raced through the red light, barreling into Anna's driver-side door, slamming her car into another, leaving the scene and abandoning her for dead? Was she hung upside down, the seatbelt all that held her unconscious body in place as the blood trickled from lacerations across her scalp, face, micro-cuts peppering her limbs from the shattered glass, bodily fluids and leaked gasoline intermingling, awaiting the spark—no. *He had to calm down.*

"Breathe, Hugo, breathe," he said, staring at his phone, waiting for it to vibrate, but it refused.

She was probably fine. Probably not cheating. Not dying nor dead. Probably, she was at the grocery store, picking up an obscure Haitian ingredient he'd never heard of and would've been unable to locate without assistance. Or, there had been car trouble, and she was just leaving the mechanic's—better yet, the Enterprise office, in a fresh-smelling rental. But if she was in an accident, how would the hospital know who to contact? Should he call the nearest emergency rooms, just in case? Wouldn't it be better to know than to wonder if they'd received an unconscious female patient with a kohl complexion and shaved head whose license plate was from New York?

The pig snorted and he swallowed the urge to stomp outside and punch it. Hose down the siding, the roof, the grass, with water, then their nests with oil—setting every guano-laden bush and tree alight. Would those beaky bastards begin invading his evenings too, with their hideous cries?! They'd already robbed him of the morning conversations he would've so enjoyed with his paramour.

The doorknob turned as he was wondering whether wetting the house would keep it from burning. Did Home Depot sell fireproof tarps large enough to cover his flat? Where did he put the lease copy? He could check the square footage.

"Hey," Anna called when she caught sight of him standing in the middle of the living room, cell phone still in hand.

"Where have you been? I texted and you never responded."

"Oh yeah, sorry. The girls and I got drinks after kompa."

"The girls? Who are the girls? And since when do you drink?"

"Ever heard of mocktails?" she asked before listing their names. "Can't see how you'd know them. They invited me out last week, too, but I wanted to finish my book. I must have mentioned then."

Hugo was sure she had not and said so.

"Oh well. Now you know."

"Anna, I was worried. You could have been dead in a ditch! I was about to start calling hospitals."

"You mean morgues?" she laughed, but grew serious upon reading his expression. "Look, I'm fine. I didn't see your text but would've gotten back to you when I did."

Hugo sighed, took a seat on the couch, leaned his head against his hands. "Okay. In the future, can you let me know when you're going out?"

Anna relaxed into the seat beside him. "Sure, if I know I'm going out. This was a last-minute get-together."

"Alright. How about next time, last-minute or planned, you text me, letting me know when you think you'll be home."

She considered, shrugging. "Sure. I'll try to remember to text you next time. But what could you have done, were there an accident?"

"What do you mean?"

"Well, let's say I was dying, or dead, in a ditch. This is a city. Someone would hear the crash, call the cops, help would come. Are you trained to apply first aid?"

Hugo admitted he was not.

"Okay. So in a medical emergency, you'd be doing nothing but offering moral support and panicking. That's fine, normal, but wouldn't it be better to wait until

I was admitted to the hospital, being treated, surrounded by doctors who could tell you my diagnosis?"

"What if you were unconscious? How would they know who to notify?"

"I've got you listed as my emergency contact in my wallet. It's pointless wondering where I am, stressing yourself out. Either I'll be home when I get home, or the hospital will give you a call. Then you can feel your feelings because you'll know, not wonder."

"That's easy to say."

"It takes practice, but start now. You'll be happier for it."

"Okay," he said. "I'll try to worry less if you answer your phone more. Cool?"

"Oh, alright. Cool."

"Great. I'm gonna whip up dinner. Did you eat while you were out?"

She had not, and he made them one of the many salads from his new Creole cookbook, *From Granmè's Table.* The recipe called for tomatoes, red onions, garlic cloves, mint, chives, and a dressing of blended olive oil, vinegar, and mustard. It also called for a splash of Merlot, but he substituted with sherry, relieved the dish wasn't sour and Anna seemed to enjoy it, finishing hers in record time. He was snapping the leftovers into Tupperware, and she was doing the dishes when a commotion erupted out front.

Hugo'd barely opened the door when a hen burst through the gap, swooping inside. Alarmed, he turned to grab the broom to shoo the pesky intruder but was distracted by a very fat little dog yipping from the stoop. Too skittish to enter their enclosed space, it backed away from the exiting Hugo while barking at his upstairs neighbors.

"How do you like it?!" Hugo called above, antagonizing the ever-present Boukman.

Watching the pig lift its head and level eyes on the fluffy assailant, Hugo intervened before the pup could get hurt. Lunging, he reached for the furball, but it scurried away, redirecting its high-pitched yapping at him.

"Anna," he called into the house, "grab some cheese! There's a dog without a tag."

She was behind him immediately, passing along cheddar chunks with which to coax the stray. Hugo spent several minutes inching near, issuing kind words, common commands, and whistles, all to no avail. Finally, Anna stepped from the doorway, barefoot, and bent down.

"Come here," she said, just once, and the dog charged into her arms, dousing her with big sloppy kisses.

"Okay, I love you too!" she said, laughing, and carried the dog in.

Hugo closed the door behind them and Anna put their new friend down on the couch. In the lamplight, they were better able to discern its features. They were looking at a mutt, Hugo assumed, or perhaps a very obscure purebred. Shaped like a Norwich Terrier, with its short body and shorter legs, the coat was reminiscent of a golden retriever, both in texture and color. Its eyes, her eyes, were small, dark, and it was certainly a she as *she* wasn't simply fat, but pregnant. Very pregnant, if Hugo was any judge.

He carried a bowl of water into the living room, then searched the cabinets for dog-friendly treats, relying on Google to tell him what was acceptable. Eggs were a safe bet, so he boiled two, peeling and delivering them with a side of peanut butter. As soon as she'd licked the bowl clean, the dog stepped back, yipped, and took to exploring. Anna supervised, the dog responding to basic commands from her.

"Did you see if that bird flew back out?"

"Oh yeah. He swung by to drop off a note from my mother, then left." So saying, she pulled a scroll from her pocket before crumpling and tossing it in the bin. "Guess she talked one of my cousins into playing the scribe. My money's on Jean. She's always spoiled him, and he has ready access to plenty of ash. Still, that's better than a message in blood. Maybe she has cooled off."

Hugo stopped walking, dually puzzled, before prioritizing his concerns.

"I thought your mom was dead?"

"What? No. I said she was gone," Anna replied without turning to face him. "She moved after I left home. I haven't kept up with her, and it's not like I have a relationship to maintain with my father."

Hugo closed his eyes very tightly and took a deep breath as he internalized this. Throughout their discussions regarding her parents, he'd always spoken of them as one would of the deceased, in the past tense. Why hadn't she corrected him sooner?

"Well, what did the note say?" He finally asked, when he could trust his tone.

"Nothing nice," she answered, her shoulders falling slack a moment before she resumed her natural poise. "She's not thrilled about my life choices. I won't be responding."

Whelmed by the news that his paramour's mother not only lived, but sent mail via unclipped fowl like a queen from some prior century, Hugo rubbed his brow. Leaving his paramour and the pup to their tour, he popped Aspirin and turned on the desktop, counting down the minutes until his headache abated.

"I'll see if there's anything online about a missing dog."

There was. Burlington being a city, there were dozens of owners whose dogs had escaped under the fence, out the door, car, from their harness, and so on, but none matched the description of their portly mutt.

"Nobody's posted anything yet, but I'll keep checking back."

He almost asked Anna if she could contact the shelter the following day, but remembered she'd be leaving for her flight in the early afternoon, and had mentioned running errands beforehand. The Learning Center was hosting a week-long drive to help refugees get settled. She wanted to drop off supplies and ask about giving English lessons.

"I'll get in touch tomorrow after work," he said instead. "What should we call her in the meantime?"

Anna was watching their guest squeeze under the bed, exploring a land of forgotten socks, belts, and cords. "I don't know. She's going to be a mom. What's a good mom name?"

"What about Carnation? Or Rose? Those are the flowers people send on Mother's Day."

"Rose? Crowned queen of all flowers due to its beauty, fragrance, medicinal uses, and flavor?" she commented, attempting a British accent. A foul odor filled the room and Anna cast an accusatory glance at the furball struggling to crawl under the low frame. "It's the perfect fit," she concluded.

Rose snarled at the sound of scratching coming from the side of the house, baring her teeth.

"Don't forget the thorns!" Hugo added, watching the pup disappear and reappear with a belt in her mouth.

"Sweet. A tough mama then. Rose, drop that."

Rose complied, letting the belt fall at Anna's feet.
"Good girl."

Chapter 13
Whelps, That's A Wrap!

It was hard to tell who was more smitten with Rose, Hugo or Anna, but they had a solid guess as to who she preferred. Rose did anything Anna said, and promptly, without the promise of treats. Hugo called the shelter the second he got home from work Thursday, describing everything from her appearance and temperament to her condition.

"Well, Mr. Atmen, we can take her, but the shelter is no place for an expectant mother. She and the pups would have to be quarantined. What she needs is attention, more than she'd receive here, and to be kept safe, comfortable, subjected to as little stress as possible. Would you be willing to hang onto her, as a foster, until after she's whelped?"

"What's that—whelped?"

"Giving birth, Mr. Atmen. Mothers being fostered tend to deliver their young more easily. In the shelter, the stress of being in a crate, hearing strange dogs, can trigger the whelping before she and the pups are ready. Complications become likely."

He looked down into the sweet brown eyes of the fluffy bundle nestled on his lap and sighed.

"And what about after the birth? Will the puppies be okay in the shelter, or will you be convincing me to hang onto those, as well?"

"The puppies must remain with their mother for a minimum of eight weeks, and it'll be easier on her and them if they aren't relocated during that time."

"Of course," Hugo agreed, palming his forehead. "So what you're getting at is I'm going to be a dog grandpa for the next two months?"

"Well Rose and all the folks here at the Humane Society would appreciate that, though nobody more than her pups, I'm sure."

"I've never delivered puppies before."

"And you won't have to. Whelping is a relatively quick process, and she shouldn't be in any major discomfort."

Hugo took a deep breath, gave his good girl a scratch behind the ears, and she readjusted herself, the better to kiss his hand.

"One sec. I have to grab a notebook. I'm going to need you to walk me through my role in all this, and I'll need the contact information for whatever vet you guys use. If there's an emergency, some major complication, you will cover it, right?"

"Yes. Rose will be the official property of the Humane Society. I am going to need you to stop in and handle the paperwork in person, but I can give you documentation to provide to our vet should any issues arise."

"Great. Should I bring Rose, so you guys can see how far along she is, how her pups are doing?"

"Sure. You have our address?"

He did.

"Great. So why don't you come now and we'll have the forms ready. Then you can talk to our vet directly about what to expect."

"Alright. Do uh—should I buckle her in? How does that work, having a little dog in the car?"

The woman, Nadia something, he thought she'd said, laughed.

"Putting her on the seat in the back is fine. Just don't take any sharp turns and keep the windows rolled high so she can't jump out."

Looking at Rose, he was surprised she could jump at all in her condition. Had he not seen her do so already, he would've believed it impossible. Her legs were so stunted, her burgeoning stomach dragged along the floor.

Fifteen minutes later, Hugo was carrying Rose into the lobby, where he was met by a plump woman with copper skin in jean overalls and a Humane Society t-shirt, her long black hair tied into a low ponytail.

"Hi! I'm Neda Bari, the Foster Coordinator, and you must be Mr. Atmen."

"Hi, yeah. And this is Rose," he said, lifting her to face Neda. His arms strained under her weight. Placing Rose on the floor, he let her roam the contained area.

"No leash yet?"

"Nope. I wasn't planning on holding onto her, but—"

"The puppies?"

"Yeah," he said, raising his open palms in defeat.

Neda nodded, then pulled a walkie-talkie from her belt and called the veterinary technician to the lobby.

"He's also going to microchip her. We won't be giving her any vaccines now. Once the litter is eight weeks old, we can start vaccinating them. If they're still in your care at that point, I can walk you through their vaccine schedule."

Hugo, who hadn't given any thought to vaccinating dogs, nodded.

"Do you have any pets of your own?"

"No. I had a dog as a kid, but not since."

"Okay. That's fine. We have packets to walk you through any issues, plus you have our number."

"Do you know what kind of dog she is?"

Neda bent down as Rose pawed at her legs, demanding to be held. In between pets, Neda suggested she was a terrier mix.

"Her coat isn't wiry like the Glen of Imaal breed, otherwise that would be my guess."

The vet tech arrived with a cheap leash, essentially a lanyard cord children make at sleep-away camp, which he looped around Rose's neck, leading her away. Docile, she didn't fight the pull but stopped to sniff every few feet until they were gone from sight. Neda moved behind a counter, pulling forth papers for Hugo to initial, including one to explain how he came into possession of Rose, and how long she was with him before he turned her in.

"Do you think her family will come for her?" he asked, flipping from one sheet to the next.

Neda sighed. "You said you found her last night, yet still, they haven't reported her missing. Rose is very pregnant, at least a month in, and either they couldn't justify the expense of getting her spayed, or they're backyard breeders. Licensed breeders sell purebreds and she isn't that. These people would barely have made back the cost of the vaccines, selling mutt puppies."

"So those puppies weren't going to be vaccinated?"

"I doubt it. And after letting her down thus far, I don't see them taking responsibility for her today. They're probably thanking their lucky stars she ran off, *if* they didn't dump her on your street in the first place. You'd be horrified at how often people ditch their pregnant dogs, their litters, right out front, here, every year. Heedless of the elements. Still, better that than into the woods, or off at some stranger's farm."

"Jesus. I'm glad she showed up in our yard. Why wouldn't a family just turn her in if they couldn't afford to keep her?"

"There is a small fee involved when surrendering a pet, but I think it's more about the stigma than the money."

"It's hard not to look down on someone abandoning a loved one," Hugo agreed.

He couldn't bear the thought of Rose's owner driving her into the middle of nowhere and pushing her out of the car, and blinked the scene away.

With the paperwork filled out, Neda handed him a stack of informational packets pertaining to everything from how much to feed a dog, based on their weight, length, and breed, to common household poisons, tick prevention, training methods, and pertinently, how to prepare for and help with the whelping process. He scanned the titles while Neda wandered off in search of supplies. The list of poisons was long. He was memorizing the contents when she returned with a folded metal crate, proper leash, and collar from which hung a name tag listing the Humane Society's address and phone number.

"Does she need a cage?" he asked, concerned, and Neda responded with the pros of creating a safe space for Rose within his home. "The house is a shared area, between yourself, your girlfriend, and Rose. The crate will be her happy place, where she can hide and be comfortable even when you're vacuuming, the blender is running, or you have a guest over that smells like cats."

A squeaky bark announced Rose and the vet tech's return, sounding from beyond closed doors before they swung open and she was racing for Hugo's feet. Bending to accept her exuberant smooches, he placed the collar around her neck. This he clipped the leash to, removing the lanyard stand-in. The vet tech warned Rose would be giving birth very soon, likely within the coming week. Hugo swallowed hard, nodding. Thanking the vet tech and Neda, Hugo led Rose out. He felt guilty walking her outside on the cold ground, the brisk wind catching her fur, instead of carrying her, wrapping his jacket around her, shielding her from the elements.

From the shelter, he went to the pet store, where he grabbed bowls and the dry food brand recommended in the "Dog Nutrition" packet. Another explained the specific dietary needs of newborn puppies, but he planned to wait until they were born to stock up. Not sure what toys were best for dogs, he walked Rose down an aisle lined with plastic bones promising bacon flavors, big plushies, little plushies, tires, and ropes, claiming those she reacted to.

Unsure what else he needed, he stopped an employee, sheepishly explaining his predicament.

"Ah. Alright then, so food, toys, bones—not the rawhide though." she said, pulling a package of manufactured bones out of his cart and putting them back in their place on a shelf. "I wish we didn't sell those. You said they gave you a crate? Good. Well, she's going to need a bed. You don't want her giving birth there, otherwise, it's gonna get pretty gross. You'll want her to give birth over newspapers. But, she's still going to need a comfortable place to sleep, and her crate won't be cozy without a bed. You'll also want a heating pad for her and the litter."

The employee took the lead, helping him fill the cart.

"You'll want her on heartworm, flea, and tick prevention medications once the pups are weaned," advised the employee before further suggesting he pick up a rectal thermometer, a tool he'd assumed wasn't used outside of sitcoms and cartoons.

"You said the shelter gave you a packet. It probably lists a normal temperature range. If memory serves, that'll drop to about one hundred degrees an hour or two before whelping. If she hasn't eaten all day and her temperature drops, it's time. You're not gonna want to leave her side then."

When Hugo left, his wallet was significantly lighter, but Rose settled into her bed behind the passenger's seat, and her comfort was worth every expense. She was snoring peacefully as he pulled into the drive. "Poor girl must be tired," he thought, his indignation at the cheap bastards who'd done her wrong reignited. She snorted when he picked her up, but made no move to shuffle from his arms, so he carried her into the house. Closing her in the bedroom temporarily, he brought her supplies inside. Awake and distressed, she took to scratching at the wood, yipping through the gap. He cringed, but there was nothing for it. He couldn't risk that she'd run outside. Having brought everything in, he freed her from the room, gave her actual dog food for dinner rather than the eggs-peanut butter combo, and figured out how to set up her crate. Popping her bed therein and tossing a throw blanket over top to make the enclosure private, he hoped Neda was right about Rose's happy place.

Of course, he also hoped she'd play with the toys she picked out, but Rose was fixated on a sock that hadn't made it into the laundry bin. Sighing, Hugo played tug with one hand, dialing Anna with the other.

"She's staying?!"

"Just for a couple of months, until the Humane Society can get her litter adopted."

"Why couldn't they take her?"

He repeated what Neda said about the increased likelihood of complications whelping in a shelter setting.

"Whelping?

"Giving birth."

"So what happens if you're at work and she goes into labor?"

"They gave us a packet. It has instructions, but we shouldn't have to act unless something goes wrong. We can call their emergency vet, but at worst, we'll probably just have to open the sac ourselves, or cut and tie off the umbilical cord."

"Sack? What sack? *Hugo, we are not vets.*"

"No, but we're better than whoever bailed on her. And we're better than a cage in a sterile room where she can hear but can't see all the other dogs, because she and the pups have to be quarantined until they've had their shots."

"I wish you would have discussed this with me. This is a huge responsibility you accepted on my behalf."

"Blame Neda."

"Who?"

"Lady at the pound. I was all ready to swing by, drop Rose off, let them take it from here, but Neda explained the realities to me, and it wouldn't have been right."

"Fine, but Hugo—I love animals and Rose is precious, but a pregnant dog? Helping her give birth, then raise her babies? I'm in, but that's a lot. I don't know the first thing about having a regular dog. Let alone puppies."

"Me neither, it turns out, but we'll do our best. She needs us."

"Alright. For Rose. But if I can identify the people who abandoned her, I'm going to find them and then I'm going to kick them in the teeth."

"You get 'em, grandma," Hugo said, but his smile faded as he recalled the moaning of a fallen attacker lying in the shadows.

Later, he shot a quick text to the gang letting everyone know he wouldn't be at Sonya's show, as he was focused on getting Rose settled. Following the birthing packet's instructions, he located a cardboard box big enough for her to fit comfortably in. This he placed in the corner of the living room before removing the top and a side, laying a garbage bag underneath, and lining it with newspapers.

What if she gave birth that very night?

No matter what, he'd have to remain present for the whelping of the first two pups. After that, if Rose was preoccupied, his job was to keep those born warm with the heated water bottle. Concerned he might forget a vital task, Hugo rotated the couch and an end table to face the birthing bed, storing the packets close at hand for the big day. Over those, in a drawer generally reserved for the TV Guide and user manuals, he placed the thermometer, a bottle of water ready for warming, scissors, thread, and towels.

Once the living room was ready, he set about training her to like her crate and box, utilizing the opportunity to get her used to her name. "Good girl, Rose," he said, handing her treats while she sat first in the box, and then in the crate. Her birthing bed gave her no trouble at all, but while she was calm as long as the crate door was open, the second he closed it she whined, pawing through the bars.

Hugo tried to woo her with treats, but she remained stressed, wide awake, and loud. The hours grew long, darkness set in, and finally, he pulled his bedding to the floor, curling up beside the crate.

"See Rose? I sleep down here, too. You're okay," he cooed.

Unlocking the crate door, he left it open a smidge, and her protestations ceased. When Boukman's posse woke them Friday morning, he found that she'd scooted her bed to the lip of the crate, as close to him as possible without knocking the door into his head. Hugo hadn't reset the alarm, nor politely asked the flock to take into account his new morning responsibilities, so he was running late by the time Rose was fed and walked. Concerned she'd give birth while he was out, he knew he'd be distracted his entire shift, but he'd already taken too much time off.

"Please, if today's the day, wait until I get home," he begged on his way out. Arriving at work, Hugo went to Nate's office and explained Rose's condition, that he'd be taking long lunches on the days Anna was out of town until he could find a dog walker. To his surprise, Nate supported his endeavor. "I've got two dogs of my own, and if my wife wasn't home with them, I'd be rushing back every day at noon, too. Are you planning to keep any of the puppies?"

Hugo said that he'd have to discuss that with Anna, that this was all very new, and they'd have to see how they handled Rose first.

"I understand. If I get word of any reputable dog walkers in the area, I'll let you know."

Esteban too, cheerfully accommodated Hugo's new pal.

"Of course. I totally get you can't come out. Is it cool if I come with you to walk her? I want to meet your baby girl!"

So it was that Esteban gave Rose booty scritches while Hugo watered and fed her. She ate quickly. The humans feasted on oversized sandwiches, giving her stomach a moment to settle before they took her for a walk. As they strode, they chatted, initially chuckling when she pulled to sniff every bush, flower, or stain on the sidewalk. The humor wore as she maintained her slow meander. She whimpered when they left her behind to return to work, and for a moment, Hugo debated hiring a pet sitter.

"She looks like she's ready to pop," Esteban commented on the ride back to the bank.

"Yup. Any day now."

Esteban asked how Anna liked their temporary roommate and Hugo shared her reaction to the news. He didn't look to see, but could tell Esteban was nodding.

"Yeah, it would have been better to talk it over with her first, but I'm sure if you had you both would have reached the same conclusion. Can't let your sweet girl give birth in a cell."

Anna seemed better disposed to their new responsibility when she returned home on Monday, and Hugo got the call Tuesday, just after eleven a.m., that it was time.

"You're sure?"

"Yup. Two down, don't know how many more to go. Look, I'm not cut out for this. *Get. Home. Now.*"

Promising he was on his way, he hung up. Nate wasn't in his office, so he tasked Esteban with updating their boss as to why he'd walked off for the day. A customer jokingly asked, "Where's the fire?" as Hugo ran through the lobby.

"My dog's in labor! I'm gonna be a grandpa!"

After a parade of red lights, Hugo charged up the walkway, reaching their open door. Anna was there, waiting, eyes wide, mouth agape. Moving quickly, she led him into the living room.

"She's had three so far, but she keeps straining, and how am I supposed to know if she's keeping them warm or not, and the packet doesn't say how pink their tongues are supposed to be, and I heard the first two whimper but the third isn't making a sound and the tongue isn't really pink but not grey either and—"

Hugo stopped listening as he neared Rose, who was indeed straining, three shut-eyed slimy pups squirming gently at her side, letting loose a flurry of whines, and what looked like a fetal blob abandoned at the edge of the box.

Swearing, Hugo lifted the blob, and with his fingers, tore the transparent skin covering the face, tugging it from the tiny limp body. Having freed the pup, he tossed the skin aside, the sac looking like a torn condom. Grabbing a towel from Anna, he wiped clean the pup's mouth and nose. Spewing a fresh series of expletives, he paused, reflecting on what he'd read. He knew there was something he was forgetting.

"Get the birth packet!" he commanded, cutting off the stream of anxious rambling he'd been tuning out. "Read me how to revive a puppy. Quick."

He was pretty sure he had to blow on its little face, and did so, warming it with his hands, but he was missing something crucial, a step. Meanwhile, Rose had pushed another pup out and was licking away its sac, which she then ate. Shit. They were supposed to have been counting those, making sure she'd expelled one per dog. Had Anna kept up? Not if she'd stepped away to talk to him. Probably not.

"—Okay, uh, place the puppy at the center of a clean warm hand towel. Gently swaddle them, being careful to keep their face uncovered. Then rub them. The towel will absorb the birthing fluids while the rubbing will stimulate breathing. Once their fur's clean and their breathing's regular, you can place them beside the mother. Be very gentle with the umbilical cord. She will clip it, but if she doesn't—"

Hugo had already wrapped the mouse-sized puppy and was massaging through the fabric. He was about to ask her to call the emergency number on the front page when the puppy let out a squeak.

"Thank God," he said, barking a relieved laugh. It tried to suckle his finger as he handed it back to Rose. Placing the runt near her face, he let her handle the cleaning. When she was done, and Hugo was moving the pup to her side, he checked to see if the umbilical was clipped or bleeding. Finding nothing wanting, he let the pup suckle, watching to make sure his siblings let him in, and left him be.

Then, sitting back, he wiped his brow, which was slick with sweat. "Fuck," he breathed, and Anna nodded, taking a seat beside him on the floor where they could better supervise Rose and her brood.

"Do you think she's done?" he asked.

Anna shrugged. "You said the shelter lady compared her to Glen of Imaal Terriers. I looked online, and those usually have litters of three to five puppies, so we might be."

After an hour of no straining, the couple was fairly certain all of the puppies had been born. Anna struggled to rise from the floor, complaining of back pain, so Hugo stood, helped her up, and sat back down to watch Rose. While Anna made tea, he picked up each puppy in turn, checking its gender and making note of any identifying characteristics. Of the five, there were two boys, three girls, and all were green. He assumed the un-usual hue was a trick of the light, so he left the lot alone for a moment and returned with two stand lamps, each equipped with fluorescent bulbs as opposed to the yel-lowed electric lights that came with the apartment and still hadn't died. He flicked them on and found that in the white light, each pup's coat was more of a pistachio green than that of a swamp, but green nonetheless. The packets didn't mention green puppies, but the birthing packet stated birthing fluids were dark and would stain anything they came into contact with. Once Rose had cleaned them all nice and proper, Hugo figured he could get a better feel for the color of their fur.

He had to call the Humane Society, give them an update, but first he wanted to delve out names. They'd be there a while. He had to call them something.

Anna returned with their tea and, gesturing for the couch, convinced Hugo to reposition himself beside her. He complied.

"Are they supposed to be that color?" she asked, and he shook his head.

"Dunno. Didn't say so in their papers. I'll mention it, see if it's anything to be concerned about when I call."

Then he relayed the gender count, asking for name inspiration. Anna pulled a pen and pad from the coffee table for brainstorming. He suggested they look to plants, as much in honor of their odd hue as their lineage, and Anna agreed that was a fine idea. Debating the pros and cons of medicinal herbs she apparently knew a great deal about and that he had only used for cooking, they reached an accord.

In the end, they figured the three girls would be called Carasee, Parsley, and Mint, while the boys would be Aloe and Thyme. Anna suggested they wait to decide which pup would get which name, as much because they didn't have a feel for their personalities yet as because they honestly couldn't tell them apart. Heck, they couldn't tell the boys from the girls without flipping them over.

Drained of the adrenaline that had coursed through him since Anna's call not two hours prior, Hugo slumped back and took a contented afternoon nap.

Chapter 14
Eleventh Hour Stitch

When he woke up, he called Neda, giving her the good news and asking about their coats.

"Well, you're right, in a way. It is a stain. Which one is green?"

"It's the entire litter."

There was a pause.

"Wow. It's not unheard of for a puppy to be born green, but all five of them? How bizarre! Well, it's not permanent. Cleaning them will eventually remove the stain from their fur."

"Okay. Should I be cleaning them? The packet only said—"

"No, not yet. Leave them to Rose. I'm going to come by with the vet tech. He can give them all a look-see, check for any defects, and we can leave a scale with you tomorrow. Will you be home during the day?"

"My uh—" Anna was sitting next to him. "—paramour will be."

"Great. So I'll swing by around ten a.m.. You should weigh the puppies daily for the next two weeks, and take note of their gains. If they stagnate or lose weight, ring me immediately. I'm going to give you my cell number if you have any issues. Rose will be a good mama, but make sure she is feeding the littlest one, too. Sometimes mamas reject the runt, and we'll help you step in, should that occur."

"Alright. Also, while I've got you on the line, can you recommend a dog walker? I work during the day, and my boss won't be thrilled if I take long lunches for the next two months. My paramour would do it, but she's frequently out of town."

"Sure." Neda paused and Hugo heard the sound of typing over the line. "Looks like you're not far from Landry Park. I'll text you the number of a friend. That's her neighborhood. She's very professional."

Hugo thanked Neda and, making sure he got the text, ended the call. Anna had been listening, but he let her know when Neda would be coming, and that he'd be hiring a dog walker.

"Oh, thank goodness. I was worried I'd have to come home every lunch."

"Are you not home during the day?"

She released a throaty laugh. "No. Why would I be?"

"I don't know. You haven't mentioned—where are you, then?"

"Depends. Why?"

"I thought you were going to start letting me know when you were going out—"

"If you'd be coming home to an empty house, assuming I was dead or kidnapped."

"I never said anything about kidnappings."

"Look, I'm not a homebody. I enjoy our evenings together, so I make sure I'm around. But during the day, you're out, and I like to keep busy. The only reason I stayed in today was because I had a feeling about Rose."

The image of that fetal blob, their unbreathing runt, flashed across his mind, and he trembled, horrified then furious over what might have been.

"So, you knew we had a pregnant dog, due this week or next, and had you not sensed the whelping would take place today, you would have gone out? What could be more important than supervising her birth?"

"Well, your job for one."

"I went to work content with the knowledge you would be here with her. Heck, I was terrified going in

Friday, and didn't leave the house again all weekend, except to walk her."

"You stayed to care for the dog *you* agreed to foster."

"We already did this. You said you were in. And anyway, if our roles were reversed, would you have made her give birth in a cell?"

"I don't know. I wasn't given a choice in the matter."

"So what would you have done today then?"

"Whatever the hell I wanted," she snapped. "You are not my keeper."

"Nobody said I was. I just don't understand how you could bail on Rose to go out, and what? Meet the girls for yoga in the park? Walk the mall? I haven't asked you to quit your job to stay home with the dog. But during your downtime, the least you can do is keep an eye on her, and the litter."

"Which I did."

"Because you had a feeling. Not because it was the right thing to do. And you didn't even stay with her throughout the birthing. Instead, you called me home, and what did I find when I got here? You, in the foyer, the dogs alone in the living room, one still in his sac, not breathing. What were you thinking?!"

"I was thinking, I didn't sign up for this. I don't know how to do this. At no point in my life did I think, gee, I sure can't wait to deliver some stray's puppies!"

Hugo massaged his forehead, biting back a swear. "Well, while she's in this house, *Rose is our dog* and so are the pups. In two months, we can adopt them out, but for now, they're our responsibility. Rose picked us. Let's show her she made the right choice."

Anna sighed, closed her fists, and opened them.

"Fine. Did the shelter lady tell you how the hell we take care of a new mom and a litter of newborn puppies?"

"There's a packet, but she's coming tomorrow if we have more questions, and we have her cell number."

Rose was a good mama. Hugo watched to make sure she wasn't prioritizing the others over the runt, but he suckled plenty. The vet tech checked the litter over and said mama and babies alike, were in good health. He also photographed them, at Neda's urging.

"We didn't believe they'd really be green!" she commented later.

True to her word, Anna took detailed notes on how best to care for the pups. She accepted supplies for their eventual transition to solid food and discussed Rose's diet with the vet tech, who gave precise instructions regarding how much and when to feed her. They double-checked that the heating pad wasn't too hot, and just in case, placed another layer between the pad and the whelping box, which Hugo had stripped and lined with fresh towels.

Anna was informed as to what ailments to watch for both in Rose and her pups, as any illnesses could prove fatal. She took the warning to heart, highlighting every other word in her notebook. There was a correlating packet, of course, but she explained about retaining information better when she wrote it down.

The dog walker stopped by in the evening, introducing herself. She stated her terms, and Hugo agreed. Walks would be kept brief, so the puppies wouldn't be alone for long.

Anna left for work Thursday morning. By then, Hugo had already let the gang know he'd be unable to partake in any shenanigans for some time. Sonya wanted to meet the puppies, so she swung by before her show, dressed in a hoodie and sweats, her braid wrapped like a crown atop her head. She wasn't wearing any makeup.

"Is this plant fake?" she asked, examining the blooming tree while she took off her shoes.

"Oh, no. That's my dwarf pomegranate tree. It won't produce edible fruit, but the flowers look nice."

"That they do. Are they usually in bloom this early?"

"They're supposed to bloom in July or August. This year we lucked out. She didn't flower all summer, and then a few weeks after I'd brought her in to escape the chilly fall weather, she was in full bloom."

"So she—your tree—has looked like this since fall?"

"Yeah, since October, I think. I was sweeping underneath daily, but I couldn't keep up. Besides, it's kind of romantic, walking in on a path of petals, right? At least, I hope so. Anna hasn't complained. Shouldn't be many there now, though. Today's cleaning day."

They moved into the living room, and Sonya squealed with delight. "They're so little! *Are they supposed to be green?*"

Hugo explained about the bile, how the color would fade in time. Before she could hold them, he reminded her they weren't vaccinated, requesting she wash her hands first, and she complied. As Sonya reached for the nearest squirming earth-toned pudge, Rose growled, but Hugo scratched behind her ears and stroked her back while Sonya snuck to the fridge. She returned with a peeled hard-boiled egg. Bribe enthusiastically accepted, Rose relaxed. Sonya gently held up each puppy in turn, asking Hugo for their names.

He explained that they were still waiting to get to know them. Once they could tell which was which, he'd figure out what name went to who. Only Thyme was named, since Hugo'd arrived in the nick thereof. She confessed she had half a mind to adopt one once they were old enough.

"Mushroom Butt could use the company."

Nate wanted pictures, which he nearly dropped with surprise at their collective hue. Nicole and her friend came by Friday, straight from Luminous. Esteban was behind at work, or he'd have come too. Joe was away for the weekend, officiating the wedding of a Wiccan couple she'd introduced, but humbly requested Hugo tell the pups good things about her in the meantime.

"That way they're almost as excited to meet me as I am, them!"

Between feeding Rose, walking Rose, and constantly checking that the puppies weren't overheating, Hugo made time to entertain his guests—easily the most he'd hosted in such rapidity since Claire'd moved out. He had a feeling it wouldn't be hard to find homes for the pups once they'd been weaned.

He was in high spirits when he called Anna Saturday night, only to hear a man's voice in the background while she was detailing the view from her hotel room.

"Who was that?"

"Who was what?" She paused. "Oh. Do you mean Zandor? I told you he lived in Philly."

"You did not mention seeing a Zandor in Philly. I promise you, I would have remembered." Who could forget such an unusual name?

"Huh. Maybe it slipped my mind, what with the puppies, and all. Anywho, Zandor is a friend from back in the day. He was happy to hear I have the night off from *nannying,* so I could see the sights with him."

A deep-throated "Hi Hugo!" erupted in the background, and for a moment, he felt cuckolded. But that was ridiculous. Were she cheating, would her fling be so bold as to announce himself? And again, there were the visions to consider. They were destined to unite, not to revel in each other's abuse. Hugo asked where she and Zandor were, what sights they'd seen and would see, but Anna cut him off, apologizing for the abruptness. They could talk later. She was entertaining her friend *now.*

He told himself she didn't want him to blow her cover, disclose her actual job to her friend, but the thought lingered despite his efforts to clamp it. What if she was covering an affair, the infidelity nearly revealed by a single ill-timed comment on the part of her consort? He loved her, knew he ought to trust her, but as the hours wore on without further texts or calls, his anxieties mounted. Sunday passed without a word, and only in the company of dogs, who he was fast learning to identify.

The runt, Thyme, remained the smallest, but he was fast putting on weight. His whine was earsplitting when he was in discomfort, or being shoved from his mama's teat, whereas none of the others were similarly loud. His nose was pink, claws darker than those of his littermates. Aloe and Mint had white splotches on their foreheads and bellies that were more visible as the green became less pronounced. Parsley's paws, belly, tip of the tail, and brows were white, while Carisee's uniform pistachio tint was fading to tan.

Rose was quick to potty on her walks, as anxious to return to her brood as he was to get her back to them, and she ate several times a day. He moved the water bowl closer to her, but just far enough where he needn't fear finding a puppy floating face down.

He slept in the living room, in case any trouble arose, until Anna returned on Monday. Throughout his shift, he kept telling himself not to quiz her on who this Zandor fellow was. If she said he was an old friend, then he was. If she said they were seeing the sights, then they were.

Except why hadn't she mentioned him prior? Why did Hugo have to find out by hearing a man's voice in her room? And at that hour, why were they at the hotel? If he was showing her the city, wouldn't they have been out, enjoying the hustle and bustle of the night life? Exactly what time did he leave? Had he slept over? Was she so naive as to assume they could share a bed without the other expecting sex? Or was that what she'd wanted, no naivete about it?

Was it Hugo who was being naive?

"I mean," he thought out loud, "she lies constantly, to everyone, even if only about work, so why not to me?"

On that note, where was she going every weekday morning that she couldn't bear to miss? Was she just going to brunch with the girls, hitting up farmer's markets, volunteering, or was she seeing another man? Come to think of it, *when was the last time she'd kissed him?*

Yes, they had sex, and with reasonable frequency, but when had she ever taken the initiative in the bedroom?

Did she really want to be with him, or was she just biding her time until the next, better, more convenient roommate came along? He loved her, but did she love him? She'd never said so. In truth, he'd been sparing with the phrase too, at first, wary of pressuring her too early, but now, sharing a bed, a roof, shouldn't she have known? And, well, she either loved him or she didn't, so did she?

"Who the hell is Zandor?!" Hugo spat in response to her cheerful greeting as he slammed the front door shut.

"What?"

"The Philly guy from back in the day. *Remember*?"

"No, I know who he is. Duh. I mean, what and why are you asking?"

"How long have you guys been planning to sight see and why wasn't I told?"

"Okay, first of all, calm the fuck down. Zandor has been a friend since forever, and I planned on seeing him as soon as I learned I had a Philadelphia posting. He manages the Ritz-Carlton there. I'm sorry if I didn't mention him sooner. It must have slipped my mind."

"Fine, but you've got to understand how much it sucks to hear some guy on the line when I'm talking to my girlfriend who is staying at a hotel in another part of the country."

"I don't like that word."

"Paramour. Whatever. My point stands."

"I didn't mean to not tell you. There's been a lot going on lately, but if you're going to be jealous or clingy, this isn't going to work. By this, I mean us. So relax. I'm with you. I will tell you if I'm not. Zandor is a friend. He thinks I'm a nanny. You're one of a select few who knows what I do for a living. And not that it matters or it's any of your business, but he's engaged. The Save The Date has been on our fridge since I moved in, and I told you who he was when I put it up."

Thinking back, Hugo vaguely remembered her naming the folks on her magnets, explaining how she knew them, where they were now, and how she missed them all. He was nearly overcome by the urge to check the fridge that instant, before she had a chance to sneak by and put Zandor's face up, but shook the compulsion. He was being crazy. Even if she was lying, there was no way she'd have made a Save The Date for this occasion, and had she that kind of foresight, doubtless it really would already be on the fridge. Besides, him being engaged didn't mean they weren't sleeping together. Hugo had to trust in Anna, and in his premonitions, or not. There was no middle lane, but telling himself that didn't change how he felt, which was like he'd been careening the wrong way and just missed being pancaked by a semi.

"I'm not being jealous or clingy. That was an inappropriate lie by omission, and it wasn't the first one. You still haven't told me where you spend your mornings."

"Oh, sleeping around, mostly. The second you're out the door, I hop into Jorge's bed. You know Jorge, next door? Then I work my way down the block, banging Ted, Jose, Ahmed, and Mark, before I finish to a parade of high fives and move on to the next street. Their wives wrote and signed a petition, trying to get me thrown out of town. There was a council meeting over it. The mayor has to sign off though, and he's been making excuses, hoping for a blowie. Hadn't you heard?"

"You're hilarious."

"And you're not entitled to know everyone I talk to or how I spend my time."

"I just don't get why you're evasive if you're not hiding anything."

"I'm not evading so much as setting a boundary and telling you not to cross it. My time is *mine*. I don't harass you over where you are, or who you're with, and I expect the same courtesy, the same trust."

"I'd tell you if I was leaving town to go meet someone. You spend half your life out of state. Which is fine. I signed on for that, but keeping me in the loop would be nice."

"You shouldn't demand it though, and maybe if you didn't, I'd tell you more. Right now, telling you anything sets a bad precedent."

"This isn't law. It's love, and if you love me, you should want to share with me."

It was Anna's turn to massage her forehead and look to an unseen sky. He followed her gaze. Had there always been that crack in the plaster?

"Hugo, I care about you a lot, but we haven't been together very long and love takes time. Maybe you love me. Maybe you don't, but I don't love you yet. I like you. I see potential here, with us, for a future. But you've got to step back and lay off with the jealousy. It's tiresome and I didn't come home looking to be tired."

Hugo took her admittance that she didn't love him in stride. He'd suspected as much.

"Look, I'm trying here. I don't get upset when you take hours to text me back, or when you go an entire weekend without calling. But long-distance is hard, consistent communication is crucial, and I feel like I'm the only one making an effort to communicate. Will you at least share with me where you spend your mornings? And please tell me before your next weekend getaway with *another guy*? So I don't accidentally find out and assume the wrong thing."

He paused, double-checking he didn't have anything else to ask.

"I think my requests are very reasonable."

"Well, you would. You're the one making them." She sighed. "Fine. If I know I'm seeing a male friend at work, I'll try to be better about telling you before I head out. As for my mornings, it varies. I don't have a set schedule. Some days I help out at the soup kitchen. Some, I hit up museums, art galleries, historical sites, hiking trails. A friend of mine teaches capoeira. I try to make it to her class once a week. Last Monday, after I landed, I spent a few hours at the Learning Center, helping refugees with their conversational English. I do what I want, when I want. You've got to get used to it."

"Thank you," he replied, acknowledging the first part. "That's all I wanted."

Without saying so, Hugo looked over the magnets and invitations peppering their refrigerator until he spotted one listing the marriage date of a Zandor and Angeline, stating that a formal invitation was to follow. He told himself to be satisfied, to swallow his suspicions, but within the hour, he found himself seated at the desktop for no reason other than to snoop.

Brushing off his rarely used Google-fu, Hugo narrowed down where Anna had to be going to kompa for her to be arriving home when she did. If she was telling the truth. She usually walked in the door at about six-fifteen, and according to MapQuest, the Carmelle Dance Studio was six miles away, a fourteen-minute commute from their apartment with low traffic. Any alternatives were too far, unless her class regularly let out early, which he doubted.

What if he drove by while she was at kompa? Just a peek, see if her antique was really parked out front, maybe stick around for a hot minute to see who she spoke to on her way out. If there were men after all, if they were reaching for her, feigning innocence with a peck on the cheek here, a hug there, so he'd know what he was up against. Should they arrive home at the same time, he could claim a late evening at work. She could hardly question him without hypocrisy.

Besides, he wasn't being jealous. Even if Anna wasn't being blatantly unfaithful, who was to say she wasn't being groomed? Women were blind when it came to the intentions of men, but Hugo—he'd know a prowler when he saw one. He'd read the sex crazed glint in their eye, watch them trace her figure, her ample bosom and buttocks, and put them in their place.

And it was up to Hugo to keep her safe. He could see the predator tailing her in the dark, and her without the means to protect herself, nor the wherewithal to recognize a threat until they had their hands around her neck, her waist, under her skirt. Hugo felt a lump in his throat, heard a slam, and looking down, found his hands balled into fists, his right, throbbing.

"What was that?" she called from the couch, a room away.

"Nothing! Just stubbed my toe."

He had to calm down, think clearly, plan. His heart was in his throat. What he needed was a drink. Hugo glanced into the living room, making certain Anna wasn't approaching before he pulled a bottle of vodka out from under the sink, where he kept his liquor supply. Digging free a short glass from behind the cups, he took two shots, coughed, rinsed the glasses, and placed them in their cabinet. Then, careful to stow the vodka away, he brushed his teeth and returned to the living room.

Anna had her head in a book, so Hugo grabbed the novel he'd been reading and, taking a seat next to her, feigned interest, turning the page whenever she flipped hers.

Hugo spent all morning distracted, telling himself he wasn't suspicious of his paramour, but of those men leering from every corner, waiting for the bar to close, to *help* the poor stumbling woman in the short skirt home. To say these men were of ill repute was to assume their reputations reflected their behavior, and Hugo didn't believe predators were always so obvious. Just because they weren't blatantly untoward in class didn't mean they weren't scheming to take her from Hugo, whether through seduction or force.

Eesteban invited him out to lunch, letting on that Nicole would be meeting them. Hugo declined, as much to make up for time lost in thought as because he feared Nicole would intuit his plans, try to change his mind.

That evening, he stayed a half hour late before pulling out, following MapQuest's directions to the studio. Sure enough, just before the light where he would turn and search for parking, he saw her car beside the meter, where a tourist with a camera-hooked-lanyard was taking a picture of the oddity. Dimly, Hugo wondered how many strangers had photographs of Anna's car, with or without her therein. The light changed and he passed the studio, its front wall a floor to ceiling window, revealing the sultry stirrings within.

Had the driver behind not honked him forward, Hugo wouldn't have ambled on, would've remained stationary, hogging the lane, engine running, until her session concluded. Instead, he looped the block before parking across the street, the better to watch his paramour's betrayal while she posed beside the glass. When she'd called kompa a dance, she'd failed to describe the motions, the swiveling of her ass, hips, the way her groin met that of her partner's, rubbed along the other man's thigh. Hugo didn't know how long he sat there, transfixed and horrified, as she thrusted into partner after partner.

Unless he was seriously misinformed, kompa was nothing like zumba.

Then, all at once, the partners split, and he saw that they did indeed grasp hands, that air kisses were exchanged between Anna and her partners, in a European fashion, though that insult paled to the previous. And she'd been doing this for months? Throughout their entire relationship.

He sped home, half expecting sirens at his back, arriving only minutes before her. Hugo'd been too shocked, too busy watching to think, to ask himself how to handle what he witnessed, and so he'd returned without a plan. Watching her getting out, locking her car and walking up the drive, he told himself to wait. To sleep on this discovery, to decide the best way to confront it tomorrow. Could he forbid this dance, request she learn another? Should he ask if it never crossed her mind that sex while dressed, with or without intercourse, was still sex? Just because she didn't orgasm back there didn't mean she wasn't cheating. Except he hadn't set that standard, but now he would.

Then Anna marched inside, her shout drowning the bang of the door in its frame.

"What the fuck were you doing spying on me?!"

"What?! I would never—"

"You're full of shit. I saw you!"

"I was at work. Then I came home. Whoever you saw, it wasn't me."

"Oh, of course. It must have been some other redhead with your face in a gold Alliance."

It was then that Hugo recalled the age of his vehicle, and the rarity of its condition. Not that he could change his story now.

"You're insane. Listen to what you're saying, how convoluted you sound. I can't be the only guy in Vermont with a vintage Renault."

"So you're going to keep lying to my face? What do you need to admit the truth? Footage of you circling the block, staring at us? They have cameras. I can get that."

"It wasn't me."

Anna breathed out, resting her hand on her stomach, before twiddling with a hem of her blouse. "Look, I don't know if we moved too fast or what, but this can't continue."

Hugo's heart dropped and his throat squeezed shut.

"What are you saying?" he choked.

"I wanted to make this work, to believe in your visions, but we are *not compatible.* I like living alone, moving at my pace—and you need structure, not just for yourself, but for your partner. I need space, you need to be held. I can't do this and I won't drag out the inevitable."

Shit! Shit! Shit! *No!*

"So"—he coughed again— "you're just going to leave?"

"I need time to figure out what's right for me, not us. I've got work tomorrow and it's too late to pack everything, but I can have my stuff cleared out by the time you get home Monday."

"This is just a fight! Aside from today, we've been doing great! Aren't we bigger than one measly disagreement? We can work through this! Don't you want to?" That last came out a whine.

"It's not one small disagreement. It's who we are, and who we are doesn't mesh. You're rigid. It's not enough that you do things your way. You need your partner to do the same and that's not me. I do my own thing, always, and I won't be pushed around. Not by you, or anyone. I was happier alone. There is no future for me here. I'm sorry."

"What about Rose? The pups?"

It was a weak pull, and he knew it. What he was asking for was two months to prove her wrong and she saw through paper flesh to the cyanide core.

"You wanted to foster a pregnant dog and her litter, so have at it. You hired a dog walker. She can handle them while you're at work. You don't need me. You only think you do."

It was obvious she intended that to be her final word, that she wanted to retreat to her room, but they shared it—so he followed her, begging her to change her mind, spewing assurances, promises, but her decision was made. In the end, to escape his pestering, she carried her mound of quilts into the bathroom, locked the door, and must've slept in the tub. Not that this quieted Hugo's pathetic ramblings any, but she had headphones, and he assumed she was wearing them, as she'd stopped responding.

For the first night in a long time, Hugo didn't sleep a wink. In his restlessness, he paced, ignoring the child's laughter that erupted around three a.m.. At the sound of shuffling on the roof, he peered out, saw first that her buggie's lights were on, and second, that hens were flying somersaults over his Alliance, peppering the gold grey with droppings. Cursing, he returned inside. After a quick internet search, he located a bag of sunflower seeds, mixed them with vinegar, garlic, and every type of pepper at his disposal. These he sprinkled over and around his car, across the lawn, patio, and backyard. To his relief, the homemade repellent worked, and the birds fled the stench of his vehicle. He wiped it clean in peace, waiting for Anna's battery to die. When he had to piss, he ducked into the back, aiming for the bushes.

Come dawn, he had a hero's breakfast waiting for her. He was ready to spend the entire morning convincing her anew when she unlocked the door, and in her bedclothes, met him in the kitchen.

"I didn't come out here to eat. I came out to tell you to go to work today and Monday, not to waste your time trying and failing to make me stay. Don't get fired over a lost cause."

That was sound advice and Hugo almost took it, more because he hoped the time away would let her miss him than because he valued his career over the tidings of his heart. Instead, he insisted on running her errands with her, driving her to the airport.

"You said you were picking up gulal today, for Holi. I'll come with."

She would have turned his offer down and initially did, but her car wouldn't start. In a foul temper, Anna plopped her bags on his back seat and allowed herself to be chauffeured to the Indian shopping outlet. Hugo reasoned with her, begged, pleaded for a chance to prove himself loyal, loving, hers, but her jaw was set, her obsidian eyes staring straight ahead.

She shushed him as they stepped into Chhuttee Ka Baajaar. Speed walking, she flagged an employee and asked where to find gulal. The man, dark-skinned with thick brows, cheerfully led her to a spiral of lofted baskets filled with different colored powders, making small talk with a thick accent. Anna thanked him before pulling thin plastic bags from a roll and filling them with select hues. Once the shopkeeper had stepped away, Hugo could bear the silence no more and resumed protesting. She couldn't leave him and she wouldn't. Not if he could prove himself. He just needed an opportunity, he thought, an instant before it revealed itself.

In her haste to leave that section, the store, and Hugo behind, Anna spun, knocking a rack with her elbow, sending it toppling into those ahead, and despite their best efforts to right the domino towers, in seconds the floor was a Pollock painting of mixed powders, baskets on their sides, and metal shelves grounded. The commotion hadn't been quiet and soon the shopkeeper was standing before them, shouting in a language Hugo did not speak. Anna struggled to apologize but Hugo, glancing at his watch, made a decision.

"There's no time. Take my car. Catch your flight. I'll handle this."

She attempted to argue but he shook his head, pointing to his watch. She nodded.

"This doesn't change anything," Anna said as she rushed past the shopkeeper, who was exclaiming English swears interspersed with what was likely Hindi.

"Sir, I apologize for my girlfriend's clumsiness," Hugo interrupted, when she'd gone. "How can I rectify this?"

The man paused, took a breath, and in broken English explained he needed to total-up the value of the damaged merchandise. Hugo agreed to wait, moving to stand beside the counter while the shopkeeper ran his calculations. In the end, he wrote an amount that made Hugo's pulse quicken and his eyes twitch.

"I don't have that much. What if I clean it up? Sort the gulal by color?"

The man said that wasn't possible, and Hugo smiled. How better to prove his love than by resolving her impossible mistake?

"Great. I'll get started now."

The man shook his head, perplexed, but he agreed.

"Fine. Do a good job," he said, handing Hugo a pair of rubber gloves and tweezers that he pulled from underneath the register. "And if you sneak out, I will call the police."

So it was that Hugo spent Thursday seated on the floor of an Indian bazaar sorting dyed cornstarch blends by color. To start, he lifted large clumps of single shades and dumped them into those baskets stained by their residue. Then, he set about un-mixing the rest, grain by grain. At noon, he took a break to check his phone. Anna'd texted the location of his car, and there were several missed calls from Nate, Esteban, Janet, and the Human Resources office-line. He smacked his forehead. Of course, on top of everything else, Hugo had forgotten to call out.

After the briefest pang of anxiety, he told himself he hadn't failed. Fired or not, Northfield never appreciated him. Going on four fucking years and they'd denied him the only promotion to come around, just to give it to their most amply endowed, best-networked employee who'd barely been around for one. Two years? Fuck 'em. Let the bastards fire him. He'd have a new job in no time, a better job, with a bank that took care of their best, brightest, and hardest working. He turned his phone off.

Observing movement, Hugo bent low. Ants were migrating through unsorted mounds, attempting to carry clumps away. Rubbing the stress from his forehead, Hugo reached down and with his pointer-finger, crushed them, one by one, before lifting their tiny corpses with tweezers and dropping them away. The shop keeper had a single album playing on repeat the entire shift. By dinner time, Hugo'd memorized the beat and syllables, though the meaning of the lyrics was lost to him. Singing along quietly, he persisted.

The sun had tucked itself into bed, but there was an hour left until closing when Hugo stood, announcing he'd finished. Wordless, the shopkeeper strode from the counter and approached the spiral rainbow of straightened racks. He laughed, complimented Hugo on a job well done, and bid him goodnight. Outside, Hugo powered his phone on to call a taxi.

When it pulled up, he directed the cheerful driver to the airport and, following Anna's instructions, found his golden Alliance in no time. Catching sight of his reflection in the side mirror, Hugo realized he'd smudged emerald gulal above his brow, oddly in the shape of a Greek cross. Perhaps that was why the shopkeeper had laughed. And, given the symmetry of his mistake, the cab driver likely thought it intentional, otherwise he might have spoken a warning. Sighing, Hugo pulled a rag from the glove compartment and wiped his forehead clean. Then he pulled out of the space, paid his way from the lot, and ambled home.

A hen slipped in as he entered the foyer. It dropped a hand's-width scroll and exited while he stood, dumbfounded. Then, remembering his unleashed, barely-trained mama dog, Hugo closed the door and picked the letter up. Removing the blue ribbon binding it, he unrolled the parchment. With flourish, rust colored calligraphy read, "Let her go." It went unsigned, the letters cracking as the scroll flexed, and could only be from Anna's mother, or Anna, pretending to be the same, except her handwriting was girlish, fun. Meanwhile the note would have been at home in an illuminated manuscript from a medieval scriptorium. Recalling that parchment was traditionally made from animal skins, he looked again to the lettering, felt their raised and dusty surface. Was that blood? Shaking his head at the audacity of a woman he'd never met, he crumbled the note into a ball and chucked it in the trash. Anna must have called her, made amends after what she believed a breakup.

Anna gave up too easily.

She said she needed space? Fine. She could have it. That weekend, he drilled holes into the ceiling, hanging curtain dividers that split the bedroom and living room each in two, the soft barrier cutting across the couch, their bed, to be moved aside at her command. In the kitchen, rather than hanging flammable material above the center stove, he halved the space with painter's tape, curving the edge from the burners. Then he moved his belongings to his side of every room, and Anna's, to hers. Nomadic, she owned less than he. So her spaces wouldn't be barren, he ran to Barnes and Noble, Target, Ikea, McMart, picking up best-selling autobiographies, a desk lamp, an end table, cookware, and food galore. To help, he brought the Creole cookbook, gathering any notable ingredients listed therein.

Anna didn't have to leave. She could have her freedom, privacy, right there with him. When she was ready to commit, she could cross the line, and he would be there with open arms.

The dogs and their bedding, he kept to his side, so as not to burden her. Esteban texted Saturday to see how his friend was doing, but Hugo wasn't ready to talk about why he'd no-called, no-showed. He was in no mood for a lecture. Anna didn't contact him again. Putting the news on as a distraction, he learned Sunday was Easter, and shot her a holiday greeting text without answering those he'd received from his folks, siblings, friends. He couldn't handle them just then, could barely handle himself.

Interrupting his introspection, Hugo heard motion in the bedroom, and rushing in, found Boukman coming out of the closet, Anna's only white dress caught in his mouth. Hugo'd had enough of that blasted pig and his pestilential posse. Leaping for it, he slammed into the floor where the damned beast had been. Fast, Boukman escaped the way he'd entered. Rubbing his smarting elbow and mourning back pain to come, Hugo climbed out the window after him.

He saw Boukman charge forward, shake himself out, and dart across the street, down the walk. Cursing, Hugo raced back into the house, grabbed his keys, hopped into the Alliance. Pulling out, Hugo stomped the pedal, shooting from zero to forty, then fifty-five, in pursuit of the beady eyed bastard. What would Anna say if her dress disappeared? Would she think him a juvenile panty sniffing thief, graduated to dresses?

He'd expected Boukman to slow, drop his prize before they'd gone a few blocks, but instead, found himself losing and regaining sight of the pig as the devil burst from behind trees, telephone poles, a handful of brownstones, in and out of yards, parking lots, until finally, several towns over, he ducked under a welcome sign, slipping into the confines of a small park. Springing up, hanging the garment over a high branch, Boukman landed in the water of a wide mosaic fountain, where he drank. Seizing his chance, Hugo rushed from his car, and with zero thought for the consequences, which was becoming a pattern, climbed the tree. Branches cracked under his weight, and at every sign of strain, he flinched, but Boukman was coming back and Hugo swore he would burn the park to the ground before he would let that pig steal Anna's dress.

Unfortunately, Boukman spotted him worming his way down, white cotton in hand, and charged. In a panic, Hugo let go of the branch he'd gripped, and judging from the resulting pain, sprained his tailbone in the landing. He heard the growling, opened his eyes, and blinking, focused, recognised those bleak slits as nostrils, the whites as teeth, the gold pearls, Boukman's beady eyes. The pig was bent, posed snout to nose with Hugo, who flung himself to the side, but not quickly enough. Boukman reared back before slamming his skull into Hugo's face, knocking him down, the dress still in his grip. Boukman flung himself at it, and in his zeal, tore a long strip from the hem.

They heard the tear and ceased struggling to stare at the damage. Boukman dropped the scrap, screamed, and backed away before shooting Hugo a look that could only have implied hate before he ran off. Sore, Hugo groaned and rose, rubbed his smarting bottom. Pocketing the sorry scrap, he carried the dress to his car, ignoring the swelling of his face. A wetness trailed from his nose to his mouth and he coughed at the taste of blood. The fast food napkins from the glove compartment served more to smear the stain, than to clear it. Catching his breath, he drove home, careful to avoid his reflection in the rearview mirror. Spotting a dry cleaner, he left what was left of the dress with them for pickup. They didn't offer seamstress services, but maybe he could fix it himself, later. He'd gotten decent grades in Home Economics.

Monday, he woke early and sat on his side of the living room, facing the front door, and waited for Anna's arrival. The doorknob turned at five to eleven, and then she was crossing the mantle of petals, her crown haloed by the midday sun. Sealing the extraneous behind her, she spotted him. He swallowed as her lips thinned.

"I told you not to be here."

"But look!" he said, indicating the dividers. "See, I gave you space! Now you can—"

"No," she said, and without another word, turned and left, heading to her vehicle.

Hugo followed, then ran ahead, blocking her, like a goalie from the net.

"Just give me another chance."

"No."

"But I—"

"I. Said. No. Get out of my way."

"But your things!"

"I'll buy new things!"

"No, you don't have to do that. I'm sorry. I'm going. See? Walking away. Go get your stuff. I'll go to work."

She sighed, brought her hand to her brow, shook her head to the tune of, "Fine," and made for the apartment.

Hugo didn't go back to work. There was no point. If he walked in now, it would be to receive his termination papers and that shame could wait. Shooting the dog walker a text, he let her know to come by at lunch as usual, and then took off without any goal, direction. He loved her, had lived with her, and believed he'd come close to making her love him, only something had gone wrong. The universe told him the what but not the how, and he'd lost her.

Hugo didn't realize he was speeding until he heard the siren. Pulling to the side, he rolled down his window, pulled his wallet out, and retrieved his registration from the glove compartment, moving both hands to the dashboard where the officer could see them. The approaching policeman was portly, with a friendly face.

"Hello. I'm Officer Metley, with Saint Abans Police Department. How's your day going?"

"Hi. I'm Hugo. Honestly, it's been terrible. My girlfriend just walked out. Yours?"

"Better than yours, or maybe worse, depending on your perspective. My wife's not going anywhere, Lord help me. Otherwise, it's not been too shabby. Workday, so same ol'. Your girl give you that shiner?"

"Oh, no. That was her mom's pig. Wish I could catch and eat him, honestly."

"I see. Did you file a report?"

"Nah. No point. He does what he wants, and I don't know where the old lady lives, to be held accountable."

"Fair enough. Do you know why I pulled you over?"

"No, officer."

"Well, you were going seventy in a fifty-five. I'm going to need your license and registration."

"Of course." Hugo pulled his license from his wallet, passing it through the window, along with the registration.

The officer accepted the documents and returned to his vehicle. Hugo waited, wondering how many points would be added to his license. Ten, and he'd be without a ride. It wasn't one point per mile over, was it? Couldn't be, otherwise there'd be no daredevils left to harass his streets and he flinched at speed demons on the daily. The officer stepped out, returning to Hugo's window.

"Look, I don't want to do this, but you were going pretty fast. There are states where I'd have to arrest you for reckless driving at fifteen miles over. Luckily, this isn't one. I'm going to give you a citation. If you fight it, you might be able to knock down the fine and the points. Drive safe. Breakups suck, but your day will be a whole lot worse if you hit somebody. Whoever she is, she's not worth life or limb, alright?"

"Right," Hugo lied, nodding. "Thank you officer," he said, getting himself organized while Metley returned to his vehicle and the road.

When he got home, his lucky coin was in his pocket.

"I guess you've lost your luck," he said, as much to it as to himself as the trinket.

Chapter 15
Bye-Bye Birdies

When he got back from drag racing, Anna was gone, and not just her, but all of her things. Gone were her two suitcases, scarf, gloves, hat, and boots, which were always by the door though she never needed them. Gone were her quilts, and her clothes, tidily hung by hue, her laptop, sketchbook, notebook, flower albums, tarot deck, incense, rosemary clippings, and avocado tree. Left behind was everything he'd purchased to make their home more comfortably hers.

Hugo swept away the petals and sat beside Rose's blond litter, not a green hair in sight. She tried to cheer him with her kisses, but the puppies, like him, cried out for Anna. That night, he slept on the couch, having brushed aside the curtain divider. It was easier than facing the desolation of their, now his, bedroom. He awoke Tuesday from a perfectly ordinary dream, but not from the clash of fowl chatter that had announced the sun since late February. There were no new petals to soften his step when he crossed the foyer, and glancing out, he found the flock had departed, abandoning rows of nests, many full of chilled eggs. Dimly, he wondered if he should throw those out before they stunk up his yard, but couldn't bring himself to bother.

Hugo applied for jobs until lunch, pretending not to notice the incoming interrogatory texts from Esteban, who apparently would not be so easily ignored. A knocking sounded later that afternoon, and his friend could see the news in his expression when Hugo opened the door.

"Shit, man. I'm sorry. Let me know if you want to talk," was all Esteban said. No "I told you so's," nor empty idioms that would have been devoid of comfort. He didn't even mention Hugo's black eye, and for that he was grateful. The last thing he wanted was to explain how he'd gotten it.

As the day wore on, the pomegranate tree withered, browning until it appeared as frail and brittle as he felt.

Hugo made a trip to Home Depot for plant food, which he added to the pot, but without optimism. For dinner, he ordered in a steak and drank warm beer. All of their fruit had turned overnight, and the apartment reeked of decay. Telling himself he'd get through this, he put an unfamiliar sitcom on, but after not retaining a single name, let alone the plot, turned it off at the sudden blare of a commercial break.

His butt and back were sore when he laid still, but the pain was magnitudes worse when he moved. To minimize the ache, or at least not exacerbate it, he slept flat on the floor, wrapped in a blanket, without so much as a pillow to cradle his head. The couch was more comfortable, but he worried about his tailbone healing wrong.

Tuesday, Hugo mourned the lack of half-full cups on every surface, missed collecting and rinsing them, putting them away. Her debris was the closest she came to leaving footsteps. Coming into the kitchen and find-ing the cabinets closed, the lids screwed on tight in the fridge, he was tempted to trash the joint himself, hoping to match an inkling of the life she'd breathed into their space. Weird, that it had never occurred to him to dec-orate the refrigerator, but now it looked naked without her celebratory magnets, links to people he'd never met and never would.

When he awoke Wednesday, he realized the walls were that soul-sucking white Anna despised. Funny, he thought. The apartment didn't reek of paint when he'd returned home with his speeding ticket, and somehow, she hadn't gotten so much as a drop on the wooden floors, nor the carpet.

Sorting the gulal, saving her dress—it wasn't enough, none of it. He'd fucked up, and what he needed was a grand gesture, *a miracle of a gesture.* The problem was, Anna wanted very little, and there was even less she couldn't obtain on her own. Reflecting, he sat on the floor, petting Rose and her pups, watching the little ones bump and nuzzle each other. He liked the smell of them. It was comfortable, homey, at odds with the stench of fermented produce that emptying the garbage failed to dispel. He was going to have to pick up air fresheners, or if that failed, incense. As it was, he had half a mind to spritz the kitchen with cologne to hold him over until he got to the store. Wait! That perfume Anna liked! He was sure he'd jotted it down.

Leaving Rose to coddle her brood, he stood, brushing fur and dust from his sleepwear. After several minutes of searching, he found what he sought in the kitchen drawer under a mound of menus and a leather-bound address book. Retrieving the water-stained notebook, he flipped through wrinkled pages listing Anna's likes, dislikes, and sparse background until he spied the name of a perfume, Bousquet's Chamonix. Then he turned to his desktop, confirming in no time at all that there still wasn't a single bottle for sale on eBay, nor Craigslist.

Hugo considered the matter from another angle. He couldn't recall ever having stolen something.

"Well how about that," he murmured, surprised.

Most teenagers went through a rebellious streak, stealing CDs, designer clothes, toeing the law. His surly phase was spent pursuing advanced English and math courses, to the chagrin of his father. In college, when his peers were story topping, he wondered at the key factor separating his temperament from theirs. They'd committed, and largely gotten away with, petty theft, violence, property damage, and in some cases, arson, while he'd been reading his fancy books and playing with a calculator. Playing it safe, in other words.

Well, no time like the present to make up for missed experiences, Hugo told himself, googling the address of the actress, Bousquet's spokeswoman, Lynnette Lewis. Unable to find the street name and number through a direct search, he examined the picture of her house that punctuated a local interview she'd given. It stood behind a tall fence, complete with a guard booth. What an absurd level of security, Hugo thought, zooming in on the large number twelve posted below the guard's window. It was difficult to tell, but the earth-tone bricks in the border wall appeared Mediterranean in style, that theme amplified by the stucco mansion front. There were even potted palm trees on display. This house had to be on the water. Pulling up MapQuest, Hugo printed a route to every road featuring waterfront properties in

Burlington. Then he set out. Checking the twelfth house on every relevant street, Hugo was halfway through the list when he found himself before the photographed gate of what was likely the only remaining residence of Bousquet's Chamonix in the states. As far as he could discern, Claude Bousquet was living in Greece.

Alright. So far so good. Step one down, Hugo thought, checking off an invisible box. Step two was finding a way in that wouldn't land him in jail. Unfortunately, he doubted security would be receptive to him waltzing up and earnestly explaining he only wished to buy a single bottle.

"Price be damned," he whispered.

This lady wouldn't want his money. She'd just want him gone, unless she thought he worked for her. But how to make that happen? Hugo made note of the street name and parked a little further down, so as to not arouse suspicion. From his perch alongside a brief stretch of trees marking the border between two large, though not ostensibly gated, properties, Hugo kept a record of the vehicles entering and exiting the Lewis mansion. Writing rapidly, he strove to catch every license plate number, make, and model. The speed limit wasn't high, but his eyesight was average and occasionally, cars passed between himself and his target. As his stomach began to rumble and he reflected that Rose was due for a walk, a van exited through the gate. Across the side was the logo for Merry Maids, brandishing a phone number underneath.

Perfect. He dialed, the receptionist picking up immediately.

"Hello. This is Donovan with Merry Maids. How can I help you?"

"Hello Donovan. I'm with security at twelve Wrightington Avenue, in Burlington. The usual guys have been called away for tonight and tomorrow. Last-minute training conference, you understand. I'm just filling in. Now, I was informed Merry Maids would be sending personnel come morning, but not at what time nor what their names are. Would you mind providing me with that information?"

Donovan supplied those details without asking for evidence of his credentials, and bid him a pleasant shift. Hugo concluded likewise and headed home, picking up the dress from the dry cleaners en route. Then, upon catching sight of his reflection in the decorative mirror posted over the foyer tree, he headed back out, much to the dismay of at least the eldest dog.

Hugo had a dim recollection of waiting, somewhat impatiently, while one of his exes had a beautician apply their makeup in a Macy's, utilizing precisely the skills Hugo both lacked and required in order to enact his loose plan. He looped the mall lot until he spotted the Macy's logo, parking directly out front. Trying and failing to silence the ghost of his father's condemnation, Hugo raced inside, heading directly to the makeup counters by the interior entrance.

"Can I help you?" asked the middle-aged brunette as she ceased adjusting the lipstick display.

"Can you teach me how to cover my black eye? I've got a job interview tomorrow."

Smiling, she assured him that was no trouble. Leading him to a selection of compacts featuring various skin tones, she pulled free a tiny purple wax crayon.

"Your bruise has a yellow tint, so you neutralize that by applying the complementary hue. In this case, purple. May I show you?"

Hugo gave his accord, closing the still slightly swollen lid. Leaning close, she gently applied the concealer with a q-tip. The bruise was browner, as a result, but hardly any lighter.

"Next up, we match your skin tone. Do you mind if I test these on your arm?"

He did not, and soon, bore stripes in several shades, all similar to that of his wrist, though not exact.

"That's alright," she commented. "Close enough is fine. We'll blend it out."

Again, she had Hugo close the offending eye, and he complied. The beautician took longer with the second layer, which she spread with a brush, fading it out at the edges.

"That looks much better," Hugo commended, as she was pulling away.

"Good. If you're worried about your eyes matching, you can apply this shade to both of them."

Hugo thanked her and, having led him to her register, she checked out his purchase.

"I hope you land the job!" the beautician said, by way of goodbye.

Friday, he awoke long before dawn and, having concealed the injury that would have cast suspicions over his character, pulled up to the gate twenty minutes before the maids were set to arrive.

"Good morning. Please state your business."

"Hello there. I'm Donovan with Merry Maids, here for the bi-annual employee audit. Shelby and Melissa should be here any minute, at which point I'll be shadowing them to report on their efforts today. The property representative will receive a copy at the end of this shift."

"Huh. Donovan—Donovan O'Hanity? It says here you're the receptionist. We weren't expecting you today."

"Oh, I was promoted a month or so ago. When was your registry last updated?"

The guard sighed. "Who knows? I'll make a note," he added, rapidly crossing out and jotting down the title. "Alright then. Can I see some ID?"

Hugo made a big show of pulling his license from the sun visor and dropping it between his seat and the door.

"Oh, sorry. I dropped it. Just a minute."

A car had pulled up behind his, and Hugo heard another following, slowing further behind. He opened his door, visibly reaching under his seat.

"Sorry. Can't quite reach it."

"Nevermind. We'll print a temp badge. Just next time, please have your ID ready."

Hugo waited while the guard printed a wallet-sized piece of card stock featuring his new name and position, popped it into a plastic sleeve, and handed it over.

"Here you go. Take a left where the driveway forks. Service entrance is in the back."

"Thank you. Take care," Hugo replied, heart pumping in his ears as he rolled his window up and eased down the drive. He pulled his car into a space beside a rusted and rundown Toyota. Traipsing around a budding garden that was abuzz with bees and hummingbirds, he let himself in.

"Hi. And who are you?" asked an older woman in a floral top and a flour-stained apron.

"Hello. I'm Donovan O'Hanity, manager of Merry Maids."

She looked from his badge to his face. "So you are. Well, you're early. The girls won't be here for a few more minutes."

"That's just fine. Which way to the lavatory, if you don't mind?"

She didn't, giving him very specific instructions on where to access the allotted bathroom. Hugo followed her route to the letter, turning down a hall of chest-height porcelain vases arranged beneath portraits of Mrs. Lewis posed in varying levels of undress. He turned at a corner table bearing an antique golden clock and followed the filigree carpet until he found a door with a brass lion's head handle and, turning it, entered. Unfortunately, being for "the help," there wasn't a single perfume present. Not by the mirror, nor under the counter. Even the toilet paper was cheap. Single ply? Hugo shook his head.

Convinced that women kept perfume in their bathrooms, Hugo crept on, in search of another.

Meandering through a labyrinth of obscene wealth, he prayed no one would take notice of his trajectory and denounce him a fraud. His pulse drummed with every step, and perhaps it was a mercy when, finally stumbling from a guest bathroom complete with a clawed bathtub, gilded molding, and Roman mosaic floors—the sought after perfume in victorious yet trembling hands—Hugo bumped into exactly the wrong man.

He was tall, balding, with faint brows, a wide nose, and a thin mouth, the only color in his face the blacks of his eyes, as if he'd been born to don that crisp suit and those shined shoes. The butler would have looked the same in greyscale as in technicolor, Hugo observed, wondering if he suffered from albinism.

"Why, hello there, Mr. O'Hanity, sir. Funny, you looked different the last time we met. *Very different indeed.*"

He waited for Hugo to confess. When he didn't, the man continued.

"I'm George, head butler here, and there appears to have been a misunderstanding." He listed how far they were from the appropriate restroom, concluding with, "but that's not what you were looking for, was it?"

The butler's eyes narrowed on the bottle in Hugo's hands.

"What? Oh, this? I tried it and thought it smelled nice. Was just bringing it to show the cook, to ask her if she knew where I might buy more."

"Come off it, Mr. O'Hanity, or whatever your real name is. You're here to rob the Lewis family and I won't have it. Come with me."

Hugo sighed, recognizing that resistance was futile, and allowed himself to be led to the kitchen, where he sat glumly beside the cook while the butler called the police, then the guards.

"What if I bought it? That's what I tried to do anyway. I wouldn't be here at all if they hadn't ceased production."

"Production of what, sir?" George asked.

"The perfume. My girlfriend walked out. This is her scent, and if I give it to her, if I can prove that I love her, maybe she'll come home."

"Sir, you broke in to steal some old perfume?"

"I've tried everything else," Hugo said, listing his previous attempts to win her heart since losing her trust, finishing his morose tale as a guard entered. "I'd give anything to have her back."

The cook stared quizzically at Hugo while George turned to the incomer, explaining that while the intruder entered under a false identity and attempted to rob them, he didn't appear violent.

"I'm not cuffing you, but if you try to stand, to leave this room, I'm within my legal rights to tase or tackle, and you won't get past the gate," the guard explained.

Hugo nodded, staring at the ornate crystal bottle that remained in his grip. He looked again to George.

"Can I buy it? Would you ask Lynnette Lewis, or her husband, if I can? I've got cash and good credit. I can afford it."

George traced his brow with a crooked finger.

"I will call Mr. Lewis. Mrs. Lewis is away for work."

With bated breath, Hugo watched as George dialed his boss and succinctly broke down the situation, calling Hugo a lovesick fool, explaining he'd engaged in an act of desperation. George nodded, agreed with his employer, and ended the call. The butler did not look at nor speak to Hugo and, crushed, he took that as a "no." Minutes later, a clean-cut fellow who could only be Mr. Lewis appeared in a silk button-down top over ironed slacks and leather loafers. Hugo could hear the sirens. The police would be up the drive soon.

"Hey, George. So, this is the guy?"

George gave his confirmation and Mr. Lewis stroked his chin, then looked to the guard. "I'll be having a talk with your supervisor later. This man should never have made it past the gate."

The guard nodded but kept silent.

Then, turning to Hugo, Mr. Lewis asked, "Alright, so who are you?"

At this point, Hugo's best bet was to appease these people. Besides, his wallet was in his car. The police doubtless had the means to acquire access. His identity wouldn't be a secret for much longer.

"My name is Hugo Atmen. I'm sorry for all of this trouble. I just needed that perfume to get Anna back. Everything else has failed."

Mr. Lewis looked Hugo over, nodding to himself before he spoke.

"Well, you can have that. We've got plenty of those floating around the house. As for sneaking onto our property—I can't let that slide."

Hugo took a deep breath but nodded his accord. "I knew the risk, but she's worth it."

Mr. Lewis raised his brows and shrugged.

"I hope you're right," he said as the police were led in by the other guard, who immediately left to return to his post. The officers conferred with Mr. Lewis.

"Good day, officers. This man trespassed on our property and I intend to press charges."

"Very well. How did he enter your residence?"

"My man George here brought him in when he found him wandering the grounds."

Hugo looked to Mr. Lewis in surprise, saying nothing to contradict the lie.

The officers took note of the narrative. Then they told Hugo to turn around and put both hands behind his back, and he complied. They took the bottle from him, closed the cold metal cuffs around his wrists, read him his rights, and led him back to their cruiser. En route Hugo looked first to Mr. Lewis, then to George, as if he might thank them with his eyes. Trespassing was a far lesser charge than breaking and entering. Once outside, Hugo asked what would happen to his car? It would be towed. And the perfume? It would be kept safe for him when they got to the station. Hugo explained that all of his IDs were in his car.

"Where in your car?" asked the paler of the two officers. Hugo told him, as well as where his keys were on his person.

"Are you granting us entry into your vehicle?"

"Yes. There's nothing illegal in there, and I want this to go as smoothly as possible. I have dogs at home. I'm fostering a litter. They're not even two weeks old and can't be alone for long. The dog walker comes around lunch, but I need to get back to feed and walk their mama by dinner."

The officers exchanged a wary look and Hugo realized the odds of him going home that day were slim.

"Alright. I'll go get your IDs. Don't move."

Hugo obeyed. He stood stock-still, his hands cuffed behind his back, beside the tanner officer as the paler locked the Alliance and returned with Hugo's wallet.

"Got it. Let's get going."

It was awkward, entering and settling in the back of the cruiser without the use of his hands. He leaned forward so as not to cut off his circulation and looked out the window, watching the curious faces that stared back from cars ambling by. None dared speed beside a cop car. To his surprise, Hugo was calm. Had anyone asked how he'd react to being arrested, he'd have anticipated a crippling, hands-shaking, word-stumbling, mind-numbing fear. Instead, his pulse slowed to a resting rate. What would be, would be. There was nothing he could do but wait.

At the station, once they were past the cage and the handcuffs had been removed, Hugo placed his cellphone, watch, belt, and keys into a plastic bin. One of his arresting officers added the perfume and his wallet. Hugo figured that was all, but the lady running the counter asked for his shoes and socks, too. He pulled them off, passing them over, and she went through his wallet, copying the contents within before showing him the list to confirm she hadn't made any mistakes. Hugo was then led to a holding cell, where he was searched. The officers were thorough. As he shivered, they commanded him to open his mouth, spread his cheeks, lift his balls, turn this way and that, but he cooperated despite the sack-shrinking chill. Apparently police didn't believe in central heating.

After what felt like a half-hour of having his strings pulled, they returned his shoes and socks to him, moving Hugo on to fingerprinting. His fingers were stained black, the alcohol failing to cleanse him of the ink, and he nearly quoted Lady Macbeth, but dared not risk the humor. From fingerprinting, Hugo was brought to a wall marked with height lines and had his picture taken from the side, then again facing the camera. The flash was blinding, but he was grateful for the concealer he wore and staggered where led, which was into a concrete room with a flat wooden bench-bed and a toilet. So, that's really what jail cells look like, he thought. Movies weren't exaggerating.

As the officer was closing the cage behind him, Hugo asked if he would be allowed to make a phone call.

"I'll see what I can do."

Hugo thanked him and sat down, grateful that he was the only arrestee—prisoner, he amended—so far that day. The slender windows didn't let in enough light to warm the air, and the bench wasn't shaped for comfortably sitting nor sleeping. His posture had exacerbated the pain in his lower back when the officer returned with Hugo's cell phone. Unable to stand straight, it was bent that Hugo approached, stopping a foot before the bars, so as to not intimidate.

"I consulted the bail schedule. Because you did not gain unlawful entry into the Lewis residence, you're only facing a misdemeanor trespassing charge. Bail is set at two thousand dollars. If you're calling someone to cosign, you guys are going to be ponying up ten percent of that, or two hundred dollars, before we can let you out. As long as you show up to court, neither of you will be responsible for paying the rest."

Hugo thanked the man again and immediately dialed Sonya, as Esteban, while an avid texter, would absolutely not pick up a call on his cell during bank hours.

"Hugo? I'm at work."

"Please don't hang up! I'm in jail."

"You're kidding."

"I'm not."

"Jesus Christ, Hugo. What did you do?"

"You know that actress from the Lamentation Song trilogy?"

"Yeah, she lives here. Why?"

"Well, she happens to be the spokesperson for Anna's favorite perfume, and they don't make it anymore."

"Tell me you did not break into a celebrity's house over a perfume."

"It was the only way."

"You have lost your damned mind."

"Be that as it may, would you mind taking care of the dogs tonight? I have a spare key under the mat. I think Anna's back in White Plains, so she's not around to do it. I'd ask Esteban, but I don't know how familiar he is with caring for dogs."

"Yeah, whatever. Wait. Did they set bail yet?"

The officer was making a winding motion with his hand, telling him to wrap it up. Hugo nodded.

"Bail is set at two thousand dollars. I need a cosigner, and to pay two hundred before I can go home."

She heaved a dramatic sigh. "Where are you being held?"

Hugo asked the officer and relayed the address to Sonya.

"Fine. I'll come by when I get out of work. Don't do anything stupid in the meantime. *And you are making that court date.*"

"Yes, I am. Thank you."

"Ugh. You're welcome, I guess. Bye."

She hung up before he could wish her a nice shift and Hugo handed his phone back to the officer, thanking him again.

"She's coming to get me when she gets out of work."

"You really did all of this for some perfume?"

Hugo shrugged, aware that confessing to more than trespassing could make his day a lot more complicated.

"I did what I did for love."

The officer stepped away, shaking his head, and Hugo was left alone to mull over his choices. He wanted to while the hours away with sleep, but the bench wouldn't allow it. Standing, Hugo paced the cell, gradually straightening his back. Though his stomach grumbled, he was grateful he hadn't eaten anything all day. The idea of taking a shit in front of those watching from afar, or over the cameras, made him cringe. Once, an officer stopped by to offer him a paper cup of water and a plastic-wrapped sandwich. While he accepted both with grace, the sandwich was frozen in the middle, and the edges of the cheese were hard, dark with age. Not long after he'd managed to down his quaint meal, another officer appeared to let him know Sonya had arrived.

The officer unlocked the cage door, stepping inside. He led Hugo out, holding the cell door open. Then he brought Hugo to the counter where his friend waited, checkbook in hand and expression somewhere between bemusement and aggravation.

"I cannot believe you. I half expected this to be an elaborate prank."

"Thank you so much for coming. I promise I'll pay you back as soon as I get to an ATM."

The officer showed them where to sign, accepted the check, and handed Hugo a receipt listing his court date. Hugo took back his belongings, asked where to pick up his car, and wished the officers a lovely evening. Then the duo left, stepping into a light spring shower.

Neither had brought an umbrella, and Sonya shivered as they stepped beyond the overhang. Outside wasn't any colder than in, and Hugo had adjusted during his wait.

"If you don't mind giving me a ride to an ATM, I'd like to pay you back today."

"Sure. You can tell me what it was like on the way," she replied, unlocking the car and moving some books from the passenger side so he could sit.

There was a shopping outlet just down the road, and he'd arrived at the house in his narrative when they parked. Trailing him to the ATM, Sonya listened to his tale as she pocketed the sum offered. She listened as she drove him to the tow lot, and as they waited for the clerk to see them. He was describing the strip search when the clerk returned, and Hugo ponied up another fifty dollars to get his Alliance back. The clerk stepped away to drive Hugo's vehicle to the exit gate, and Hugo sped through detailing the remainder of his day.

When he was done, Sonya repeated the same question Mr. Lewis asked.

"Was it worth it?"

"Anything for Anna," he said.

Sonya rubbed her chin, which was partially concealed behind her popped collar. "Gonna call her? Tell her what you did?"

"Yeah. Got to find out where to send it. I'm not sure where she's staying."

Sonya sighed, called him an idiot, wished him luck, and split.

No sooner did he arrive home that he texted Anna a novel, detailing his trial with the gulal, besting Boukman to save her dress, and the moderate success of his perfume heist. Where should he send the dress, perfume, and anything else she left behind? He asked, but she didn't respond. "Well, maybe she didn't see it," he thought. "Or she could be busy with work."

Friday, Esteban, Nicole, and Joe all shot him texts, wondering where he'd been for comedy night, asking if he was okay. Saying only that he was sorry to have missed it and that he wouldn't be around that weekend, Hugo let any further messages from friends and family go unanswered. Neither Sonya nor Anna attempted contact. Before he hit the hiring pages, Hugo wrote out his official letter of resignation, wherein he apologized for the manner in which he'd abandoned his position, citing struggles with his heart, mental and physical health. That last was an exaggeration but nor was he well. His inbox pinged a moment later, and checking, he found an automated response from Human Resources confirming they'd received his message.

Hugo looked to his phone, imagining a buzzing pocket, but Anna still hadn't gotten back to him. The homey scent of the pups hadn't spread beyond their nest, and the sickly sweet odor of rot had grown sour despite the absence of greying produce. It reminded him of Anna's bizarre cabbage, carrot, and squash sandwiches. What he wouldn't give to taste those again.

That night he slept in their bed, inhaling the coconut residue still saturating the comforter, sheets, and mattress—praying it wouldn't fade away, and then promising himself that he wouldn't wash them until she came home, for she would be coming home. They were fated to be together, and forgetting, acting against that faith, was a transgression akin to sinning.

Monday, Hugo awoke impatient for her to land, to text or call now that she'd be returning from her weekend post. He fed Rose, walked her, played with the pups, applied for unemployment benefits, jobs. The walker arrived at lunch and he debated letting her go. He couldn't justify the expense when he didn't have an income, but he thought better of it. With his experience, he'd be getting calls back in no time, interviews sooner rather than later, likely hired on the spot. Then he'd have to formally enlist her services all over again. Better to save himself the hassle, he told Rose after the walker left.

He opened the book he'd been neglecting, only to put it down again. There was nothing on TV, but he left it on to drown out the silence while the litter napped. At dinner, when she still hadn't called, Hugo drank a bottle of wine, then dialed, ready to plead his case, or at least to hear her voice, but after the first ring, he was routed to voicemail. Either she was quick to decline the call—unlike Anna, given her propensity for ignoring notifications for hours on end—or he'd been blocked.

That night he did not sleep. After hours of lying awake, he took to circling the block around Carmelle's Dance Studio, debating waltzing up, punching the first guy that walked out, or going in and inquiring as to whether her instructor, or classmates, knew where she was, ultimately deciding against both. His restraint was rewarded Tuesday morning when the phone rang and *Sweet Mother of God*—it was her!

"Hello?" he answered before the first ring subsided for the second.

"I made some calls. The charges have been dropped. You should be hearing from the precinct later today, letting you know," Anna said, bypassing the usual greetings.

"Wha—how? You didn't have to do that."

"Doing what I do, you make connections," she said. "I can't have you in jail. Now, what you did was very, *very* stupid. Please don't do anything so hair-brained ever again. The Lewises would have been absolutely right to charge you with breaking and entering, trespassing, and attempted burglary. You should be very thankful they did not press all of those from the get-go. Had they, and there would have been no way to fix this mess. Breaking and entering charges can't be dropped. Did you know that?"

Hugo confessed he did not and assured her he had no intentions of ever getting arrested again.

"Glad to hear it. Now Hugo, for the last time—I get that you believe we're destined to be together." He nodded, well aware there was a "but" coming. He assumed it would be followed by "I need more time," or "we are going to have to set some boundaries before we can get back together." What he did not anticipate was the ax to the chest in which she stated, *"you're wrong."* Yet that's what she said, and her tone left no room for argument.

"I'm sorry, but you misinterpreted your premonitions. We're not soulmates. We're not even star-crossed. *I do not love you.* I never will. This is the last time I will ever speak to you."

Hugo's heart dropped and he sank to the floor, babbling in a manner he hoped expressed that their love was forever.

"Now I wish you all the best," she continued over his vehement, though perhaps incoherent, protestations. "Take care," Anna said, hanging up. He immediately tried to call her back, but she declined his calls, again, and again, and again, until his cell battery flashed a warning. The device was on the brink of death and for a moment, Hugo envied his phone.

Chapter 16
Poppet Master

The precinct called to relay the good news and Hugo feigned positivity, but even Rose's kisses failed to make him smile. He went through the motions of playing with the pups, feeding, walking their mama, and applying for work in Burlington and beyond. Even after their trip to Windsor, he had savings. He could buy his way out of his lease if necessary. Thursday, he got a call back from a top bank in Champlain, New York and set an interview for the following week. To reward himself for doing something, anything at all, right, Hugo poured himself a glass of Jack Daniel's. Finishing that, he poured another.

By his fifth glass, he'd run through the gamut of breakup emotions. He'd gone from denial, convinced that by now *she must miss him,* to guilt, shame. What the hell had he been thinking, spying on his girlfriend? Paramour. Whatever. Digging his nails into the soft flesh of his palms until blood rippled forth, pooled, he cursed his folly. *The universe had spoken!* She would be his! Yet he'd gone and fucked it all up. Because he was a fuckup, just like his dad always said. A man, *a real man* with confidence from being accomplished, from being strong and capable, wouldn't have doubted her fidelity. A real man would've taken it for granted that he deserved her, and she, him. She'd have remained at his side, a happy foster grandma beaming at squirming quintuplets.

Then he redirected his anger at her. Why didn't she see he was doing his goddamned best?! He'd tried since day one with her. Tried and tried again. She wanted an apartment in Burlington, and who found her one? She would have spent Thanksgiving and Christmas alone if not for him! What kind of woman didn't have a single close relation to provide welcome for the holidays? And what the hell kind of excuse was that, blaming work for lying all of the time? To everyone? Her clients were loaded! It wasn't like they ran in the same circles as her friends, him, or his family. She'd never needed to lie.

The bitch just liked it, keeping secrets, telling tall tales! That was it! She lived in a fantasy, maintaining a man-ufactured aura of mystery, probably lying to herself, too!

It didn't matter. None of it mattered. She was gone. At that, Hugo shotgunned his sixth glass, then doubled over, coughing. Catching his breath, he poured another glass, spilling some, rewetting the crimson crescents in his hand.

No! This wasn't over. Yeah, he'd fucked up, and badly. Obviously. But then he'd extended olive branch after olive branch, trying to mend things, convincing her of his love. And he did deserve her! He did! He'd given her everything, shared his bed, home, even his family when he thought she had none of her own. He'd given up his job. Hell, he'd gotten arrested for her! And what had she done for him? What?! She wiped his record? So what? He hadn't asked her to.

Hugo deserved Anna and *he would have her*, he thought, eyeing the poppet propped atop the book-shelf. That would do very nicely. Having seen, foretold the coming of his perfect lover, who was he to say voodoo wasn't real? She sure believed in all that occult stuff and he'd never considered her dim. If there was something to it, to tarot, energies, magic, there was no better time to find out. Locating the certificate of authenticity, without considering the hour, Hugo called the voodoo practitioner whose number was listed on the inside slip.

On the third ring, a male voice answered.

"Oungan Martin at your service. How can I help you?"

"Hello, Mr. uh, Oungan Martin. I'm Hugo. My girlfriend ordered a doll from you a while back."

"Oh, Oungan is my title. No mister necessary. And great! How's your effigy working out? Do you require a blessing renewal? They're buy one, get one this week. Or I can give you a discount on a second poppet. They make great gifts for friends and family!"

"Well, my girlfriend walked out, and I'd like her to come home. How do I go about making that happen?"

"Ah! What you need is a love spell. If you have a credit card, I can mail you a kit."

"I do, but is there any way we can make this happen faster? I would rather have the spell cast tonight if possible." Hugo hoped to catch her while she was "crashing" with friends, before she signed a new lease all her own.

"Tonight? I can instruct you on how to cast it yourself."

He offered a price which Hugo agreed to, pulling free his credit card and reading the numbers out. When he was finished, Oungan Martin took down his email.

"Perfect. You should receive the instructions in your inbox. Give me twenty minutes. I've got to type it out. If you don't see it, check your spam folder. If it still isn't there, call me back and I'll make sure I didn't type your address wrong."

The call ended and Hugo bandaged his bloodied palm, wiping clean the red smear across the cell phone while waiting for the notification. His desktop pinged not ten minutes later and he set to work. First, he had to link the existing poppet to himself. Pulling out his little-used sewing kit, he ran thread over his lucky coin, knotting it tightly to his doll's chest.

Then he set about building hers. For a cross of sticks, he bound two pencils. Cornhusk was the recommended fabric, but linen or similar would do in a pinch. Reaching for a coffee-colored satin throw pillow, he sliced it open and pulled it over the frame. Spanish moss was the preferred stuffing, but without the foggiest as to where to find any in the middle of the night in Vermont, he let the cotton balls be. Squeezing the pillow into a head and limbs, he tied off the joints at the torso and sewed her up. The doll was to resemble the subject, so Hugo dug through his closet until he found a top with shiny black buttons. Snapping two of them off, he sewed them onto her head, admiring how they caught the light.

To connect the doll to Anna, he required something of hers. Hair would have been great, but alas, she kept a shaved head. Furthermore, in a moment of perceived strength, he'd cleaned the drains, swept, dusted, and now even her clippings were gone. She'd packed her things, not forgetting so much as a pen. Even the prim was missing. Still, she must have overlooked something, Hugo told himself, running a hand through the shirts hung in his closet by formality, rather than shade. He checked the living room for autobiographies, but she brought those from the library, rarely buying her own. He examined the bathroom drawer that she'd taken over after Claire, and unlike her predecessor, left bare. It was when he was checking under the bed that he recalled the scrap of fabric from her dress. "That'll work," he said, fiddling through jean pockets until he found it. This, he stitched to her torso before grabbing a red sharpie and drawing a heart on her front. Coloring it in, Hugo looked to the next set of instructions.

To purify her poppet, he placed a large bowl of water on the kitchen counter, stirring in salt. Then he was to light incense. Oungan Martin didn't specify what kind, not that it mattered. Hugo didn't own any. That had been Anna's thing, and as with everything else, she'd left him none. Sighing at the delay, Hugo hit the web, searching for incense ingredients. Other than the main spice or herb for scent, incense was a mixture of bamboo and charcoal or wood paste for an easier, longer burn. Cinnamon being the most popular fragrance, he pulled his shaker from the pantry. Shrugging, he laid chopsticks on a plate, shaking the spice over top. So they'd catch, he poured a shot of Everclear, wetting the pile, struck a match, and dropped it. The flame was blue, spreading quickly to the edge before dying, leaving only the cheapo chopsticks lit. Their light was weak, but the smell, strong.

"It'll do," Hugo said, placing the printed script before the bowl for easy readability.

When the fire died, he performed her baptism. Lifting the doll, he cradled it in the crook of his arm while making a cross with his fingers.

"I baptize you, Anna Petro, in the name of the Father, the Son, and the Holy Spirit. You are who I wish you to be. All that is done to you will happen to Anna Petro in the world as I command it. You, Anna Petro, are mine."

Concluding his proclamation, he dunked the doll in the saltwater.

Next, he needed a red candle and ribbon. The candle he actually owned. Power outages were common during Vermont winters, and Hugo had plenty of varying shapes, sizes, and shades, scattered throughout the bathroom cabinets and under the kitchen sink. It took him some minutes to find a red one, but find it he did before carrying it out to his poor excuse of a backyard, where the new moon offered no illumination. According to the Oungan, a new moon lacked the immense power of a full moon, but was suitable for love spells, offering a fresh start.

Placing the dolls before the candle, Hugo returned inside in search of ribbon. He'd adopted his mom's habit of saving gift bows and bags, so he had a collection to pull from for any occasion. Locating a long stretch of burgundy polyester, he carried that and the print-ed script to the spell site. Lighting the candle, Hugo thanked Papa Legba for opening the crossroads so that he could make his request known. Then he called upon Manman Ezili.

"Manman Ezili Freda, I ask you, please bind my love to me. I seek the heart of Anna Petro, for her to shed unjust enmity."

This he chanted as he wound the ribbon first around the effigy of Anna and then around that of himself, tying the two together with a simple bow. As he repeat-ed his mantra, the words taking on a rhythm of their own, he saw her dancing the kompa, except now, rather than thrusting against another man, she rubbed against Hugo. They merged, standing, crying out in ecstasy as wave after wave passed over them both under the starry night and fiery day. Lost in passion, Hugo ejaculated and was suddenly ripped from his trance by a voice. Terrified, he opened his eyes, searching for the source. Had a neighbor born witness to his antics? It had to be after three a.m.

Then his panic twisted from social anxiety to bone-deep mortal fear as the voice came from every-where at once, surrounding him, multiplying, until he was swept along by a sea of tongues he couldn't under-stand before he pinpointed one he could.

In English, it said, "The child gifts you protection and you *dare* slap her with chains! Repent, you fool!"

At once, his feet hit the ground with a jolt that left his knees bent, his fists knuckle deep in mud. Righting himself, catching his breath, Hugo saw a spark leap from the candle. As if lifted by a conscious breeze, the wisp touched the very edge of the bow, where it caught, flashing bright. Hugo's face and hands blistered from sudden heat as the fire consumed the ribbon, leaving both dolls intact. Inching back, he touched his split, peeling lip and flinched at the sting from face and fingers both.

"That can't be good," he rasped.

Hugo consulted the instructions, rereading the final step. Once the candle blew out, he was to place the dolls in a box, to be tucked away in a space easily overlooked, forgotten, to be part of the home. The instructions did not mention ephemeral voices, possessed flames, or a burnt ribbon. Hugo lacked a background in chemistry but he was fairly certain the plastic-based fabric should have melted, rather than been reduced to ash. Hours had elapsed since he'd called the Oungan and he hoped the man was still awake. Holding his breath, Hugo punched in the number, waiting through the first ring, then the second.

"How did it go?"

Hugo told him, leaving nothing out, in case the ultimate deviation was his fault.

"Wild! That's one hell of a 'no.' Nah, it wasn't your pronunciations, and none of those substitutions would have offended Manman Ezili. Every Oungan does things a little differently, and nobody would expect you to be an expert on voodoo. At worst, the substitutions might have weakened your connection to the loa, but it sounds like you had a *fine connection*. That said, the spell bombed for a reason. You've really pissed somebody off. Somebody important. Fuck. I'd mail you some myrrh, but you need it *now*. What's your address again?"

Hugo told him, looking nervously around in case these loa, whatever they were, attacked.

"Cool. Got MapQuest up. Just checking out your neighborhood. Ah—here we go. Adder's Fork is like ten minutes from your house. I'm gonna leave them a message after we hang up, but tomorrow—first thing—get your ass there. Pick up myrrh resin. Light it over the dolls, wherever you cast your spell tonight. In fact, do not touch your setup until then. Now, it shouldn't stay lit for long. Looks like you're in for high winds. That's fine. Don't be a moron about it. Wet the grass if it's dry, so it doesn't all go up. That's basic fire safety. When it burns out, you bury the dolls. Hang on to the myrrh, though."

"Why? Am I going to have to burn it more than once?"

"What? Not for this. It's just really handy to have around. You never know when you'll have to break a spell or rid yourself of the evil eye."

The second his watch read nine, a heavy headed and nauseous Hugo was out of his car, crossing the pavement, echoes of last night's voices igniting a tremble in his extremities. A woman eased the glass door open, holding up her palm so he would go no further.

"Hugo, right?"

He nodded.

"Look, I'm happy to help but I can't have you inside until after you've lit this stuff. Bad juju. You understand. That'll be five dollars." He tried to hand her the money but she shook her head. "Oh no, if you can put the money on the ground, I'll put down the myrrh."

"Uh, okay," he said, putting a five-dollar bill on the concrete walkway and reaching for the paper bag she'd kicked forward.

"Nice doing business with you and good luck. I mean it," she said, rising to her feet, a crisp five in her grip as she returned to the safe confines of her shop.

Hugo continued to quiver as he carefully laid the myrrh over the dolls, along the soot lining their middles, evidence he hadn't imagined the sentient spark. Wordless, mouth dry, he dropped a lit match. A pungent aroma, not unlike figs, filled his nostrils, and he watched as the flames licked, blackened, and nibbled away the fabrics, feathers, shrouding the beads black, until the fire died. Their faces were burned through, the ashes blown away. With his hands, he dug a shallow grave, as much to bury his hope for otherworldly assistance in his butchered love life as for the dolls themselves. Relieved the Oungan hadn't suggested giving a eulogy, Hugo placed each doll in its hole, his throat too tight for speaking. He sprinkled soil over their charred remains until nothing was left but the smell of myrrh and a single half-melted red candle, which he threw away.

So that was it then. The universe might have drawn him to her, but it would pull her no nearer, and by now, she was in White Plains, living with friends she'd never bothered to name. The loa, whatever they were, wanted him to give up, pretend every lover he'd ever bed was half the woman she was, though inevitably, they'd be much less. The voices wanted him empty, unfulfilled, for neither he nor her to bask in the glory of love. The loa were evil. They opposed fate, the proper order. They were a blockade, set against him on this path.

It had been two weeks since she'd left. Reaching her dial tone anew, Hugo turned to the web. He wished, for the first time, that Anna shared the superficiality of their peers, that she had a Myspace or a blog to stalk. That she frequented chatrooms with enough regularity that he might find her there, but she wasn't the type.

Instead, he used what he had to track her down, which wasn't much. First name, surname, last known city of residence, and that prior. He even included her number, but all he found was her phone carrier. Fat lot of good that would do.

Then he checked for her employer, Maitresse Matchmaking in Manhattan. Imagining himself convincing some secretary that he was Anna's brother, or a lawyer perhaps, seeking her out over an inheritance, he tried various spellings and search engines. Unfortunately, if they had a website, it was obscurely named. Hugo was unable to find any record of Maitresse Matchmaking in Manhattan or anywhere else. There were a few small businesses featuring the name Maitresse, and even more offering matchmaking services, but not one matching her description.

"I guess they really are that hush-hush," he sulked.

He was falling apart. His tail bone was sprained, his back sore and eye swollen, but now his face and palms were likewise inflamed, he had a pounding migraine, and the tidal waves of heartburn refused all medication. Yet nothing compared to the rejection. How could she just shut him out? Pretend she couldn't love him? There was nothing else for it. He would go to White Plains and find her. Calling the dog walker, he promoted her to sitter.

"I have to go out of town for a couple of days," he explained.

She was reluctant, but he offered to pay her hourly rate to stay over. The walker replied that she only offered daytime services, but would make an exception just this once on account of Rose having just had puppies. He thanked her, and while she refused to spend the night, she drew up a schedule that would suit the little ones' needs fine.

At dawn he hit the road, having caffeinated long before. White Plains was a good five hours away, but he didn't have anywhere else to be. Traffic stalled and the crowding worsened as he entered New York. Twice he passed accidents that warranted ambulances. The second was just wrapping up, EMT's pulling a tarp-covered stretcher.

As lines blurred and the sun seared his retinas, Hugo considered how he was going to convince Anna to come home with him. He loved her, and even if she didn't believe so, Anna would come to love him, if she didn't already. He'd fucked up and he would admit to it, be better. No more questioning where she was, who she was with, getting frustrated when she didn't respond. Anna was a busy woman and no pushover. She demanded freedom, to act without question, without delays, and would accept no less.

Recognizing her needs was half the battle, and now, so armed, he could better provide. Those distractions pulling her away were temporary. Not like him. He would stand by her forever. One day she wouldn't have to answer to a boss, clients. Hugo would be so high on the totem, raking in such an income, she wouldn't work.

Then Anna could see the world, and he'd join her for weekend getaways, vacations. He'd get his numbers up the second he found a new position. But first, he had to make amends. Without her, what did money matter? Why kill himself, slaving over a desk, without his beloved to share in the meat of his labor? The unknown distance between his heart and hers was a drain on his motivation, his concentration, and with only one possible cure, he drove on.

Arriving in White Plains, Hugo recalled that Anna had been living with a group of college students before moving in with him. What if she'd returned to them? A gas station attendant let him know that the university district spanned northeast from their position. In fact, they weren't far from Empire State College. With thanks, Hugo set out on foot. As decent a starting point as any without an address to work from, he parked off Central Ave and the hunt began.

Knock! Knock! The door opened, and a harassed-looking woman, two boys shouting and wrestling at her back, acknowledged him.

"Who are you?" she barked, scowling at the sight of him with his swollen eye. As evidence of his battle against Boukman, he'd decided not to conceal it. In retrospect, he could have simply removed the makeup before meeting her, but he hadn't anticipated the importance of leaving a positive impression on strangers in pursuit of Anna.

"Hi! I'm Hugo Atmen. Would you happen to know Anna Petro?"

"What? No. You must have the wrong house," she said, swinging the door shut.

Knock! Knock!

"Hello?" croaked a raisin of a man who looked older than the United States, and Hugo wondered how his grape stem arms could budge that formidable door.

"Hello, sir! Do you know a woman by the name of Anna Petro?"

"Who?"

"Anna Petro."

"I don't need petrol!"

Mystified, Hugo shook his head. "Glad to hear it. Thank you, sir. Have a great day!"

And so it went. Many asked what he thought he was doing, going door to door, asking after some girl, and he told them the truth. Reactions were mixed. A few older women found his grand gesture romantic, the sort of behavior they'd expect from men in one of their soaps—especially when he explained his bruises were earned reclaiming her property from some creep. The younger women ranged from coolly polite to openly hostile, all pointedly telling him that he should leave this Anna-person alone, to respect her decision, several adding that he should consider therapy. They remarked what he was doing wasn't healthy and verged on illegal. The men, what few demanded an explanation before shutting him out, were sympathetic but ultimately unhelpful.

Hugo was on his fifth block, in the process of meticulously crossing off another leadless address, when for the third time in recent memory, he was approached by police. Two officers, a man and a woman, conferred, pointing, before striding his way.

"Hello, sir. I'm Officer Bashaw and this is Officer Shorthall," said the woman. "We received a call about a man attempting to harass a woman. Are you Hugo?"

"Yes officer, I am. However, I believe there has been a misunderstanding. I'm not harassing anyone."

"Would you please describe what you are doing on this street, then?"

A car drove by, blaring a pop ballad through open windows, and Hugo had to repeat his response as it had gone unheard.

"Of course, ma'am. No problem. I've been going door to door to find out if anyone knows where my girlfriend is."

"That sounds a great deal like stalking, Mr. Atmen," she replied.

"Is your girlfriend missing? Have you filled out a missing person's report?" Shorthall inquired.

Thinking on his feet, Hugo said, "Yes she is, and no I have not. You see, Anna and I have been living together for about a month. She works weekends, generally out of town. However, she should've come home before I'd returned from my Monday shift. Meanwhile, it's Sunday and I haven't seen her for most of a week."

"She's been missing for a week and you're only just worrying now? Did you guys have a fight, or what?" Bashaw put in.

"We did, yes." The officers exchanged a look. "But it was just a minor disagreement! Nothing to leave over, not for this long. I figured she might still be mad, and that's why she's stayed away, but days have passed. I mean, we even got a dog—dogs really. Who up and leaves their pets over a petty spat?"

"When specifically did you last see your girlfriend?"

"Monday morning, but only for a few minutes."

"And when you saw her, Monday morning, did she seem angry? Was she behaving at all unusually? Were her things gone when you got home?"

"She was angry, and her things are gone, and I know how that sounds, but I can't believe she'd stay gone on purpose. Not like that, there one minute, gone the next."

Shorthall raised his brows, looking to Bashaw, who sighed, shaking her head. Shorthall nodded, spoke.

"We're not going to write you up for harassment or stalking, okay? We're going to let you go with a warning as long as you leave right now, and *do not touch* another door. You're right. It sounds like she left on purpose and you need to back off. Leave her alone. You are welcome to come to the station to log the missing person's report, but I have a feeling you'll be wasting your time and ours."

Hugo thanked them for their lenience and defeated, backtracked to his car. Rather than the police station, where he assumed filling out an actual report would only hurt his chances of Anna hearing him out, were she to learn of it, he circled residential neighborhoods, just in case, by some fluke, she was walking back from an outing, or sitting on the porch, maybe thinking of him too, but probably not. What if he hired a private investigator to track her down? Even if she wasn't on the lease, wherever she'd ended up, she had a phone bill, and Maitresse had to send her checks *somewhere*. Could he afford a PI? *Did he have a choice?* Hugo drove aimlessly, finally settling on a side street beside a sprawling park.

The first warm spring day, and a Sunday to boot, it was packed. The vast lawns were stamped flat by families flying kites, the pond afloat with crumbs for overfed ducks, and at every angle dogs pulled to sniff this or that bush, greeting passersby. Hugo eyed the multicolored diamonds, prisms, and even the couple of dragons whose lines crossed above. The part of him that didn't learn dallied over how Anna would've joined in the youngsters' fun, yanking her own, doubtless imported or artisanal, kite along. Mid-stride, forcing a smile for the benefit of a particularly vocal husky, Hugo mistakenly lowered his foot onto a soda can and slipped.

When he righted himself, skull ringing a symphony of pain, the wind picked up, and the clouds merged, thickened, casting the park in shadow as the temperature dropped. Appearing at first like a storm front, the clouds gained definition, splitting into human figures standing tall as highrises. Their expressions, hands, hair, and even sparse clothing shifted like children commanded to sit still for a daguerreotype, though there was nothing childlike about the chill of their eyes upon him. The ground was dry, warmer than the air, but the distant chatter of picnickers, barking, chirping, and quacking ceased. Hugo pushed himself up, ambling on, confirming that those celestial gazes followed him.

Finally, he laid down, stretched over the mowed grass lining a small hill which rose devoid of tables, grills, and foliage. He would rest and listen. Quieting his mind of words, the raw hurt, love, Hugo focused only on his breathing. The universe had spoken to him once, and now, he needed it to do so again.

He was about to close his eyes when he looked up to a cloud that resembled his lover, were she older, fuller bodied, with two scars marring her face. Where obsidian irises should have sparkled, catching the light, grey windows pierced his soul. Those eyes were older, wiser than he remembered from his dream. What had her mother's name been? Danto? Dantor?

"Where is she!" he tried to cry, while thinking "What in god's name?!" so that both became garbled, lost in his throat.

She shook her head, the hem of her dress trailing off in lenticular waves.

"You will never see her again. Move on," came a contralto from above, but Dantor's lips never moved. Hugo thought the command was voiced by another, one of the women beside her, and no sooner had they spoken than the wind picked up, pulling the ephemeral figures to pieces.

"But what of my visions?!" he called out, turning from one cloud to the next, as they dissipated. No sooner could he pick out eyes, a nose, mouth, than they would flutter by, until the heavens were cleared of drifting features.

Never had a blue sky caused such anguish.

Hugo sat up, wiped his eyes, looked to passersby for their dumbfounded skyward stares, but their eyes met his. His mind was silent as he stood, staggered on as one drunk. Later he asked himself if he hurt more after knowing she was real and unattainable, or when he believed he'd invented a love that could never be? In the moment, he didn't think, his legs carrying him of their own accord.

On his way back to his car, Hugo knocked down a little girl whose eyes were as glued to her kite as his weren't to anything at all. He opened his mouth to apologize as her parents rushed over, dusted her off, but he didn't trust himself to speak and walked on, mute. They muttered at his back, but he didn't care to hear. Hugo continued his introspection-less retreat until he couldn't see to watch the road. Then he pulled to the side and put the Alliance in park. There was no choice but to wait out the deluge.

Chapter 17
Thyme Heels

Hugo spent that week and the next applying for any position vaguely related to accounting, in his state and those neighboring. His friends called and texted with increasing frequency until he forced himself to respond, to say he needed time to himself. While his family proved less than understanding, he figured out how to mute their ringtones. When he left his flat, it was to walk Rose. There were no errands. His appetite was gone, in the physical sense and in relation to his interests. Hugo barely ate, and when he did, he ordered in. Reading went nowhere. He was unable to sympathize over fictional perils facing the heroes on the page. His problems were real and he would have no happy ending, which wasn't the case for the prince and his princess, no matter how many warlocks or dragons they came up against. Every act in his fantasies served a greater purpose, and even when the heroes died, they dragged the monsters to hell with them.

What had Hugo accomplished? He'd lost his job and his soulmate, back to back. What was left but to trudge on, follow his dad's advice as he rode the capitalist conveyor belt to oblivion?

When interviewing, he sounded lackluster even to himself. Of course, he'd gone through the motions preparing, shaving the burgeoning tufts of a beard, leaving his jaw raw, itchy, irritated. He got a fresh haircut, ironed a silk button-down and slacks for the big day, stepping through a cologne mist the morning of. When the hiring manager, a ginger as well, reached for his hand, Hugo's grip was comparatively slack. Listing his qualifications, he hadn't stumbled over his words, nor forgotten details of importance, but he droned. Never one to play-act, Hugo didn't know where to begin to muster a facade of enthusiasm, and he knew without being told the hiring manager would inevitably offer the position to another candidate. Perhaps Hugo was the more qualified, but he couldn't be the more likable, and that was the quality interviewers measured. Had either he or the other candidates been underqualified, they wouldn't have been met with at all.

Upon exiting her office, he heard the woman sigh with relief. Barely glancing at his competition, Hugo let them know she was ready to see them, nearly congratulating them on the spot, but thought better of it. Who was to say she wouldn't be interviewing others?

Shutting himself in, faced with the sour stench of his flat, he decided it was time. He'd wallowed, but now he had to climb out of the rut he'd dug. What would his father have said, or his mother for that matter, looking at the fast-food wrappers littering his coffee table, kitchen? He imagined them wrinkling their noses at his long unwashed sheets, the toilet he hadn't bothered to flush since the day he stopped putting the seat down.

"Who am I trying to spite?" he asked himself as he bent down to pick up newspaper scraps the pups had torn and strewn across the floor.

The universe had spoken. He wasn't to look for Anna, and so he tried to forget her, scrub his mind of her angular face, mysterious eyes, rounded lips. Of her smooth skull, love-marked bosom, soft waist, softer thighs, slender hands, and feet, nails always neutrally painted. He tried to forget her voice, her laugh, the liveliness with which she brightened, and cluttered, every room.

Hugo shook his head, commenting, "She never needed any paint," the fluid thought gaining definition. "It wasn't the white that drained her. It was me. Anna has all the energy in the world, and I add nothing, not one quality to make her better." And wasn't that what couples did? They complimented each other, supplying what skills, traits, the other lacked.

She'd done him a favor, taking all of her things. "The better to forget you without, my dear," he joked, bitter-ly.

"There will be other women," came a whisper that sounded more like Esteban than himself, but Hugo knew better. Anna Petro was *the one,* his one and only. Another woman, any other woman, would be but an effigy to what was. Like the poppet, Hugo could see himself manipulating his someday wife to experiment with her spirituality, put her health first, shave her head, and oh—wouldn't she just love to travel more? Turning her this way and that, asking for a nip here, a tuck there, until he had a life-size Anna-Petro-shaped doll, all for his benefit—and would she even know? But of course, she would. Women always do.

Tears pooled, though for himself or his future lovers, held to an impossible standard, he couldn't say, and didn't want to. Dabbing at his eyes, Hugo told himself to strip the bed. Those sheets wouldn't wash themselves, and the smell of her coconut lotion, like the produce she'd left behind, had grown rancid. Her residue was staining the sheets a blueish grey. Tossing the bedding in the wash, he set the cycle to heavy-duty.

Then Hugo emptied the garbage and, shuffling from room to room, he gathered litter, rapidly filling another trash bag. That carried out and another liner in the bin, he progressed to boxing anything that had been Claire's, Riga's, or Evelyn's. Unlike his beloved, they'd left ample evidence of the overlap between their journeys and his own. Rather than sorting for every coupled headshot, Hugo gave the photo albums their own box, ridding himself of every past there pictured. What smiles were genuine, if any? Had Evelyn wanted revenge after leaving him, had she prayed for an interlife karmic exchange—like that of the Wiccan she'd been for a minute or two—*it had come.* They were even. He'd destroyed her and then destroyed himself, or at least the him he could have been, with Anna. At least she'd been put back together again, if living in a haunted house and helping youths talk to the dead counted as having healed.

His eyes were dry when he labeled the package with his parents' address. His mom would have a place for it. The remaining mementos he piled high in the backseat and trunk of his Alliance, fabrics swaying from cardboard edges, beads rattling as he swerved, hitting potholes, ambling along backroads, until he'd returned to Pebble Beach and wandered on, past the crowd, the lifeguard, along the trees and shore. Finally alone, he got to work. With doilies, floral curtains, throw blankets, and love notes both written and received as fodder, Hugo built a bonfire where the remnants of another beckoned from a pit, lined with stones. He fed it Claire's upcycled kitchen mat, watched woven grocery bag strips twist, blister black, staining the flames blue, the tips flickering yellow. Then he added a hand-sized painting of a tongue layered with seeds, perhaps a homework assignment of Evelyn's, forgotten heels, sandals, and any number of women's gloves, hats, scarves, magazines. Hugo's gaze burned, imprinted with seared words in bold fonts as pages curdled. Bits of canvas, cloth, lace, wool undulated with the breeze, as if in escape, before being consumed by the sparks they carried aloft and landing defeated, deceased, as ash, their present very like his own.

Through the flames and the snaking smog, Hugo peered across the bay to where Red Rock Point should be, and where instead, he saw himself on the edge of the treeline, no fire at his side. He could cross Malletts Bay, had done so before, but for what? Waving to himself, Hugo asked himself again, was he better for having known her?

Were the memories worth the loss of his job? His new criminal record? And what of his reputation? Did Sonya think him insane? Esteban? He put his hand down, turned from the past, another future.

"Well, I guess I have my answer."

Not that he was happy about it. Hugo drank and burned and burned and drank, until he fell asleep in the mud. Shaken awake by the chattering of his teeth in the chilly spring air, he remembered the dogs and, judging himself sober, retrieved a thermos from the car. Filling it with lake water, he let the contents wash away what embers remained. Most of his trash had been reduced to earth, but not the metal, which he collected, tossing springs, buckles, pins, and cords in his trunk. Returning home, he gave Rose and the pups a late-night dinner, then took her on an even later walk.

When morning came, he took his time filling out job applications, caring for the pups, purposefully avoiding those fleeting images of she who was not to be sought. For all he spoke of need, without her, he walked on.

Neda kept in touch, letting him know which pups had been applied for and would be going to happy, healthy homes as soon as they were weaned. The news brought equal measures of joy and sadness. He'd come to adore them all, to recognize from whom every whine or squeal originated, and so too, what they indicated.

When Neda informed him that all but Rose and Thyme had new homes prepared, but not to fret, several candidates had expressed interest, Hugo couldn't stand the thought of losing them too, and offered to adopt them both.

"If you're sure, I can have the papers ready by tomor-row."

Hugo was sure. He set the appointment and was at their counter ten minutes early, signing one dotted line after another. Neda asked if he wouldn't mind emailing her a picture of him with the puppies so she could share their success story on the Humane Society's website. That night he posed beside the litter until the timer flashed, taking a handful of shots before the role ended. These were the first pictures he'd taken of his new life, and he rushed to have them developed. When Hugo handed the film to the teenager running the photo counter at CVS, the young man was sorry to report that most of the pictures were blurry. Of all the pictures Hugo had taken in the past year, only those of the dogs and himself were in focus.

"That's for the best," Hugo sighed, choosing a favorite picture and having it blown up, reprinted.

Later, he scanned it, emailing Neda the digital copy before framing the original and hanging it in the living room. After downsizing his possessions, that picture was the only wall decor in his flat, unless he counted the calendar, and he didn't.

Thyme was a silly yapping testament to Anna's imperfections. Had Hugo arrived home any later, the little guy might have inhaled the sac's fluid, or worse yet, never breathed at all. It was despite Anna's inaction that Thyme scurried, yelped, thrived. Anna wasn't perfect either, Hugo was reminded by the enthusiastic pawing of his ankles, yips for attention, and puppy kisses.

Admitting that the woman he'd relentlessly pursued for months was flawed didn't loosen the noose around his ventricles, but it made the idea of one day meeting someone lovable less farfetched. In contrast to Anna's absentmindedness, Hugo commended himself for every half-empty cup he didn't abandon, every cabinet he closed, and the schedule he planned to the hour, telling himself *it would be okay.* Loneliness wasn't so bad. The world's most successful men peaked in solitude. Would Sir Isaac Newton have invented calculus were he distracted by matters of the heart? What of Julius Caesar? Hadn't his first wife, who he'd been mocked for loving, died before the First Triumvirate? Leonardo da Vinci never got married, and look at all he'd accomplished! Considering the world's best singles while ignoring the source from whom he'd learned each bit of trivia, Hugo swore not to be a failure. He could starve himself on her love, cling to memories sparse with joy, or he could acknowledge his heart beating on, lungs pumping, the small comforts of the everyday.

There was still his career. To his immense shock, his next and best opportunity arrived at the mercy of Nate, who called Hugo at home from his office, alerting him to an opening on the commercial loan team of a sister bank. Nate was ready to write that recommendation if Hugo had gotten his act together.

"All I can do is vouch for you, and hopefully they'll decide you're the best candidate for the position. But between you and I, my word holds water and I believe you will be offered the role. If you want it."

"Thank you so much. That means a great deal," Hugo said, blinking back moisture, swallowing a lump in his throat.

"Don't thank me. Thank Esteban. He explained the troubles you've had, why your productivity slipped, why you needed time to yourself. As for the team, should they take you on, you'll be a fresh hire. There will be a three-month probationary period during which you will prove yourself to be punctual and efficient."

"Of course. I promise to be an exemplary employee. Everything that kept me from work is gone now. There's nothing to distract me from what's important."

"I'm glad to hear it. Now, speaking not as your ex-boss but as a friend, I suggest you consider therapy. I can recommend someone if you like."

Whether Hugo wanted help or not, he wouldn't risk offending the man who put his word behind the no-call, no-show employee who'd quit not a month prior.

"If that's what you think is best, I'd love their name and number. Thank you."

It was halfway through May when Hugo was formally offered and accepted the position, an event that cast the week brighter, as saying goodbye to four pups had otherwise tainted it. Likewise, as he'd predicted, Sonya had applied for Mint, and Nate, Aloe. The Humane Society found their homes fit, and neither puppy cried at being taken from their mama. Hugo was relieved that with regards to those two and his own, arranging playdates wouldn't be an ordeal. Esteban invited him out, to celebrate Hugo's new job.

"You'll be great. Nate knows you're the best guy for the gig or he wouldn't have told you about it. He's seen what you can do when you're focused."

"Thanks. I just had to get my priorities straight, I guess."

"That's the spirit. Make sure to eat before your orientation. Don't want them thinking you're an addict, or trying to get into the modeling biz."

"An addict? Why would they think that?"

His friend pointed and Hugo flinched, seeing himself in the mirror behind the bar. At first glance, he thought that wraith was somebody else.

"Wow. I'm rail thin."

"Oh, you're thinner than that. Let's get the onion rings. Hell, wings, too." Esteban smiled in punctuation, but without the telltale crinkle of his eyes.

They cleared both dishes. As they were leaving, Hugo promised to make comedy night. He'd cheer Sonya on with the best of them.

Arriving home, a peal of young laughter cut through the gloom. Turning on the lights, Hugo's gaze caught on the prim atop the bookshelf. "What the fuck?" Hugo gasped, wondering how he'd missed it during the cleansing.

"So she did leave me something. Well, too late to burn it now," he commented, midstride, before losing his balance and landing on his finally healed butt. Rising, he spotted the obstacle, a hand-sized ruby-hued pomegranate, and it wasn't alone. There were a dozen below his suddenly and shockingly flourishing little tree, another several nestled in its short, twisted branches. "How—" He'd had that tree for years, and while it annually produced what could very technically be called *fruit,* those miniature pomegranates were so small, the seeds so plentiful, that after his first tentative bite, he'd never ventured another. Yet these looked large, ripe—and slicing one open, turning it inside out over a bowl—he found they were juicy. Popping a few seeds in his mouth, Hugo was satisfied that they tasted as they should, which was to say, sweet, verging on tart. In fact, they were the sweetest pomegranate seeds ever to grace his tongue.

Then Rose whined, and he put the bowl aside, dressing her for a walk. Leaving his cell inside, it wasn't until after she'd concluded her official doggy business, and he was settling down to eat the miracle fruit that Hugo noticed his messages.

"Well, that's weird."

There were notifications from Sonya, Nate, and another of the adopting families. As he was accessing his voicemails, the phone rang again, caller ID denoting the identity of the fourth family.

"Hello? Hugo speaking."

"Hi! Yes, this is Diane. I adopted Parsley on Monday."

"Hey, Diane. Is everything okay?!"

"Well, I don't know. See, I just got home from a long shift, and well—Parsley is green! I called the shelter but their phone is down or they're closed or something, and it went straight to voicemail. I just don't—"

"Slow down, Diane. It's probably okay. The whole litter was green when they were born. It's—"

"They were born green and you guys didn't tell me? What's the matter wi—"

"Diane! Stop. It's not a big scary deal. Sometimes puppies are born green. Ask Neda about it tomorrow. It's unusual, but not unheard of. It just means their fur was stained while in the womb."

"Well *Parsley wasn't in the womb* while I was at work today."

"Yeah. No idea what's up with that, but I missed three calls from—can you hold on a sec? I need to check something."

He'd been so distracted by the wonders of the full-size pomegranate and then walking Rose that he hadn't played with Thyme. Following the sound of little footsteps, Hugo found him under the couch.

"Come here, little guy. Into the light."

Thyme ignored the request, and Hugo returned with an offering of cheese. The pup scampered out, and Hugo used the opportunity to hold him up for a better look.

"Yeah, Thyme is green, too. I guess it's the entire litter."

"Well, what does it mean?"

Hugo tilted his head, stroking his chin. "Maybe nothing. Might be worth seeing the vet tomorrow, but Thyme is hopping around. He seems fine."

Checking the wee pad, he folded and tossed it, laying another in its place.

"Aside from the color, he seems normal. How's Parsley? Has she been crying much? Low energy at all? Eating okay?"

"Oh, her energy is plenty high. I didn't think they zoomied at ten weeks, but she's been running circles around her gate."

"Okay. Definitely take pictures, and call Neda tomorrow, but don't kill yourself worrying, alright? I'll call too."

Diane let him go, and he got in touch with each adoptee in turn, explaining that he was aware of the oddity but ignorant of the cause. The next day, Neda was alarmed.

"Reverting to green? I've never heard of such a thing." She put him on hold while presumably double-checking with the vet tech, then returned. "It's the entire litter?"

"Yes. Have you checked your voicemails? Diane left a message."

"No. The phones went down last night. We didn't know until we got in this morning. The Fairpoint technician only just left. I'm sending the vet tech by. Are you home now?"

Hugo was. Not twenty minutes later, Thyme was squealing and Rose barking in response to a knock at the door. Hugo let the man in and made tea while Thyme was examined.

"Find anything?"

The man shook his head. "Nope. Other than the coat, there's nothing amiss."

He asked about Thyme's diet, energy levels, whether the little guy was stressed, and if Hugo was walking him outside yet.

"Too many dogs in this neighborhood. Neda said to wait until he's fully vaccinated, to stick with the puppy pads until then."

The vet tech nodded. "Good. Well, aside from the discoloration, Thyme appears to be in perfect health. I'll contact the others and let you know what we learn."

As the day wore on, the only news Hugo received was that they all seemed fine, but to be safe, he brought Thyme to his vet the following week for a second opinion. Diane kept calling him with that quiver in her voice, passing her anxiety along, but while his vet was confounded by the color, he agreed with the vet tech.

"If anything changes, call me immediately, but I think Thyme is okay."

The next time Diane or any of the other adopters rang, he gave them his vet's number, and gradually, they calmed. In days, texts of fear and concern shifted casual as they discussed which were the best dog parks for later, when it would be safe for the pups to interact with other dogs. How long until playdates were possible? Sonya too, couldn't wait until Thyme could meet Mushroom Butt, but in the meantime, she relayed how Mint's training was going.

Hugo tested all of the basic commands on Rose in English, then in Spanish with Esteban's help, before concluding she hadn't been trained at all. So it was, he set about teaching her and Thyme both. "Sit" was a breeze, and they got the hang of "stay" over a day. "Leave it" and "heel" proved more challenging, especially the latter. Even in their small backyard, the pups needed serious bribing to stick to his side, but they were making progress.

Home, teaching claimed his attention, but at work, he was learning. He was accustomed to the software, but the file management system was in no way intuitive, and he needed to become better acquainted with their forms, so as to help clients fill them out. When he wasn't dealing with numbers or customers, Hugo was memorizing the names and faces of his team members. He hadn't made any friends, and doubtless wouldn't for some time, not being naturally sociable, but Esteban worked a block away, so lunches weren't lonely.

It had been a long week, and he planned to sleep in Saturday, but the dogs had other ideas. Rose hopped on the bed, pawing at Hugo's face and whining, while Thyme squeaked below, his cries almost a bark. The poor little guy couldn't yet reach mattress height, though not from lack of trying. Instead, he scratched at the frame. Unfortunately, Hugo hadn't succeeded in breaking them of that habit. No longer feigning unconsciousness in the hopes they'd follow suit, Hugo sat up, brushed Rose gently aside, and stood. Stretching, he stepped past Thyme on his way to the kitchen, where he fed them. Then, on autopilot, he changed out the used wee pad. With coffee brewing, he dressed and walked Rose who, despite her enthusiasm to leave the house, wasn't eager to go to the bathroom so much as to pause and sniff every sidewalk stain.

Returning home, Hugo was careful not to trip over the freshly fallen fruit. Bending low, he unlatched her harness and scratched behind her ears as she slumped beside Thyme, who tugged at her ear while pawing at her face, demanding play.

"Good luck with that," Hugo laughed, abandoning Rose to her son's antics while he claimed and sliced a pomegranate for breakfast. He'd just turned the flesh inside out when he heard a sound in the bedroom. It wavered, the air grew still, and Hugo thought he'd imagined it, but then the trilling trembled, erupting anew.

That better not be Boukman, he thought, touching the flesh beneath his finally-healed eye.

Rising, Hugo crossed the living room, eyeing the prim for any sign of activity. He passed Thyme, who was failing to engage his mama in play. Then Hugo turned, entering the bedroom, where he found the source of the warbling. In the center of his bed was a woven basket, the handle and rim inlaid with a blue ribbon. Swaddled within was an infant, barely a week old if Hugo was any judge, given their complexion was closer to mauve than brown. The child stared at him with round obsidian eyes, their tiny mouth agape, and let loose a fresh whimper. Their brow rose ever so slightly as they scrunched their soft features, and the whimper became a cry.

Unresisting, Hugo leaned across the bed, withdrew the bundle, and pulled the child to his heart.

Once upon a time, there was a young graphic designer named Jessica Ferrara. She had a passion for creating beautiful designs that could captivate the eye and stir the soul. After graduating from the College of Saint Rose with her Bachelor's degree, Jessica spent three years honing her craft as a tattoo artist in Albany, New York. But Jessica's thirst for adventure could not be quenched by her artistic pursuits alone, and so she set out on an epic journey across the great continent of Europe. She backpacked through ancient cities, explored exotic cultures, and gathered inspiration from every corner of the world. And when Jessica returned to the United States, she found a new home in the heart of Texas. She began a new journey of blogging on her website and reviewing books on Instagram with her return to the States as a way to chronicle her life and open the imagination of potential readers. Here, she could be found writing and painting, pouring her passion onto the canvas and into the written word. Her designs were bold, imaginative, and always spoke to the soul of the viewer, which can be found on her website, Instagram, Facebook, and TikTok . You can also reach her via email at JessLynnStudio@gmail.com.

Also by Jessica Ferrara

Stem & Stone
YA Dark Fantasy
CW: violence, gore, hints of drug addiction

9 781957 893815